BECAUSE OF YOU

PLAYING WITH FIRE, #2

BY

T. E. SIVEC

Cover art by Okay Creations
www.okaycreations.net

Editing by The Polished Pen
www.polished-pen.com

Formatting by Fictional Formats
https://www.facebook.com/pages/Fictional-formats

TABLE OF CONTENTS

PROLOGUE   1

CHAPTER 1   4

CHAPTER 2   24

CHAPTER 3   39

CHAPTER 4   54

CHAPTER 5   71

CHAPTER 6   84

CHAPTER 7   102

CHAPTER 8   116

CHAPTER 9   134

CHAPTER 10   149

CHAPTER 11   154

CHAPTER 12   166

CHAPTER 13   179

CHAPTER 14   193

CHAPTER 15   209

CHAPTER 16   229

CHAPTER 17   245

CHAPTER 18   250

CHAPTER 19   264

CHAPTER 20   277

CHAPTER 21   294

CHAPTER 22   308

CHAPTER 23   327

CHAPTER 24   339

CHAPTER 25   348

CHAPTER 26   359

EPILOGUE   380

ACKNOWLEDGEMENTS

Thank you to Max – the best editor and friend a girl could have. You put up with a gazillion texts on a daily basis and my complete stupidity when it comes to tenses without wanting to stab me (I think) and I love you for it.

Thank you so much to my awesome beta readers: Madison Seidler, Amanda Clark and Tressa Sager. You are the best cheerleaders and I love you all so much for taking time out of your lives to help me.

Thank you to Tiffany King and Ana Ivies for reading this early, being amazing and boosting my ego without me having to pay you!

Thank you to my Street Team for all of your hard work and support, especially my head honcho, Angie West-Ellis, who never hesitates to jump in and help me out. I love all of you and I'm so glad to have you on my team.

Thank you to Trish Patel-Brinkley for practically being

my own personal signing planner! You are wonderful and I can never say enough good things about you for all of the hard work you've put in to each of the events this year.

Thank you to Rose Hunter for the quick, last minute legal advice!

Thank you to my "Wicked Girls" for being the best friends ever and for GOAT SCREAM.

Thank you to Jasinda Wilder, Katie Ashley, Raine Miller, RK Lilley and C.C. Wood for dealing with my swift ninja skills and knowing just the right words to yell to bring me to the yard.

Christina Collie – this one's for you. And you better finish it, bitch! I love you!

April 25, 2012

Dear Layla,

Great performance tonight in Chicago! Once again you blew me away with your talent. I'm so glad I was able to get tickets to the show at the last minute. See you in a few months in New York – that's where you'll be in July, right?

Sincerely – Ray, your biggest fan

July 4, 2012

Dear Layla

Another job well done, my
beautiful lady! I did notice
that your bass player had a
bit of trouble in the 2nd set.
You really should make sure
he checks his instruments
carefully before each show.
It doesn't pay to be
unprofessional like that.

The fireworks at the end
were a nice touch, though.

Until next time - *Ray, your biggest fan*

September 22, 2012

Layla,

I was a little irritated that your show in Minnesota was cancelled tonight. I stood outside in line for hours before the show hoping to get a picture of you getting off your bus. Did you know the great songstress Rachel McIvers went on six hours after giving birth? And Amanda Vandell performed two hours after being involved in a car accident. In their entire careers they never had to cancel a show. Gives you something to think about. Take care of yourself.

Ray - your biggest fan

November 10, 2012

Layla,

You weren't really enjoying the show this evening. I could tell. As a performer, you really need to make sure your audience believes you enjoy what you're doing. Your eyes looked tired, like you were just going through the motions. I really expected better from you. I'll be seeing you again in Cleveland. Hopefully, I'll see some improvement. Otherwise, I'm just not going to be happy. It wouldn't be wise for you to make me mad.

Ray - your biggest fan

January 1, 2013

Layla,

It's a new year and it's time for you to turn a new leaf. I had really hoped my previous letter would have given you the incentive to improve upon yourself. Obviously I was wrong. Nothing changed with last night's New Year's Eve show at the Rock and Roll Hall of Fame. I saw the same robotic girl from Detroit – lifeless eyes, a smile that wasn't believable, and no joy whatsoever on your face. It makes me angry that nothing I say has gotten through to you. I'm only trying to help you. I think we should sit down and talk about this when you're back home in Tennessee. I'm assuming you'll be staying in your apartment in Nashville? I know you have a home elsewhere in that area, but it's been extremely hard to pinpoint exactly where it is located. I guess it doesn't matter. I'll find you wherever you are.

Ray – your biggest fan

PROLOGUE

Present day...

In the dark, cold room, I blink my eyes to focus, but all I can think about is the pain. It hurts to breathe and every inch of my body feels bruised and battered. Probably because it is.

Oh God! Why is this happening to me?

I try to move, to get up off of the hard floor, but my broken body isn't cooperating. I need to find a way out of here or I won't survive this. I know with every part of my being that if I don't leave this room, I'm going to die here. Alone.

The tears run down my face, and I can't even move my arms to brush them away; something is holding them in place.

I slowly turn my head to the side, trying not to throw up from the pain that rushes through me with that one simple movement. I'm tied down to something, but I can't make out what it is. The only light in the room comes from a street lamp right outside, which throws a thin ray of light through the small window close to the ceiling.

With all of the strength I can muster, I try to pull one of my arms free from whatever is holding me in place, the bindings cutting into my wrists and pain instantly shooting up my arm that's most likely broken in several places.

My scream echoes through the empty room and my throat aches from all the screaming I've already done...yesterday? The day before? I'm losing track of time.

Oh God, this is the arm I play with. This is the arm that cradles the guitar to my side and the fingers that strum the notes that take me away to another place. Notes and melodies that bring me back to life and allow me to be who I really am.

I know I'm going to pass out again soon. My vision is swimming. Spots flash before my eyes as I struggle to remain conscious.

Flashbacks of the past few months run through my mind like someone flipping the pages of a book, and my heart shatters at the memories. I should have seen what was happening. I should have listened to him from the beginning, but everything about him scared me. The force of what I felt for him shouldn't have been so strong so quickly. He had my heart and my soul from the very first touch, the very first moment. But he didn't want it. He didn't want any of it. I trusted too quickly, gave too easily.

Trusting someone is what got me into this mess. I trusted the wrong person, and now I'm going to pay for it with my life. Someone who should have been there for me and protected me...it was all a lie from the very beginning. Deep down I knew it. I'd always known it. I just never wanted to believe the hatred ran that deep.

I let the darkness wash over me, knowing it's the only way the pain will go away. I close my eyes, thinking back over the last eight years and wondering about all of the things I should have done differently, the choices I made that have led me to where I am now. If I had never let *her* control me, never succumbed to the undeniable connection I had to *him*...if we hadn't experienced that initial pull towards each other, maybe things wouldn't be ending this way.

I hear shouts and the pounding of footsteps in the distance, but I can't force my eyes open no matter how hard I try. They are probably just coming back to finish the job, not satisfied with how much they have already broken me, how much they have already taken from me.

Maybe if I had realized sooner, listened earlier, put away my pride and the belief that everyone has some good in them deep down, I wouldn't be where I am now—fighting for my life and wondering if the person I love cares enough to save me from this hell.

CHAPTER 1

BRADY

Three months ago…

Even though my mind is going a hundred miles a minute, worrying about how I'm going to pay the growing pile of bills in my hand and keep a roof over Gwen and Emma's head, I'm still one hundred percent aware of my surroundings, a blessing and a curse given to me by Uncle Sam.

The four-door, blue sedan parked three spots down from me has a rear tire that's losing air and will most likely blow a flat within three days.

The wind is blowing from the southeast at around five miles per hour.

Fireside Bookshop, the store across the street, is three minutes and twenty-seven seconds late opening this morning.

Mr. Jensen, the owner of the building I rent, has a yappy, shit-kicker dog named Mitzy. They live upstairs from Marshall Investigations, and on nice days like today, he leaves a window open so Mitzy can get some fresh air.

Pushing open the door to the office with my shoulder, I sort through a stack of mail as I make my way inside, blindly reaching one hand out to the wall and flipping on the light switch as I walk by. Mitzy manages to bark thirty-five times from the moment I open my car door to when I reach the quiet tranquility of my office.

My dark fucking office.

The fact I can barely see what's written on the envelopes in my hand now that I'm inside the building and out of the bright, early morning Nashville sun can only mean one thing.

"Son of a bitch!" I angrily mutter to myself, shaking my head in irritation. I back up a few steps and feel across the wall with my hand, flicking the switch up and down a few more times and cursing under my breath once more just for the hell of it.

When the florescent lights from above fail to blind me, I smack the pile of bills and junk mail down on the closest desk with a loud snapping noise and make a move to touch the light switch again.

"Playing with it over and over is not going to miraculously pay the electric bill."

The flat, unenthusiastic voice stops me mid-step, my hand in the air just hovering over the switch. I roll my eyes at Gwen as she walks into the office area from the kitchenette in the back. Every time she walks into a room, I can still feel my jaw drop slightly. My baby sister's always been the quiet one, never doing anything to draw attention to herself until she showed up on my doorstep one night looking like she'd gone ten rounds with Mike Tyson.

My parents live in a world where the country club dictates their every move. If what they're doing doesn't make them look good to snobby friends, they don't bother doing it, and unfortunately, that affected our childhood—Gwen's more than mine. She's always been the picture perfect daughter: shy, well-mannered, wearing clothes and her hair just as Mother insisted.

When Gwen burst through my door that night and headed straight for the bathroom, I didn't know what to expect. A few minutes later she came out holding her long blonde ponytail in her fist, her tiny shoulders shaking with fury.

"Never again, Brady!" she half-cried, half yelled. "That woman is never going to tell me how to live my life again." A little while later, we were slumped against the wall, and after I managed to calm her down, she laughed through the tears. "Guess I won't be catching the eye of a good man ever again without my beautiful long blonde hair and impeccable social etiquette."

I gently ran a hand over her freshly battered skin and thought maybe that wasn't such a bad thing considering the "good" man she found had done that to her. Once the bruises faded and she stopped jumping from her own shadow, I took her to some fancy hair place down the street from my office, and they waved their magic wand over her hack job haircut and color from a box.

Standing in front of me now with her hands on her hips, impatiently tapping her foot, waiting for an answer, I don't even recognize her. Her hair is still short. Chopping it off with my straight edge razor didn't leave the stylist with much to work with, but they turned it into some type of edgy reverse bob or whatever it's called.

I squint my eyes and try to make out her hair color in the unlit office. "Is that purple and blue?" I ask, slightly shocked.

"Pretty bad ass, huh?" She smiles proudly.

Shrugging, I say, "At least you don't look like an emo asshole anymore. The black made me feel like you were going to start worshiping the devil any minute."

The sun starts to filter through the wooden venetian blinds, and I notice something sparkling on her face. "Gwen..." Protective big brother is starting to kick in, and it shows in my voice, but then I see her smile and I change my tone. "Is that a nose piercing?"

"Don't even start, Brady..."

I smile and admire the tiny diamond stud. It suits her, but I'll never get used to my five-foot-two, one-hundred-pound tiny wisp of a sister and her new found confidence.

"That's a pretty cool stud," I tell her, leaning back in my

chair and kicking my feet on my desk so I can watch her annoyance turn to relief. "The nose ring isn't bad either."

My smirk puts the irritation back on her face, but I can see she's trying to hide a smile by the way she's fighting with the corners of her mouth.

"It's really sad that you think so highly of yourself," she tells me good-naturedly.

We both let out a laugh as she rolls her eyes at me and starts sorting some of the open case files on my desk.

It's good to see her smile and laugh again. Real good.

When I finally pulled myself out of my six-month drunken bender, tired of filling my days and nights with cheap whiskey and even cheaper women from every strip club within a fifty mile radius, I decided to open up my own security specialist/private investigating firm. Gwen jumped at the chance to help me out. She had her own baggage, her own rough couple of years. She'd been working a dead end job as a waitress that was more trouble than it was worth ever since she showed up here, so it made her decision a no-brainer.

Her six-year-old daughter is in school full time now which gives her more freedom to come and go during the day. Managing the office side of my business lets her finally put that college degree in Business Administration to good use. Gwen is two years my junior, and is still the only member of my family who has never given up on me. I've been to hell and back this past year and never thought I would make it out alive. I put her through the fucking ringer when she first got here. After the life she left behind, she didn't deserve that shit from me. She deserves more, so much more. It's only been recently that I've realized how much she's done for me, how much she's always done for me, and just how much I've let her down.

Throwing the last few items from my dresser drawer into the camouflage duffel bag on my bed, I zipped it closed and slung the pack over my shoulder, hustling out of my room and down the front stairway before my father could get another word in to criticize me. Ever since I made the announcement I was joining the Navy over dinner two months ago, I was met with nothing but anger and shame from my parents. The shame came from my mother.

"What will everyone at the club think when I tell them you aren't going to law school?" she asked in a horrified voice.

My father had always been an angry person, but he hid it well behind the twenty-five-year-old scotch and fancy suits. It wasn't until I dropped the bomb that I'd be leaving after graduation that his true colors came out. Apparently, "only poor people with no future and no direction go into the military. Not bright young men from affluent families with a reputation and a name to uphold."

Little did he realize, I fit perfectly into his "poor and directionless" category. I had no money to my name because I would be damned if I took one penny from him. Ever. Even if I wanted to, he made it perfectly clear he wouldn't support my frivolous dream of "goofing off on a boat and playing with guns."

The day I got the results from my SATs, my father popped open a seven thousand dollar bottle of Perrier-Jouet Champagne and called up his good friend, the dean of students at Harvard Law, and asked him what kind of a donation would get me early admission. My future and the direction of my life suddenly began to choke me. I thought about going to work every day wearing a three-piece suit and arguing the innocence of people I knew were far from blameless. I thought about kissing the asses of Circuit and Supreme Court judges every single day like my father did and playing eighteen holes with opposing counsel and joking about the sad, underprivileged people who came to us for help.

I couldn't do it. I couldn't live my life like that. I wouldn't.

"You take one step out of that door, don't you dare think about coming back here."

The stern words spoken from the top of the stairs didn't even cause me to falter as I continued to the bottom step. He had made those same threats to me every single day for the past sixty days.

"Don't worry, Dad. I wouldn't DREAM of coming back here," I replied as my steel-toed boots clacked across the marble floor in the foyer, refusing to turn around and look at him.

No matter who or what I was leaving behind, I had to leave—before it broke me.

"Brady! Wait!"

The panicked shout from the library stopped me in my tracks, kept me from the freedom just within my grasp. It was the ONLY voice that could stop me at this point. I dropped my duffel on the floor and turned just as my sixteen-year-old sister threw herself into my arms. With her face buried in my shoulder, she choked back tears and I wrapped my arms around her tightly and held her close.

"It's okay, Gwenny, it's okay," I told her softly as I rubbed my hand against her back.

"Please, don't leave. Don't leave me," she whispered.

"I'm just going away for a little while. I will never leave you. I promise."

But I did leave her. I left and I never looked back. She did everything my parents told her, so in my mind, she became the enemy.

I will never forgive myself for leaving her behind, for walking away and letting that monster get his hooks in her and turn her into someone I hardly recognized. Gwen doesn't blame me. She would never blame me. But I know better. She SHOULD blame me. She should scream and yell and curse at me for walking away from the one person who really, truly loved me. She had come back into my life so I could save her, but she's saved me in more ways than she will ever know.

When she found out how I'd been spending my days and nights before she showed up on my doorstep, she took action. The dead, lifeless eyes that looked up into mine and begged for a place for her and my niece to stay, if only for the night were suddenly filled with determination. For someone who had lived in her own private hell for seven years, she wasn't afraid to call me out on my bullshit. It only took six little words from her one night three months ago to make me pull my head out of my own ass.

When the fuck did I put a tilt-a-whirl in my house? And when did tilt-a-whirl employees start smacking their riders?

"Brady! You son of a bitch! Wake up! God dammit, wake up!"

Gwen's screams made the room stop spinning so I could

finally focus, but too bad the spinning was now replaced with an ear-splitting headache.

"Jesus Christ! I'm up, I'm up. Stop smacking me," I complained with a groan as I rolled over away from her and tried to get comfortable in my bed.

My eyes flew open when my hand smacked down in a puddle of vomit two inches from my face. I looked around and realized I was sprawled out on the kitchen floor wearing just my boxer briefs and the phone number of the stripper I was pretty sure I banged tonight written in black pen on my forearm.

"Where's Emma?" I croaked, wincing at the raspy, worn-out sound of my own voice as I avoided the puke on the floor and pushed myself up to my feet, trying not to wobble but being unsuccessful.

Gwen quickly wrapped her arms around my torso, supporting my weight and helping me over to the sink to wash my hands and splash cold water on my face.

"She's next door with Mrs. Nichols. I decided to come here first after my shift to check on you before I picked her up. Thank God I did. What a great way for your six-year-old niece to come home from the babysitter. Finding her uncle facedown in a pool of his own vomit, smelling like a hooker."

Between the stale whiskey and the disgust in her voice, my stomach started to churn.

Still dripping with water, I squeezed my eyes shut as I

13

turned the faucet off and flung my arm out to the side blindly as Gwen smacked a dry dishtowel in my hand.

"I don't smell like hooker. Stripper maybe. Probably. But never hooker. That's just gross," I said with a laugh as I wiped the towel down the front of my face and chucked it into the sink.

"Don't you dare," she whispered, tears forming in her eyes. "Don't you DARE make light of this. Do you honestly think it would have been fun for me to walk in here to find you dead? Do you think I like working my ass off at a job I HATE, spending too much time away from my baby who asks every day when she can see Daddy? Do you think it's fun for me to worry all day, every day, if today is the day I'm going to have to plan your funeral?" She swiped angrily at the tears that poured down her cheeks. "You need to stop this, Brady. Right now. Nothing that happened was your fault. Not in the Dominican, not here in Nashville, and certainly not my marriage. None of it."

I didn't know what to say. I didn't know what to do. I couldn't stand to be in my own fucking skin half the time, and I honestly didn't know if I COULD stop what I was doing to myself.

"You promised me, Brady. You promised you'd never leave me," she whispered.

Those six little words from Gwen that night were all it took to end the self-destruction. I said goodbye to the booze, goodbye to the random hook-ups with all the nameless, faceless women, and I said goodbye to the worry I saw etched all over Gwen's face every single day when she looked at me. Unfortunately, the guilt and the nightmares that ate away at me every night wouldn't be dismissed as easily. But I cleaned up my act, opened my own business, and made sure I would never, ever break that promise to Gwen again.

Except now I may have to if I can't figure out a way to pay the bills.

"Please tell me there's a few checks I can deposit in that stack of mail so we don't have to work like the cavemen did. I am not in the mood to chisel stone instead of use the computer," Gwen states as she walks up to me and leafs through the mail, tucking a blue strand of hair behind her ear.

"Bill, bill, bill, meet interested singles in your area, bill, bill..." she turns the envelopes over one by one and places them face down on the desk "...increase your penis size in just five days." She purses her lips and lets out a sigh. "Awww, Brady, did you send away for something to enhance your teeny tiny

15

weenie?"

Gwen laughs at her own joke while I stand there staring at her with my arms crossed over my chest and one eyebrow raised.

"No, I'm pretty sure that came free when you signed up for the *Itty Bitty Titty Club*," I deadpan.

"Oh, you're such a riot. Now tell me, what are you going to do about getting this electric turned on? Because hey, I've got a *great* idea. There's this awesome job where you can get paid up front—"

"No," I interrupt before she's finished.

"Brady, stop being so damn stubborn." She's starting to whine and I'm losing my patience. "They called again and raised the price. All you have to do is—"

"NO." My feet slam back down to the floor, and I raise my voice, letting her know this isn't up for discussion.

"You don't even want to know how much they want to pay you?" Gwen asks in a high pitch voice that makes me want to stab a pencil in my ear as she follows behind me like an annoying puppy—like Mitzy, but yappier.

"No amount of money is enough for me to follow around some pop star diva princess who has more money than she knows what to do with and probably invented this little stalker because her name hasn't been in the tabloids in at least three point two days. Sorry, no."

I press the power button on my computer, completely forgetting about the whole no-electricity dilemma.

"Hey, Einstein, last time I checked, computers run on electricity," Gwen says cockily.

"It's too early for this," I mutter, scrubbing my hands over my face. "I need coffee."

"In case you weren't aware, coffee pots also run on electricity," Gwen says with a smirk before she turns and walks over to her desk and takes a seat, turning her chair so she can stare at me and smile.

I ignore her gaze and pick up the phone to check my messages to see if any new clients had called overnight.

"Oh yeah, remember that new phone system you said would be more efficient? Guess what it runs on?"

I grind my teeth together and exhale loudly through my nose, counting to ten in my head before I do what I really want to—pick up the phone console and heave it across the room, preferably at my sister's head. My mood instantly sobers when I remember the kind of life she's lived for the past seven years.

I slam the receiver down in its cradle and sit silently at my desk, tapping my fingers on the wood.

If I only had my well-being to worry about, this wouldn't even be an issue. I'd decline the job and figure out another way to pay the bills. There's a cheating spouse job I had put on the back burner because it's boring as hell, but that would only last a day or two. It may pay the electric bill, but it won't pay Gwen's salary. Asking her to quit her full-time waitressing job where she was guaranteed a paycheck puts added pressure on my shoulders. I'm still kicking myself in the ass every single day for being too caught up in the Navy SEALS, and then the police force, to notice what was going on with my own sister. I'll do right by her and make up for everything she's gone through if it's the last thing I do. Even if it means taking a job that goes against every single moral, ethical, and personal belief I've ever had.

When I first left the Navy SEALS a little over a year ago, I spent a few months with the Nashville police force. I experienced my fair share of celebrity craziness from arresting the spoiled daughter of a hotel mogul for a cocaine bender that left one of Nashville's most popular restaurants trashed beyond recognition to turning down "tips" handed to me on the sly if I just did the collagen-injected, silicone-enhanced country music star one "teensy tiny favor" and *not* put that she was having sex with her underage back-up dancer when her husband came home and died of a heart-attack in my police report. I couldn't make that shit up if I tried. I was quickly tiring of the outlandish, overindulgent, spoiled rich kids. After my last SEAL mission where my best friends had been injured, and an entire team of SEALS I'd known since the Naval Academy were all killed, I thought maybe the hustle and bustle of the Nashville police force would keep my mind off of the dark thoughts and endless guilt. All it did was make things worse.

Three months after moving to Nashville, I went out on a routine domestic violence call. Everything should have been cut and dry: separate the victim from the supposed attacker and get each of their statements so we could sort things out back at the station. I had no idea we were walking into a hostage situation and the husband had no intention of letting anyone live.

That night, my partner, a thirty-five-year-old father of four, a twenty-two-year-old mother, her little girl, and a very disturbed twenty-five-year-old young man all lost their lives.

How I managed to make it out alive is still a mystery.

My parents, world renowned doctor, Beth Marshall, and Supreme Court Judge, Patrick Marshall, incorrectly assumed their prodigal son would come running back home and do their bidding by becoming a son they could be proud of and brag about over mint juleps and games of Canasta once I left the Navy SEALS. They wrote me out of their lives once again when I chose to become a cop instead. My parents' blatant disapproval of my life choices and their constant need to remind me about how I wasn't living up to their expectations pushed me further and further away until the only contact I had with them was the occasional greeting card on birthdays and major holidays.

Unfortunately, the distance I put between myself and my parents over the years also affected my baby sister. Gwen never agreed with their opinions of me, but at that time in my life, contact with her just brought the pain to the forefront. In order for me to excel at my job, I needed to remove all the negativity. I had thought Gwen was well taken care of and that was all that mattered. Even though I cut off contact long before that fateful SEAL mission, I still kept up with the news. I read all about her famous plastic surgeon husband and saw pictures of the smiling, happy couple at events throughout the years. I never really cared much for my brother-in-law the one time I met him at their wedding seven years earlier. He was pompous, had no sense of humor, and our parents treated him like the son they always wanted.

"What time does your flight leave?" Gwen asked, looking up at me while I spun her around the dance floor, trying not to trip over the train on her Vera Wang wedding gown.

I removed my hand from her waist and checked the time on my black, waterproof tactical watch required by the SEALS.

"In about two hours. I need to get going. Don't want to miss my first mission as a big, bad Navy SEAL," I told her with a smile and a wag of my eyebrows as the song we were dancing to slowly came to an end.

My father's loud, booming voice echoed through the vaulted ceilings in the ornate banquet hall. "Son! My favorite man in the room. Come over here. There are a few people I want you to meet."My shoulders tensed as I turned my head in his direction. We hadn't spoken one word to each other since I flew in the day before for Gwen's wedding. I should have known he wasn't talking to me. My eyes narrow in undisguised irritation as I watch my father throw his arm around Gwen's new husband's shoulder as they shared an obnoxious laugh, continuing to walk past us and towards a group of men I had never met.

"Hey, look at me."

Gwen's soft voice forced me to tamp down my anger, and I turned around to meet her bright blue eyes.

"Nothing he says or does means anything. Your happiness – that's all that matters," she told me with a smile as she pushed a stray piece of long blonde hair behind one ear.

Swallowing the lump in my throat, I smiled. "That's a two-way street, Gwenny."

"I know. Don't worry. I'm happy. I found my Prince Charming, just like mother always wanted me to."

Not wanting to place any type of wedge in Gwen's relationship with our parents by forcing her to choose sides or clouding her happiness by voicing my opinion of her husband, I spoke to her less and less until one day we just weren't speaking at all anymore.

I felt like shit after the SEAL mission—physically and mentally. After losing my partner and watching two young people die right in front of me a few months later, I fell into a black hole of booze and women that I still couldn't remember half of.

Three months ago, Gwen showed up out of the blue at my townhouse at four o'clock in the morning. Aside from the initial shock at seeing my sister standing on my doorstep after she'd traveled over a thousand miles in the middle of the night, the two black eyes she hid behind dark sunglasses, the cast on her broken wrist, and the way she gingerly held her hand against her side to protect her two broken ribs threw me into a murderous rage. Not to mention the curly-haired, towheaded six-year-old little girl that stood next to her sucking her thumb and looking up at me with the same big, bright, curious blue eyes my sister used to have before that asshole broke her.

To ward off the memories of that dark night, I close my eyes and take a deep breath. The guilt still overwhelms me every time I think about all of those phone calls I never returned and voice mails I deleted without listening all the way through. If I only got off my high horse and returned just one of those calls, I might have been able to save Gwen from the monster she married. If I'd listened to her voice mails, I might have been able to prevent my niece from witnessing her mother having the shit kicked out of her on a weekly basis for the first six years of her life.

I open my eyes and stare across the room at Gwen as she mirrors me, drumming her own fingers on top of her desk. She still isn't one hundred percent healed from her years in an abusive marriage, and I fear she might never be, but at least the spark is back in her eyes. I would do anything to make sure it remained there.

"Fine. Whatever they offered for this stupid ass job, call them back and add twenty percent. If they agree, I'll do it."

I rock back in my chair, confident in the fact that they'll turn down my obscenely high request. I mentally calculate how much money I have left in my savings and how long it will last while Gwen lets out a squeal of delight, turns around in her chair, and pulls out her cell phone to make the call.

CHAPTER 2
Layla

With my eyes closed, I reverently wrap my left hand around the neck of the guitar, letting the weight of the instrument rest gently on top of my jean-clad thighs. I drape my right arm over the wide, flat side of the hollow piece of wood and rest my palm against the strings. With my head tilted to the side, I listen quietly, half expecting to hear a pulse or some other sign of life—something to break me out of this funk I'm in.

My name, Layla Page Carlysle, practically screams amazing musician thanks to my father naming me after his favorite Eric Clapton song and his most beloved guitarist, Jimmy Page, twenty-four years ago. Lately, I've spent most of my alone time pulling this guitar out of its hiding spot from the back of my walk-in closet, buried underneath clothes and boxes of shoes, and cradling it to my body in the hopes that the nineteen-sixty Gibson Hummingbird will bring me back to life, breathe *something* back into me so I don't feel so empty. I long for the sixteen inch wide, flat top, mahogany acoustic guitar to play something with meaning, something with substance. Something to help me belt out the chords of a song *I* wrote that will shake my fans to their cores and call to their souls.

But just like every other time I have a few minutes to myself without the shrill, ear-piercing scream of adoring fans, the incessant questions thrown at me from curious journalists, or two dozen members of my management team, production team, wardrobe consultants, and every other well-meaning member of the entourage that's paid to hover over me, the guitar won't do anything other than sit in my lap waiting for *me* to wake it up.

I can't do it. No matter how hard I try, I can't get my fingers to strum the Hummingbird. I can't produce even one note and haven't been able to since my father, Jack, walked out the door. The guitar had been a gift from him on my tenth birthday. That was the year I discovered the one thing in the world that made me happy, aside from him.

"Where's my little hummingbird?!"

My dad's booming, happy voice carried through the house even though I was down in the basement in his home recording studio.

Despite the fact he knew exactly where I was, he'd still shout for me when he came home from work and walked through the door. Every day since my birthday, I'd go straight to the studio and play the guitar he gave me after school. I loved my guitar and I loved my dad. It was his guitar, given to him by his dad when he was a kid, and now he had given it to me.

He had showed me where to place my fingers on the frets and how to strum a basic chord progression.

"Okay, the first chord you're going to learn is the C major chord open. Put your ring finger on the fifth string, third fret," my dad explained as he took my hand and placed it in position on the neck of the guitar. "Then put your middle finger on the fourth string, second fret," he continued, once again finagling my fingers to the right spot. "Lastly, put your pointer finger on the second string, first fret."

He moved his hands away from mine as soon as they were exactly where he wanted them, stood back, and smiled down at me.

"Now, strum down from the fifth string twice, slowly."

I could never forget the look on his face when I strummed the guitar those first few times. Within a half hour, I could play every note without having to look down and make sure my fingers were in the right spots. His face lit up with the biggest smile I had ever seen, and he immediately started teaching me how to read music and play songs.

We'd spend hours down there together every single day, and I couldn't think of anything else I would rather do than spend time with him. Plus, it made Mom mad and that was okay with me. Mom didn't like anything that made me happy, but Dad said I should just ignore her.

"Layla Page! You are supposed to be working on your speech for my charity event at the children's hospital!" my mom yelled angrily down to me. Her order was drowned out by the sound of my dad's footsteps coming down the stairs.

"Oh, leave her be, Eve. That event is weeks away, and all she has to do is talk about her two-day stay with them last year when we thought she had pneumonia," my dad yelled up the stairs to her as he walked off the bottom step and gave me a wink. I immediately stopped worrying about how irritated she would be when we finally surfaced from the studio in a few hours now that my dad was there. I had a surprise for him, and I was too excited to care about my mom yelling at him, complaining he spends all his free time with me and never pays attention to her.

"There's my beautiful girl! How was school today?" Dad asked as he rushed over to my side and placed a kiss on top of my head.

"It was boring. But I got an A on my spelling test."

My dad laughed and pulled up a chair next to me, resting his elbows on his knees.

"Never tell anyone I told you this, hummingbird, but school never stops being boring," he said with a smile. "Now, show me what you've been practicing."

I tried to hide my excitement, but it showed all over my face with a smile that stretched from ear-to-ear and my eyes dancing with anticipation. I could barely sit still.

"Well, I got tired of playing *Leaving on a Jet Plane*. I know you said it's good for beginners because it only uses three chords, but that song sucks and it's depressing," I told him honestly as I positioned my fingers on the right frets and concentrated on what I was about to do.

"Well, alright then, show me what you learned!" my dad told me with another laugh.

I immediately closed my eyes and began strumming the first couple of notes to the song I'd secretly been teaching myself every day after school. One of my dad's favorites. I always forgot where I was when I played. I forgot who was in the room with me and couldn't hear people talking or anyone making noise. I forgot about everything but the music and how it made me feel—like I was free.

I finished the song a few minutes later and opened my eyes to find my dad staring at me with his mouth open and tears in his own eyes.

"You just played *Wonderful Tonight* flawlessly," he whispered.

"I know," I told him nonchalantly with a shrug of my shoulders as I looked back down at the guitar and fiddled with the strings.

"That was amazing, honey. I don't even know grown men who have been in the industry all their life that could pick up a guitar for the first time and play something like that after only a few weeks," he told me in awe.

"That's probably because their guitars don't take them away. Mine can take me anywhere I want to go if I just close my eyes."

He continued to stare at me while I started to play the song again for him. I kept right on playing when he spoke next. I was already lost in my own world of music, but I could still hear him. I could always hear my daddy when he spoke.

"Don't you ever forget that, hummingbird. You can go anywhere you want to go, be anything you want to be. Play because you love it and for no other reason. The day you stop loving it is the day it becomes a job. Making music should never be a job."

I stopped loving it the day he walked out on my mother and me. I could understand why he would want to leave her. That part had never been a mystery to me. Even as a teenager, I knew he felt trapped. I could see the unhappiness etched on his face. He was tired of the arguments, tired of the guilt, and tired

29

of not being happy.

"You look sad, Daddy."

"Don't worry about me, hummingbird. I'll be okay. I have you and that's all I'll ever need to be happy."

I didn't blame him, really. I was the stupid, naïve one who thought that I could be enough for him.

My mother never wanted children and she made that perfectly clear to me on a daily basis.

"You are more trouble than you're worth. I always knew having a child would ruin everything."

She never wanted to ruin her body or have another human being share my father's time and attention. I lost track of how many times she and my father fought over me. I was an accident, something that never should have been. But he begged and pleaded with her not to terminate the pregnancy. He promised her he'd do anything she asked if she only did this one important thing for him. The first time I heard that argument I was six years old.

"I knew promising to go through with having that child was a bad idea. All of your stupid promises you made me when I was pregnant about how you'd do anything for me if I kept it were all lies. All you care about is HER!"

At least back then he wanted me. He really wanted me.

The majority of my early life, my mother ignored me unless she felt like she wasn't getting enough attention. But after

I learned how to play the guitar, and my father taught me how to harmonize and sing as well, she could no longer pretend like I didn't exist. Especially when strangers stopped her in the grocery store to tell her how beautiful my voice was the previous night during a school concert. Teachers, faculty members, and the women she spent every afternoon at the club with pulled her aside to tell her how amazing my natural talent was and how they'd never seen anyone so young play a guitar with such passion. My mother knew at that moment she'd finally found a way for me to pay her back for the misery she endured as my mother. I could never forget the fight they had the evening he died. It was long and loud and things were said that could never be unheard.

"I HATE her! Do you hear me, Jack? I can't even stand to be in the same room with that ungrateful brat! And all you do is coddle her. She can fiddle around on an instrument and carry a tune. Why the hell shouldn't she finally pay us back for all these years of putting up with her?"

My mother wanted to capitalize on my talents. My father just wanted me to be a kid for as long as possible. He knew I had more talent than anyone he'd ever seen, but he also knew what the pressure to be something more could do to that talent. It would turn it into something you worked your fingers to the bone for, something you sweat blood and tears for, instead of something you loved. In his career, as the owner of

Hummingbird Records, he saw that happen to more than one person over the years. He didn't want that for me, his little girl, not now, not ever. He wanted the choice to be mine when I was old enough to make it, not when I was just learning how to become a woman.

As I sat in my room that night, with the journal I wrote songs in resting on my lap, I heard the words I had always wished my father would say to her when she was going off on one of her tirades.

"I can't do this anymore, Eve. I want out. I want a divorce."

My heart had sped up and I held my breath when he said those words. I wanted to jump up and down on my bed and scream with excitement. He was leaving her and he'd take me with him. No more fighting, no more unhappiness, no more guilt.

When he walked out the door that night to supposedly clear his head, he had no way of knowing that all of his hopes and dreams for me would be erased within the hour. He would never know that even before his SUV wrapped itself around a tree, events were put in motion and choices were made to guarantee his opinions never saw the light of day. Someone else's dreams and someone else's wishes were piled so high on top of my teenage shoulders that each and every day, I grew weary from all of the pressure to be what someone else wanted.

Even though I never heard him say it during their fight, my mother told me he wasn't planning on just leaving her. He hated every aspect of his life, and as much as it pained him, he needed to leave me as well.

"Your father said he needed a clean break and a new life. Music just didn't make him happy anymore, and I guess neither did we. I told you, he explained it all in the note he left."

My mother's weak attempts at comforting me when other people were in the room fell short. She didn't lie about the note. She'd showed it to me plenty of times to prove I wasn't as special as I assumed whenever I would question her about my father's motives.

The day my father walked out the door and never came home, coincidentally, became the day that music became a job for me—the one thing he never wanted. But he didn't want *me*, so why did I care anymore? I'd read the note; I knew how he really felt. I took up too much of his time, and he felt weighted down, like he had nothing left for himself. Everything he had to give went to me, and he was tired of it. He wanted to live for himself for once. The first time I read the note, I signed on the dotted line my mother put in front of me without even caring what I was doing. I was fifteen years old and just lost my best friend—the one person who had always protected me and stood his ground for me and who suddenly decided I was too much to handle. I had nothing on my side at that point except for my music, but after a while, even that left me.

I wasn't free anymore. On days like today, I feel like I never will be.

At the sound of footsteps coming up the porch of my log cabin, my eyes fly open and the past disappears from my thoughts. I nestle the guitar back into its red velvet cushion in the case laying open by my feet and quickly snap the lid shut. With the heels of my well-worn, cowboy boots, I slide the guitar case under the couch and out of site before getting up to greet my guest.

The door pushes open without the formalities of a knock and my mother, Eve Carlysle, waltzes into the room looking every bit like the diva she is. Her perfectly highlighted and trimmed strawberry blonde hair hangs poker straight and ends just below her chin.

"New suit?" I ask her. I don't really care, but I know if I don't point it out right away, she'll have something to say about how I'm always too concerned with myself to notice anything about her. It's a fight I'm definitely not up for having today.

"Chanel. No one else really does perfectly tailored suits like they do. It fits me like a glove, doesn't it?" she asks, turning this way and that to show off the new outfit my latest single helped her buy. "Look at how tiny the white trim makes my waist look."

I cringe slightly as I get a close-up view of the white, perfectly creased dress pants. Only Eve Carlysle would have the balls to wear white after Labor Day. She thinks it's okay because it accentuates the long legs she sculpts and tones with a personal trainer every other day, also courtesy of my royalty checks.

She looks just like a show business mother, minus the mothering part.

When she's satisfied with my perusal of her outfit, she breezes past me. The click of her black, four-inch Louboutin heels across my hardwood floors echo through the cabin, and the sickeningly sweet fragrance of her signature Gloria Vanderbilt perfume wafts through the air, the scent cloying and making me sneeze.

I slide my hands into the pockets of my jeans and stare at the woman I barely even recognize anymore. My mother's not the June Cleaver type, never one to hug me when I scraped a knee or soothe me when I had the flu, but the coldness that has come over her ever since I've made a name for myself in the music industry is astounding. She takes the role of being my manager very seriously. Nothing and no one can ruin the empire she's painstakingly built brick by brick. My mother will never be ashamed of the way she's gone about things: coercing her young, impressionable teenage daughter into signing an ironclad deal when she'd just lost her father and found out he had grown tired of her. How could she feel even a moment's worth of shame when she has everything she's ever dreamed of? I'm exactly where she's always wanted me—under her thumb, doing everything she dictates.

"I have a few photographs you need to sign for the fan club and the list of radio stations you'll be doing call-ins for tomorrow morning starting at six," my mother states a she pulls a stack of black and white glossy photos out of her Birkin bag along with several sheets of paper.

I make my way across the room to my kitchen table so I can stare out of the floor-to-ceiling windows that overlook the woods surrounding the cabin while she methodically organizes the stack of photos next to a black Sharpie marker, standing there with her arms crossed in front of her waiting for me to do as she wishes. Just like always.

I pull out a chair, the legs scraping across the floor, and sit down with a small sigh, wishing—not for the first time—that I can say no to my mother. These three days are supposed to be vacation days for me and the band, time for us to regroup and take a break from the back-to-back touring schedule Eve booked the year before. For six months, I've done nothing but think about these three days, dreaming about not having to set my alarm in the morning and being able to take my coffee out onto my wrap around porch so I can watch the sun rise over the hills of Tennessee. Three whole days without my mother telling me what to say, what to wear, and what to sing.

I should have known it wouldn't be that easy. It never is with Eve. She's always working, always thinking about new ways to make a buck and increase my value. I've tried many times over the years to defy my mother, to do things on my own time, my own terms. But it never ends well. My mother controls every aspect of my life, and I've allowed it to happen.

Sure, I was young at the time, and I'd just lost the one person who I thought truly cared about me, but I should have known better. Eve made me promises and dangled dreams in front of me that could be mine if I just reached out and took them. I signed every paper she put in front of me the day of the funeral, thinking I'd finally done something to make my mother proud of me, make her love me. It didn't take long for me to realize it was all a lie.

It comes as no surprise to me as I sit down at the cedar table that the promise of vacation time was a sham. I should have known better than to dream, even of something as small as a few uninterrupted days alone in my cabin. Nothing good ever comes from dreaming except disappointment.

I pick up the black marker and begin the tedious process of signing my name to hundreds of copies of a picture of me smiling straight into the camera with a cowboy hat on my head and my long, blonde hair hanging in waves around my shoulders. I don't even pay attention to the name I scribble. As I flip picture, after picture, after picture, all I do is stare into the eyes of the woman in the photo and wonder why it looks nothing like the one I see in the mirror every day.

CHAPTER 3

BRADY

She's late. Of course she's fucking late. God forbid she realizes the world doesn't revolve around her.

Reclining comfortably in my chair, my booted foot resting on one knee, and my fingers tapping a steady rhythm on top of the conference room table, I'm sure I look like the epitome of calm and cool. Inside, I'm about to punch the God dammed wall. Leave it to the princess to not give a shit about a meeting regarding her own personal safety.

I watch as her mother, Eve, glances at an expensive diamond and gold watch on her slim wrist and huffs in irritation.

Right there with you, sister.

Gwen had made all the arrangements with Eve Carlysle about the job, so I have yet to talk to her, aside from our initial introduction when I first got to Hummingbird Records a half hour ago. She seems nice enough, concerned about her daughter's safety and all that crap, tells me I have full access to Layla, and she'll make sure this whole thing is my call. Whatever I need, whatever I ask—it's mine. She says her daughter most likely won't be happy about the whole thing, but I expect that. And I don't give a shit.

As soon as I got over my initial shock that the twenty-percent increase I demanded to perform this job was accepted, I began doing research on the twenty-three-year-old singer. Google was like the Great and Powerful Oz in all things relating to Layla Carlysle.

Pulling out the few printed pieces of paper I'd stuck in the inside pocket of my black leather jacket, I open them up and scan the words probably for the twentieth time while the small handful of people in the room talk amongst themselves quietly.

To say Gwen was irritated with me that I clearly had no idea who this person was is an understatement.

"Layla Page Carlyle, born to loving parents Eve and Jack, led a pampered upper class life," I read aloud from the screen of my computer while Gwen perched on the edge of my desk. "Father started up one of the largest recording labels ever to hit the music scene in Nashville. Mother worked as a secretary for him. Layla attended—"

"How do you not know all of this information already?" Gwen questioned as she swung one of her legs back and forth, her foot banging against my desk over and over.

I reached over and placed my hand on her knee, squeezing my fingers just enough to get her attention. She scowled at me and I removed me hand, not really giving a shit if I pissed her off. At least she stopped making all of that racket against my desk.

"Why in the hell SHOULD I know this information about her?"

I continued to scroll through the article once I knew she wasn't going to go back to annoying me with her foot pounding. Now she was just going to annoy me with her talking.

"Oh, gee, I don't know. Maybe because she's only one of the biggest recording artists in the country? She's been around for years; she's grown up in the public eye. EVERYONE knows all about Layla Carlysle," Gwen informed me.

"Well, sorry to burst your bubble, but I've never heard of her. And from what I found on YouTube, I'm pretty sure there's a reason for it. That shit is straight up Britney Spears, God awful—make-your-ears-bleed—shitty dance club music," I told her with a slight shiver as I recalled the few minutes I had spent listening to a couple of her songs last night. Time I could never get back. I should add another ten percent onto the bill just for that shit.

"Oh come on, it's fun! It's great to dance to. It's feel-good music. Emma loves her. She always makes me play her newest

CD when I drive her to school in the mornings," Gwen said with a smile.

"That is NOT feel-good music. Feel good music is *Back in Black* by AC/DC or *Blaze of Glory* by Bon Jovi."

"Whoa, slow down there, Grandpa. You might bust a hip." She raised one of her eyebrows and asked with a laugh, "You do know you're only twenty-nine and not fifty-nine, correct?" Gwen shook her head at me. "You really need to expand your musical horizons."

She jumped off of the edge of my desk and walked over to her own, sinking down in the seat, crossing her legs, and folding her hands in her lap.

Gwen started to ramble facts off from memory. "Layla went to the best private schools up until she started singing professionally and enjoyed your typical high society life while growing up. She lost her father at fifteen when he went to run some errands and wrapped his car around a tree. From what I heard, though, he was packing up and moving out. Wanted a divorce and wanted to get the hell out of doge. Anyway, Layla's mother immediately took over Hummingbird Records, and within a few short weeks, Layla was signed to the record label and producing music."

I clicked on the print button while Gwen took a breath. Who needed the internet when I had a sister who was addicted to tabloid magazines. While the printer whirred to life and spit out the pages of information, Gwen continued.

"Layla was an instant success at fifteen. She had that whole sweet girl-next-door demeanor going on, and she really does have a solid singing voice, although in my personal opinion, she doesn't stretch it like she should. Anyway, within two months of its release, her first album went platinum and a month after that she was singing to sold out venues across the globe. Her first couple of songs, *I Love That Boy*, *Girls Night Out*, and *Wishing for the Weekend*, went straight to number one within hours of their release. Totally crazy how much her fans adore her and will seriously buy absolutely anything she puts her name on. *Wishing for the Weekend* was at the top of the charts for a record breaking seventeen straight weeks, beating the competition that held that record previously since nineteen-ninety-five."

I got up from my desk and walked over to the printer to grab the pages that pretty much contained all of the information Gwen rattled off. I folded them up and stuck them in my coat so I could go over them later when Gwen wasn't looking at me like I'd been living under a rock just because I couldn't have cared less about some Britney wannabe that had probably never even heard of Led Zeppelin.

I skim the pages one last time and the information on the last page jumps out at me, just like it had every time I read through this shit.

Layla was an overnight star and through the years her fans have remained loyal and enthusiastic, embracing each new record with mounting fervor. Given her overnight success and increased net worth, Layla has remained humble and close to her roots.

I snort to myself at that last line, knowing full well either Layla herself or someone in her camp came up with those carefully constructed words. No one born with a silver spoon in her mouth and worth more money than I will ever see in my lifetime could still be humble.

YOU were born with a silver spoon in your mouth.

I ignore the words my conscience screams. Sure, my parents have money, and Gwen and I had grown up well-off, but we didn't take advantage of that shit, and we didn't stick around long enough for it to change us. We are normal, everyday people who have to work hard for the money we earn, and we don't take handouts from anyone. We are grateful for what we've been given, and Gwen and I have been through more hard times than this Layla Carlysle could even imagine. I may not have been in the private detective business for long, but what I see doing this job and my time as a cop in Nashville has given me enough real life experience about just how the world's rich and famous behave: always a good show for the public—all sweet and innocent—and then as soon as the cameras are off and no one is looking, they turn into man-eating sharks ready to chew up and spit out anyone who got in their way.

I quickly refold the papers and shove them back into my coat pocket as the door to the conference room opens. I keep up my *I'm-bored-to-death-and-don't-give-a-rat's-ass* attitude as an entourage of five people enter the room, ending with the object of this meeting.

Google image search and YouTube don't have anything on Layla Carlysle in person. She stalks into the room wearing a tattered jean skirt that clings to her hips and ends not much further down, showing off smooth, toned legs that look a mile long with the four-inch fuck me heels on her feet. The click of her shoes on the tile floor as she rounds the long table forces my gaze away from the naked legs I so desperately wanted to slide my hands up so I can feel if they're as smooth as they look. She tucks them away behind the glossy mahogany table, which is probably for the best. The first thing that strikes me about her is that she's not all done up in pageant hair, make-up, and sequins like she usually is in all the pictures I've seen of her online. The black, long-sleeved Jimi Hendrix concert T-shirt she's wearing looks out of place with the image I had in my mind of how she'd look in person. That thing looks like it's swallowing her whole. It isn't molded to her body like the get-up she normally wears in the tabloids, but it does hang loosely off of one arm, and I can see a glimpse of the skin of her shoulder. There is a major contrast in public Layla and private Layla, ending with her hair. The wild, wavy blonde mane that is usually always around her shoulders and trailing down her back is pulled away from her face in some kind of messy knot thing at her neck, some of the strands escaping the knot and framing her face. If I didn't know what kind of person this chick was, I'd have to say that she had been hand-picked for me with the concert t-shirt, the long legs, the natural face without all that gunk on it, and the blonde hair that isn't a fire hazard from all the hairspray...in other words, perfect.

Fuck, stop ogling the client. And absolutely stop picturing her naked.

As Layla takes a seat directly across from me, I stare her down until she removes a pair of black sunglasses with a band of crystals near the temples that probably cost more than my townhouse.

Startling, crystal blue eyes look at me from beneath the longest eyelashes I've ever seen as everyone else that has entered the room with her takes their seats and calls out greetings.

She eyes me with a small hint of annoyance on her face, her eyebrows furrowing as she studies me and her full, heart-shaped mouth pressed tightly in a straight line with no sign of a smile anywhere.

Good. Let her be pissed. It will make this job so much easier when she starts acting like a bitch and I can put her in her place when she realizes she's not the one calling the shots this time.

"Thank you, everyone, for coming in on your day off," Eve says to the room from her place at the head of the table. "I've called you all here to discuss a concerning matter that, as of late, has forced me to take some extreme measures."

Eve is cut off suddenly as the conference room door flies open and all eyes turn and see a tall, brown-haired man waltz in. I groan internally as he smirks, watching all of the women in the room sit up straighter and begin fidgeting with their hair and clothing. I can only assume the six foot-one, a hundred and seventy pound, lean-muscled man who makes his way over to the empty chair next to Layla is Finn Michaelson: current bodyguard to the diva. And if the tabloids and Gwen are to be believed, Layla's on-again, off-again lover. I have a dossier on every single person who surrounds Layla on a daily basis. I know Finn Michaelson used to be a Marine before receiving an honorable discharge five years prior for being wounded in action in Afghanistan. The bullet he'd taken to the left shoulder meant he's no longer fit for combat, but he is still an excellent marksman and could disarm and overpower a threat faster than you could blink.

On paper, I figure I could get along quite well with Finn Michaelson, even though on principal, the fact that we were Navy/Marine should mean we remain archenemies. But sitting here, watching him eye-fuck every female in the room and smirking at the irritation on my face I can't manage to mask makes me rethink my opinion of the ex-Marine. I don't have the time or the patience for some pretty-boy who can't keep his dick in his pants. As a bodyguard, this guy should be more concerned with who he's protecting than who he's going to take to bed later that night. The number one rule in this business: never mix it with pleasure. Finn Michaelson has a lot to learn.

With a fist-bump to one of the production managers as he walks by, I watch closely as Finn gets to Layla's side and leans down, pressing his lips to her offered cheek with a loud *smack* before pulling out his chair, momentarily diverting her attention from me.

"Hey there, gorgeous," I hear Finn whisper to her, his eyes straying to a woman across the table from him as he blatantly checks out the cleavage popping out of her shirt.

He flops down in his chair and clasps his hands behind his head, refusing to break his eyes from my glare.

"As I was saying," Eve says irritably, shooting a nasty look in Finn's direction, "Layla has been receiving some very troubling correspondence the last few months. I've decided to hire a third party to investigate the issue and help make sure everyone on this tour, not just Layla, is safe and secure. Mr. Brady Marshall will be with us twenty-four seven to make sure we are doing everything we can to protect ourselves and to find out just how big of a threat the person sending these letters seems to be. Whatever questions he has, you answer them as honestly and thoroughly as possible. Anything he tells you to do, you do it without question. And that goes for every single person at this table."

Eve stares pointedly at Layla, most likely knowing full well that her daughter will be the most difficult one to get on board with this plan.

Oh this is going to be too much fun.

Everyone goes around the room introducing themselves to me, and I nod at each person in return. Even with memorizing everyone's names and faces while they say hello and tell me what their job titles are, my eyes remain trained on Layla as she glares at her mother the entire time.

"I know you aren't happy about this, but I'm only doing it to make sure nothing happens to you," Eve pleads with Layla, a hint of an emotional quiver lacing her voice.

Finn covers up a small snort of laughter with a cough and a hand over his mouth, and my eyes flash to his face with a stern glare. I turn my gaze back to the woman across from me and watch a muscle tick in her jaw as she stares at the older woman standing at the head of the table.

I find it pretty interesting she obviously knows nothing about me being hired to protect her. And by the looks of it, she isn't too thrilled.

Even from this distance, I can see tears pooling in Eve's eyes. She is genuinely concerned about her daughter, and this spoiled brat better take notice of that real quick and cut back the attitude she's giving the older woman.

Picking her sunglasses up from the table in front of her, Layla slides them back on to her face and covers up those gorgeous blue eyes.

Jesus, what is wrong with me? She's just a woman. An insanely hot woman whose legs I can just imagine wrapped around my waist while her blue eyes stare up at me as I pound into her.

"Fine, whatever you need to do. If that's all, I need to get to sound check and go over the new set list with the band," Layla states in a quiet, bored voice as I readjust myself after the mental image running through my brain.

Eve nods in Layla's direction, a look of pleasure on her face, obviously relieved her daughter has gone along with the plan without too much of a fuss. Everyone else at the table stands up and starts to leave, waving their goodbyes and saying their nice-to-meet-yous to me as they walk out of the room. Layla, Finn, and I are the last to stand. The three of us walk down our respective sides of the table at the same time until I'm standing in front of the door, blocking Layla's exit with Finn standing close behind her.

Layla comes to a sudden stop before she barrels into my chest, the top of her head stopping right at my chin so she has to look up at me. Even with her eyes artfully hidden behind her dark sunglasses, I can see the irritation all over her face. She crosses her arms protectively in front of her, and I can't help but smirk down at her as her eyes trail up and down, taking stock.

The head in my pants that does most of my thinking for me tries to prove he's in charge when once again, my brain is filled with images that have no right being there. I suddenly have the urge to yank her hair out of its knot so all of those soft waves are sliding across my thighs as she takes me in her mouth or maybe just clutch a handful of her hair in my fist as I bend her over the desk in the corner and slam inside of her. The photos on the internet and the videos Gwen made me watch don't do this woman justice. Saying she is beautiful and has a body made for sin is an understatement. Her blatant perusal of me makes my dick twitch and my mood sour.

"Can I help you with something?" Layla asks with just the right amount of attitude in her voice, a voice that practically flows out in song form even with the arrogance in it. No wonder she became a singer. That voice is silky smooth with just a touch of gravel in it that's practically made for singing rock ballads or belting out the blues. She could be the next Lita Ford or Janice

Joplin. So why the fuck is she wasting time singing teeny-bopper shit? Because that's where the money is, obviously.

I force myself back into professional mode and remember who it is I'm dealing with: a spoiled bitch.

Feeling in the mood to play with her a little to gauge just how many buttons of hers I can push without even trying, I lean my head down until my mouth is close to her ear, breathing in the soft, floral scent, from what I assume is expensive-ass perfume probably harvested from diamonds and shit.

"I'm sure you can help me with a lot of things, Miss Carlysle. But for right now, you can get me a list of everyone you know who doesn't like you."

I move back away from her a few inches and watch as the breath she'd been holding slowly leaves her lungs.

Well isn't that cute. Little princess is affected by my close proximity. Good to know.

I look down at her and smirk, totally enjoying the movement at the corners of her mouth as her full lips began to form a small, friendly smile, and she lets down her guard just a little bit.

Perfect. A *little bit* is all I need to make her realize she isn't running this show anymore.

"I'm sure that list is pretty fucking long, so you might want to get busy," I finish with a wink.

The partial smile dies from Layla's face, and with a huff,

she brushes past me, slamming her shoulder into mine.

With a chuckle to myself and a wink to her boy toy as he follows close on her heels, I pull my own sunglasses out of my inside coat pocket and slip them on before turning to follow the woman who's most likely cursing my name.

CHAPTER 4
Layla

"That arrogant prick. Who the hell does he think he is?" I ask Finn angrily as we walk out into the bright sun and over to his black Chevy Tahoe.

"I think he's—"

"*I'm sure that list is pretty fucking long, so you might want to get busy,*" I say in a deep, scruffy voice, mimicking said arrogant prick and cutting Finn off as I carry on with my tirade.

I wince as I sit down on the scorching hot leather seats, but even having my thighs and ass on fire right now doesn't stop me from continuing.

"What kind of a guy says that to his *client*? A pompous asshole, that's who. What a piece of work. He's not fooling anyone with that leather jacket, tight T-shirt, and dark stubble. Talk about having a long list of people who don't like you," I complain angrily as Finn starts up the SUV and blasts the air conditioning before pulling out of the parking lot. "That guy probably has a list that could circle the globe twice and still have enough names left over to make it to the moon and back."

My outburst comes to a stop when I realize Finn is completely silent, which is pretty unusual for him. Finn always has something to say, especially when it comes to me.

"Are you even listening to me?" I ask, glancing over at him just in time to see a smirk disappear. "Were you just *smirking* at me?"

Finn lets out a small laugh as he hits the turn signal at the first intersection.

"Layla, I have been listening to every single word you say. Listening *and* taking notes. You think Billy Badass is pretty, and you want to play with his gun," Finn states sarcastically, dimples forming on his cheeks as he presses his lips together in irritation. His bright blue eyes are swimming with anger hidden just below the surface.

"Are you high? You haven't listened to one word I've said since we got in this car. I thought I'd give him the benefit of the doubt even though Eve hired him, and surprise, surprise, he shows his true colors."

I turn my gaze to the front window and cross my arms over my chest with a huff.

Why the hell did he have to smell so good? From a distance, the jerk seemed bored and like he hadn't showered or shaved in days. Up close, he was all chiseled jaw hidden underneath day-old stubble, and I had a fleeting thought about what that prickly hair would feel like scratching against my inner thighs. A recent shower was evident by the clean, soapy smell with a hint of masculine body wash that came from him and surrounded me, tickling my senses since I stood so close.

I almost sniffed his fucking shirt. I actually looked him up and down like he was a piece of meat, which he obviously noticed. Son of a bitch!

"We don't know anything about this guy yet. Just because Eve hired him, doesn't mean he's all bad. Although, I have to say, a little bad might do you some good," Finn says with another smile aimed my way while we wait at a stop light.

"If he's on my mother's payroll, he's the enemy. If there's one thing I've learned over the past year, it's that. With the exception of you, of course," I tell him, pasting a fake smile on my face to hide the pain my words bring.

I can feel Finn's eyes on me, but I refuse to look over at him. I can't stand the look of pity that I know is on his face.

"Not every guy you meet is going to be like Sam," Finn says softly.

I bite down on my bottom lip and squeeze my eyes closed to ward off the memories that name brings, but it's no use. They overwhelm me and I can't help but succumb to them, just like I do every time I think of him.

Stepping into the bathroom at the Los Angeles Staples Center during a commercial break at the Grammys, I rush into an empty stall while Finn stands guard just outside the door, and Sam waits for me back in our seats. As I secure the lock on the bathroom door, a sparkle catches my eye, and I glance down at the six carat, radiant-cut diamond on the ring finger of my left hand. After seven months of dating, Sam dropped down on one knee and proposed last week. It was fast, I was young, and Finn wouldn't stop listing all the reasons why it was a bad idea to marry Sam Stettner, a twenty-eight-year-old rising star in the country music industry. Sam liked to call me his lucky charm. He'd been trying to make a break in the industry for years, and a few weeks after we started dating, his new album went to the top of the charts, and he'd been in high demand ever since.

Finn just didn't understand how lonely I was. Finn had never been lonely a day in his life; women always wanted to be close to him or love him. The small handful of relationships I'd had over the years always fizzled quickly. The guys couldn't handle my tour schedule or other people demanding my attention. Mostly, they couldn't handle the fact that I was a huge star, their egos often getting the best of them and the green-eyed monster of jealousy rearing its ugly head. But Sam was different. He was happy for all of my success, and since he was in the business, he understood everything that being a singer entailed. He supported whatever decision I made, and for the first time, my mother and I were actually civil to one another. She liked the idea of Sam and I together and fully supported our upcoming marriage. Normally, the things my mother wanted me to do made me cringe, and I attempted to do the exact opposite just to piss her off. But I couldn't do that with Sam. I loved him too much to be petty.

As I hung my red sparkly clutch, that matched my Badgley Mischka dress perfectly, on the hook behind the door, two female voices broke the silence in the spacious bathroom. Instantly, I recognized them and smiled to myself. Chloe and Aubrey were my two back-up singers. Both had been with me since the very beginning. They were three years older than me, and growing up on the road as a teenager, they helped me with my homework and gave me advice on boys that I couldn't or wouldn't ask my mother for. They were good friends, and I was glad to have them in my life.

"Did you get a look at that gaudy rock he stuck on her finger? Jesus. Talk about obvious. I'll take 'I'm Trying to Buy Your Trust' for two-thousand, Alex.'" Chloe laughed as I heard the faucet turn on.

"She is so damn clueless it's sad. I almost feel bad about

fucking him last week while she was at the studio, but then I remembered how much money she makes in just one fucking weekend and it doesn't seem to bother me anymore," Aubrey added, the contempt obvious in her voice.

I held my fingers still against the door lock where they froze seconds ago when the conversation began. I had begun to leave the stall to say hello, but now I couldn't do anything but stand here holding my breath with my heart beating out of my chest.

They weren't talking about me. There was no way this could be about Sam and me. They wouldn't do that to me.

"It's not her fault her mother bribed him to go out with her by guaranteeing his music would see the light of day, and he got a bonus for scoring a 'yes' when he popped the question. With a ring her mother bought using her money, no less," Chloe told Aubrey with obvious fake pity lacing her voice. "But really, have you ever met anyone so stupid?"

The water turned off and the sounds of purses unzipping and compacts opening and closing took its place.

"Layla walks around here like she's such hot shit. I'm so sick of it. If you ask me, she deserves to marry that greedy dick," Aubrey added with scorn. "But oh what a dick it is!"

The two women cackled together like witches while they finished touching up their make-up and walked out of the bathroom, never noticing Finn standing guard around the corner, completely oblivious to the devastated occupant in the bathroom.

I faked a stomach bug once I was finally able to pull myself up off of the bathroom floor that night. With one look, Finn knew I didn't have any kind of bug. He could read it all over my face.

"I would never say that to you. Unless of course you completely lose your mind and take that idiot back. At which point, I might have to give you some harsh, strongly worded pieces of wisdom. "

I forced out a watery laugh and burrowed my face deeper into Finn's neck as he tightened his arms around me.

"I'm so sorry, Layla. I can't believe Eve would do that to you. That heartless bitch is getting a piece of my mind when she gets home tonight," Finn stated angrily.

"No!" I exclaimed loudly, pulling my head away from the comfort of him so I could look at his face. "You also have to promise me that you'll leave it alone. Leave Eve alone. She's already threatened to go to the tabloids about your past and—"

Finn reached a hand up and covered my mouth with his fingers. "Hush. I'm not afraid of Eve. I'm sick and tired of her doing this to you. I can't just stand by and let it continue to happen.

I pulled his fingers away from my mouth and put on an air of confidence that I didn't feel.

"I'll be fine. I'm strong. I can handle whatever she throws at me, you know that. You're my best friend, Finn. I would never forgive myself if she went through with her threats. You finally have some peace in your life. You've forgiven yourself for the things that happened in Afghanistan. You've moved on with your life and all of that is buried now. I will not let her bring everything out into the open and ruin that for you."

Finn pulled me in closer and placed a soft kiss on the top of my head.

"We'll find a way. I swear to God, someday we will find a way to make that woman pay," Finn promised.

When Sam called to check up on me a few days after the Grammys, I told him I didn't love him, and I kept the ring. Sam sure as hell wasn't getting it back. I figured since it came out of my money, I might as well pawn it and give the proceeds to charity. My mother was beside herself when I told her I called off the engagement, saying I always ruin everything and that I should be ashamed of myself for hurting a perfectly good man.

I could have thrown it all back in her face, told her exactly what I overheard in the bathroom that day, letting her know I was finally finished with her manipulations.

I know exactly how far that would've got me. I know what happens when you defy my mother, and I will never make that same mistake again. I'm still paying the price for the one time I dared to stand up to her, still fielding questions from reporters who just won't let it go. I'm struggling to not feel ashamed for being so weak and backing down so easily when she won't budge just one little inch in regards to my music. All I want to do is record one song of my own. One. Just to see if it will go anywhere. Eve Carlysle doesn't let anyone make decisions like that but her. If it were just about me, I'd take her wrath again and again without hesitation. But it's not just about me. Finn's life and his well-being are at stake as well. Eve would crush him and the progress he's made since the war without batting an eye. She made her intentions known the first time he even hinted at exposing her and what she's done to me over the years. Finn told me all about the fight he had with her when he was first hired as my bodyguard. How she threatened to tell everyone that he wasn't the good guy he claimed to be. She had found out about how the war and PTSD finally caught up to him one night overseas. He had killed innocent civilians and did things he was ashamed of, things he couldn't even bare to share with me they were so ugly. He was dishonorably discharged from the marines because of his actions, but Eve made sure those files were sealed so she would always have something to hold over his head. She changed the past, altered his records, and used the information she'd garnered to keep him close and make sure he did exactly what she told him to do. I know Finn is a good person and he didn't mean to hurt anyone. It was all just too much for him, and he lost it for a little while. But he came home, got help, and healed himself and his wounded soul. As much as Finn and I love and care about each other, there's nothing we can do to change things. Finn has kept his promise these last eight months and never once said "I told you so" or tried to stand up to Eve again. I owe him everything and I will do whatever it takes to make sure he is never on the receiving end of her wrath again.

"I know not every guy is like Sam, but every guy will do exactly what Eve says," I remind him as we pull around the back of the Nashville Convention Center to get ready for the sound check for tonight's performance. "I mean look at this whole stalker thing she's contrived. A few weird letters from some guy over the course of a few months and suddenly she feels the need to act like a mother for the first time in her life and hire some thug off the street with a bad boy complex to step all over your toes. And of course she looks like a saint for doing it," I complain, my arms gesturing around me wildly as I grow more and more agitated when I think about my mother's actions.

"It was disgusting watching her stand at the head of the conference room table earlier and stare me down with all that fake compassion and concern," I continue, venom dripping from my voice as Finn puts the car in park but doesn't kill the engine. "That stupid, 'I'm an excellent mother' persona she only exhibits in the company of others. Everyone around that table ate it up and believed the worry she had for me was actually genuine. There was nothing I could do but concede; otherwise I would just look like an ungrateful bitch."

Finn nods his head in agreement but remains silent. "Especially when I swore I saw the makings of tears in her eyes—the perfect ruse to get everyone in the room on her side as she worried for her poor daughter's safety. Give me a fucking break."

We sat quietly for a few moments, listening to the hum of the engine, both of us staring straight ahead at the huge arena in front of us, lost in our own thoughts. Finn is the first one to speak.

"I've seen those letters, Layla. They were weird as hell. This guy travels to every single concert you ever do. He's made personal assessments about your performances that even the tabloids haven't caught on to. He's watching you really closely, and I have to be honest, that scares the shit out of me. And it should scare you as well. You have no idea what this creepy fuck is capable of. You have no idea what else he already knows about you. I agree with Eve on the fact that we need to be extra concerned when it comes to your safety. I just don't understand why she felt the need to go behind my back to make that happen."

I clench my jaw in anger and take a couple of deep, calming breaths before I reply.

"Okay, so you've read the letters that we still aren't even sure are real. But while you were busy doing that in her office before we left to come here, my lovely mother cornered me right outside the conference room. It's pretty obvious what her intentions are."

"Was it really necessary to hire a stranger to look into those letters? Finn is perfectly capable of doing his job," I told my mother as we stood outside the conference room after everyone had left the building and Finn disappeared to check on something before we followed. "Don't be so naïve, Layla. Finn is okay at what he does, but he doesn't have eyes in the back of his head. It never hurts to have someone else looking into this thing," she told me distractedly as she scrolled through emails on her Blackberry.

"Finn is more than *okay* at his job and you know it. There has to be another reason you're doing this, and it doesn't have anything to do with being concerned about my safety."

Eve finally looked up from her phone and threw an annoyed look my way, her eyes narrowing and her lips pursing together.

"If you're not safe, we don't make money, plain and simple. And obviously, having a stalker is always good for publicity. It makes the fans concerned for you and feel sympathetic towards you. By hiring outside help, there's no way it can be kept a secret. It will be public knowledge by this time tomorrow, and you'll have everyone eating out of your hands," she explained, glancing back down at her phone.

"I am not going to deceive my fans. They respect me and they believe in me. What happens when they find out this was all a hoax just to make them feel sorry for me?" I questioned angrily.

"It's all part of the business, *Hummingbird*."

I visibly winced when she used my father's nickname for me and said it with such scorn in her voice. She knew how much I hated it when she called me that.

"And if you know what's good for you, you won't question my decisions again. Otherwise, your precious fans will have a field day when they find out you suddenly went back into rehab," she said maliciously as she tossed her phone inside of her new Louis Vuitton purse, crossed her arms in front of her, and stared me down. "That little pill problem of yours was a pesky one to put a positive spin on, but I did it. And it can be done again. You think the reporters hound you now about your little stint at Betty Ford, imagine what kind of rabid dogs they'll turn into if you go back. Obviously, this would all work in my favor because publicity is publicity, and it still sells records. But do you really want all those questions to start again? 'Why did you want to kill yourself, Layla?' 'How could you possibly leave your poor mother behind when she's done so much for you?' 'You have it all, how could you hate your life so much?' Now, get your ass over to the convention center and stop trying to act like you're in charge. I own you. I will always own you and you better get used to it, *hummingbird*."

I block out the conversation with my mother that was entirely like all the rest of our conversations over the years as Finn finally shuts the car off and we leave the cool comfort of the air conditioning.

"I know we have a right to question Eve's motives about everything. I'll quit bugging you about the stalker thing, but in the meantime I'll do some legwork on this Brady guy and see what his story is. I still have military connections, and they can tell me if he's on the up and up or just another one of your mother's puppets. In the meantime, don't give him any ammunition to use against you. Don't do anything stupid and tone down the diva 'tude just a notch when you're around him," Finn says with a cocky smile.

"This 'diva 'tude' is essential to my well-being, my little minion," I throw back at him, trying to lighten the mood as we knock on a back door to the arena that says *Performers Only* and wait for it to be answered.

Finn and I both know that pretending to be a music diva is the only thing that keeps me sane most of the time. I can don the fancy clothes and the expensive jewelry and take on an air of sophistication and thinly veiled annoyance with those beneath me like it's a second skin. I have perfected that act over the years, and it's turned into a perfectly constructed wall that keeps my heart and mind intact and barely bruised. I can pretend like I don't care what people say about me, ignore the hate my mother surrounds me with, and act like my life is one big deliriously happy ball of parties, awards shows, and concerts. Finn is the only person in the world who knows the real me, who knows all of my hopes and dreams and the pain that eats away at my soul every time I get up on stage and fake a smile and happiness I never feel. Not even Sam, the man I thought I loved and wanted to spend the rest of my life with, had known the real me. The fact that I never even thought about showing him my father's guitar should have been a warning sign that I didn't really trust him. We were doomed from the start, and that's the only thing that makes all of it easier to handle.

A big, burly man with a bald head and skull earring hanging off of one ear finally answers our knock and shares a head nod with Finn before opening the door wider and letting us in.

"Miss Carlysle, it's good to see you again," the man says, his voice pleasant and soft and the complete opposite of his appearance.

"Thank you, Bones. It's good to see you too. Is the band already here?" I ask as we step through the door and follow him down a long, dark hallway.

"Yep, already setting up on stage. Some dude who said he was with security just got here a few minutes ago too. Name's Brady. He's on the list your mom gave me so I let him in already. He's sitting in the back row."

I thank Bones and Finn shares a handshake with him after he escorts us to the back stage area where I can already hear my bass player running through the scales and my drummer warming up with basic rudiments.

"Oh goody, Brady's here!" I exclaim to Finn with fake enthusiasm.

"Don't even try to pretend like the idea of him sitting there in the dark, in the very back row, with his face all broody and stubbly doesn't get your panties all in a bunch."

Finn gets a punch in the arm for that comment and my middle finger in his face before I walk away from him and up the stairs leading to the stage to warm up my voice and try NOT to think about the man at the back of the auditorium, watching my every move, and wondering if he's the enemy.

CHAPTER 5

BRADY

Like nails on a fucking chalkboard.

This music is going to drive me right back to drinking, I swear to Christ. All of this techno-electric shit is giving me a headache. Whatever happened to just sitting down at a microphone with an acoustic and a kick ass drummer?

Even though my ears are bleeding with all the synthesizing going on and the top forty, cheesy lyrics, I can't help but notice how amazing Layla looks on stage. She lights up the whole damn place as she rocks her hips to the beat and struts back and forth from one end of the stage to the other, making sure to use up all available space so the audience who will see her tonight will get their money's worth. Her choreographed moves are sensual without being over the top and fun without being too campy. I can tell they'll be just enough to get the younger members of the audience excited and have them jumping in unison with her while the older male members, probably forced to bring their daughters to the concert, wish they knew what she looked like naked. She's the perfect blend of entertaining and hot on stage.

Too bad she doesn't look like she's enjoying one minute of it. The band has just finished their eighth song in the set, and even sitting in the very last row in the twenty-thousand-seat arena so I can observe unnoticed, I can tell she dislikes every minute.

Why the hell is she doing it then?

Pulling out my cell phone, I send a text to Gwen asking her to look into every record she can find, public or private, about Layla Carlysle and her entourage, specifically Finn Michaelson and her mother. I want to see if any of them have a history of making up stories or hey, even stalking. I don't care if Finn pestered his sixth grade girlfriend with love notes; I want to know about it. I'm still not sure I completely believe that Layla has any kind of a deranged person after her since she's only received a few notes so far and no real threats have been made, but it's better to be safe than story. More often than not though, these rich assholes feel the need to invent drama when there isn't any, just to put the spotlight back on them. With the amount of enthusiasm I've seen on Layla's face today, I'm going to guess the little princess is just board as fuck and needs some excitement in her life.

I'm still getting paid, so it's no skin off my back, but she damn well better not be wasting my time just to give herself a little thrill. There are plenty of other ways I could give that blonde beauty a thrill, and it would involve less time researching and more time with her skirt up around her hips and moans floating past those full lips of hers.

Focus, Brady. Jesus, it's like you've never seen a hot chick before.

I really need to get laid. I need a mindless fuck to get this thing, whatever it is, out of my system. I don't need any type of distraction on a job, even if it *is* a pointless waste of my time. Distractions only get the people around you killed.

"I need an ETA on SEAL team four. They were supposed to touch base at twenty-one hundred. I've had nothing but radio silence from them, over," I spoke softly into my earpiece as I rounded the corner of one of the villas, my gun drawn.

Garrett couldn't find Parker and his worry and anger about that situation had transferred to me. I shouldn't have left them with Milo. Even though I called it in, and was assured they had cover, I still had an uneasy feeling when I walked away from the three of them. Parker could be anywhere right now having God knows what done to her. I knew she was a pretty bad ass CIA agent, but anyone can be broken.

I switched channels on my wireless mic and tried contacting the back-up SEAL team again. Earlier, distracted by what was going on with Parker, I had rattled off coordinates to the south side of the resort for Captain Risner to give them so they could touch down and start their own clearing of the area to eliminate any threats. I didn't have time to clear the area ahead of time, but I figured it didn't matter in a resort this size; they'd be okay no matter where they landed. They were SEALS for Christ's sakes. They knew how to do their job without me babysitting them.

"Dragon, King, Maxwell. One of you assholes come in, over."

I moved beyond the last villa in the row and headed towards an outcropping of palm trees and other exotic foliage that made up a good couple of acres of ground cover—the perfect place for someone to hide.

Ignoring the silence in my ear, I bent down to a crouch and slowly inched my way into the tropical forest, using the small tactical flashlight on the barrel of the gun to light my way, moving it from left to right as I checked for threats.

A few feet into the brush, my foot smacked against something on the ground. I whipped my gun and flashlight down and my eyes landed on a boot. A Navy SEAL issued, black, hot weather jungle boot.

"Oh Jesus. Fuck! God dammit, Garrett! Why the fuck did you come out here alone?" I moaned to myself in horror as my flashlight and gun slowly made its way up the woodland-camouflaged pant leg and across the torso bearing the same patterned T-shirt. Then I reached the face.

King, not Garrett.

It was King's pale face and lifeless eyes that stared up at the Dominican night sky. It was King's forehead that bore a bloody hole—a kill shot that took his life the instant it was fired. Jared King: a thirty-year-old husband and father who made us all laugh constantly back at the academy with his actor impersonations and shitty karaoke skills.

A pain shot through my chest when I realized the main emotion I felt right now was relief that it wasn't Garrett on the ground, and I instantly felt guilty. King was a friend. A good friend. One with a new baby at home that he showed everyone pictures of before they even asked.

I pushed aside every emotion inside of me, erecting a wall to block them out, and continued with the job. It was only one person. He knew the risks when he signed on to be a SEAL. There were still two more men on his team that I needed to find and get them the fuck out of this ambush.

Stepping over the body, I continued on, pushing palm leaves and wildlife out of my way. Just three meters later, the wall came crashing down when I found Dragon and Maxwell in almost the exact same positions as King: unmoving eyes, chests still from taking their last breaths, and a gunshot wound blossoming from between their eyes.

I should have researched the location better before I gave them the coordinates. I should have made sure the area was clear before I dropped them down right in the middle of a trap. They trusted me to lead them into a safe area, and I led them right into hell. I was going to have to tell their wives, girlfriends, and mothers it was my rash decision to get them here as soon as possible for back-up, so Garrett and I could find Parker, that got them killed. They would never celebrate another anniversary with the women they loved, never hug their mother on her birthday, never watch their children grow up.

I knew better than that. I knew not to let anything distract me from a mission.

I blink a few times and shake the dark memory from my mind, forcing myself to remember that I'm not in the tropical landscape of the Dominican anymore. The sudden quiet from the stage brings me back to reality, and I watch as Layla, with her back to the seats, speaks softly to her band members. After a few minutes, she turns and makes her way back up to center stage, pushing the microphone she's been holding into the mic stand. The drummer counts off with a few smacks of his drum sticks together, and the lead guitarist jumps in with a slow, soulful sound. This isn't the music I've been listening to for the last hour. This song isn't something made just to shake your ass to. It's heartfelt and gentle. I watch as Layla stands with one arm behind her back and the other gripping the microphone on the stand tightly. Her eyes close as she starts to sing the first verse. Her voice still has the typical pop music feel that the rest of her songs do, but there is a little more added in—a little more feeling, a little more belief in what she's singing about: a love gone wrong, regrets, and mistakes. It's a good song as far as this kind of music goes. It's not something I would blast in my car, but I wouldn't make the effort to change the channel if it happened to come on.

Halfway through the chorus, the sound of high heels echo through the arena as Eve marches from the right side of the stage. The floor microphones pick up each *click* and *clack* as she walks with purpose directly up to Layla. The band tapers off when they see their boss in front of them, but Layla, with her eyes closed, continues to belt out a few more lyrics until she finally realizes the band isn't backing her up anymore. The two women stare at each other for several minutes before I hear Eve ask the band to give them a few moments. Without hesitation, everyone puts their instruments down and hustle off stage left.

I lean forward in my seat, resting my elbows on my knees so I can concentrate on what's going to happen next. I'm sure it's going to be your typical manager/client pep talk or some shit, but I'm still on the clock and might as well watch the two women and how they interact so I can get a better feel for them.

Eve glances around the stage and arena, making sure everyone is gone, before she starts to speak. Thank God I'm far away and hidden in the dark seats where they haven't turned the lights on yet.

"What the hell do you think you're doing?" Eve asks Layla angrily.

"I'm warming up, just like you told me to," Layla replies in a monotone voice, her face blank, not giving away any emotions.

"That song is not on the set list and you know it."

Eve crosses her arms in front of her and takes on look of authority. Layla finally removes her hand from the mic, dropping both of her arms down to her sides, and I can hear her deep, frustrated sigh through the sound system.

"I know it's not on the list, but it's a song from the new album, and I think the fans will want to hear it," she explains softly.

"I don't give a shit *what* you think. You don't get any thoughts when it comes to this. You sing the fun, upbeat songs you're supposed to and that's it. The only reason that song even made it to the album is because Sam wrote it and he demanded credit for it."

I can practically see the smoke coming out of Layla's ears when Eve tells her that last part. I have to admit, now I'm invested in this conversation, and I can't pull myself away even if the building goes up in flames.

"He wrote that song? Tell me you're kidding. You told me you hired a songwriter to give me a song with a different kind of vibe to switch things up a bit," Layla states with barely concealed fury, a quiver in her voice giving her away.

"It doesn't matter what I told you. I don't need to explain myself to anyone, especially you. What I do is no concern of yours. You screwed everything up when you left Sam. You owed him a little something, even if it was just singing one of his songs on the album," Eve tells her, pointing her finger in Layla's face to make her point known.

"I don't owe him ANYTHING and you know it. You let me give him everything, and it was all just a joke," Layla fires back.

"Oh, don't kid yourself." Eve laughs cruelly. "You didn't give him anything. You have nothing to give *anyone*. I should have known better than to try and do something nice for you. You have absolutely no redeeming qualities to make ANY man happy. God knows you've done nothing but make my life miserable for twenty-four years."

Jesus Christ. This woman makes Joan Crawford look like a fucking saint.

"Keep your trivial opinions to yourself and do as your fucking told. Sing the set list I gave you."

Layla doesn't have any more fiery comebacks for her mother after her last parting remark as she stands with her shoulders drooped and watches Eve turn and walk away with her head held high.

If that bitch was my mother I would tell her exactly where to go and even buy her a fucking express ticket to get her there faster.

"What in the hell was that?" I mutter to myself as I continue to stare at Layla down on stage. She looks nothing like the diva with an attitude I witnessed earlier and everything like a puppy that was just kicked in the teeth.

"Shocking, isn't it?"

The quiet voice directly behind me has me tensing my shoulders and spinning around in a protective stance with my fists clenched at my side calculating the threat and waiting to strike.

"Whoa, easy there, rough rider. It's just me," Finn says with a smile, his hands held up in the air like I have a gun pointed at him. He's lucky it's down in my ankle holster or I would have already had it pressed underneath his chin, threatening his pretty face.

I relax and tip my head in Layla's general direction. "So, is that the norm around here? Eve smacking the shit out of Layla with her words and Layla just taking it?" I ask.

Finn shrugs and slides his hands in the front pockets of his jeans. "That? Oh, that wasn't even the tip of the iceberg. Eve is actually in a good mood today."

I shake my head in confusion. If that was Eve on a good day, how the fuck does she act on a bad one?

"Why the hell doesn't Layla tell her where to stick it? This is her career, her life."

Finn laughs but it's not meant to be a cheerful one. It's a laugh filled with disdain and irritation.

"You would think, wouldn't you? Layla is the star. She's the one bringing all the money in and has people falling all over themselves to make her happy. One would naturally assume that she's the one who makes all the decisions, *Chief* Marshall," Finn says with a raise of an eyebrow.

"I'm not with the Navy anymore. It's just Brady."

Finn cocks his head at me, a pensive look on his face as he holds his chin in between his thumb and forefinger and furrows his brow.

"Oh, my bad. I just assumed once a SEAL, always a SEAL. The kind of person who shoots first and asks questions later, someone who follows orders no matter who gives them and never thinks for himself. You know, someone who makes snap judgments about a person before they really know anything about them."

I want to be mad. I really do. I want to punch the smug look off of Finn's face, but I can't because he just described me to a T. I can't even pretend to be offended. Not twenty minutes earlier, in the text I sent to Gwen, I called Layla a "self-centered attention whore." "You know what happens when you assume, Brady," Finn adds with a smile.

"Alright, you made your point," I concede.

"Judge not, lest ye be judged."

I roll my eyes and shake my head. "Seriously. Shut the fuck up. I get it. Stop talking in idioms. There's more to her than meets the eye. Understood."

A banging noise breaks into our conversation, and we move so we can see the stage. The mic stand that previously stood front and center is now rolling in a giant circle at the far end, and Layla stares after it, her hands on her hips and her chest heaving with what I assume is the remainder of the energy she used to angrily chuck it in that direction.

"I better go check on her," Finn says quietly, his voice filled with concern as he starts to walk down the aisle behind me.

"You're her friend. Why haven't you done something to stop this?" I ask, my words making him stop in his tracks.

"What makes you think I haven't?" he replies with his back to me.

I watch as he walks out of the row and makes his way down the center aisle to the stage. After a few minutes, making sure he gets to Layla before I go, I head the same way he does, but instead of turning left to the stage, I make a right and head out of the arena.

Pulling my phone out of my pocket, I and dial Gwen. "Hey, change of plans. Put Finn Michaelson's background check on the back burner. Focus on Eve Carlysle. Get me everything you can ASAP."

CHAPTER 6
Layla

"You really need to find another hobby. This waking up at the ass crack of dawn to go running is getting on my nerves."

I ignore Finn's complaints as I concentrate on my stretches, extending my arms over my head and clasping my hands together, tilting from side to side to work out the kinks in my back. We're standing at the beginning of the Bryant Grove Trail in Long Hunter State Park, my favorite place to run when I'm home. It's eight miles round trip, but with Finn's constant bitching and moaning, we usually only complete half. Running is part of my strict fitness regimen that I have to follow in order to keep my stamina up for the concerts, but I'd still do it every day. It's the one time I can shut my mind off. The only thing I need to focus on is my breathing, my heart rate, and the distance I've traveled. I don't have to think about how trapped I feel or how if I have to spend one more day living this life, I'm going to keep losing piece after piece of myself until there is nothing left but the robot my mother has created.

"You were in the Marines. Didn't you have to run in your sleep?" I question as I step onto the trail and set the timer on my watch.

"Yes. And that's precisely why I don't want to do it anymore. People shouldn't run unless someone is chasing them," he tells me.

Finn likes to complain, but I know he enjoys this as much as I do. He might not be too fond of the physical requirements, but the peace and quiet in his head is as important to him as it is to me.

Finishing up a few windmills with my arms, I whip my head around. "That's the fifth time in the last minute you've looked back towards where we parked the car. What's with you this morning?"

"Nothing. Nothing at all. Just checking to see if there will be any other runners out here with us this morning. You know, since I am your bodyguard and all," he says cockily.

"I'm sure it's just going to be the two of us, just like every other time we run here," I remind him, turning away from him and getting ready to really take off.

A snap of a branch close behind us has me stopping and quickly turning to the noise.

"What the hell are you doing here?"

I can't hide the shock or anger in my voice when I see who's standing a few feet away from Finn, dressed in black

85

nylon Nike shorts, a pair of running shoes, and an old AC/DC concert T-shirt that's just tight enough to show off all of the contours of his sculpted chest, and the short sleeves put his muscular arms on display.

"Thanks, but I've already got Finn here with me." I try not to stare at his strong arms or the hint of a tattoo peeking out from under the edge of one of his shirt sleeves, instantly curious about what it is, in spite of my irritation with him.

"Yeah, we're good here. This is our routine when we're home. We've been doing just fine on our own without some stranger sticking his nose where it doesn't belong," Finn arrogantly tells Brady.

"That may have been fine in the past, but sticking with the same routine is what gets people killed," Brady states as he walks closer to Finn, getting in his face.

"Are you trying to tell me I don't know how to do my job?" Finn asks him heatedly, his hands clenched into fists at his sides with barely concealed rage.

Brady casually crosses his arms in front of his chest and uses the two inches he has on Finn to stare down at him, subtly trying to tell him that he could probably kick his ass without even blinking.

"I'm trying to tell you that your *relationship* with Layla might be clouding your judgment when it comes to protecting her."

The way Brady spits out *relationship* proves that he's done his research, at least as far as the tabloids go. For years they've hinted at an affair between Finn and I. Of course Eve made it known that we shouldn't disparage those rumors. Any press is good press and all that bullshit.

"You're a real piece of work, you know that!" Finn shouts.

I grab onto his arm and pull him back towards me. I've never seen him so worked up like this. His body is practically vibrating with fury. I don't want anyone to get hurt, even if I do think the ex-Navy SEAL standing in front of us could use a good punch in the face right about now to wipe that smug look off of it.

"Alright, that's enough. Both of you. If you guys are through with your pissing contest, I'd like to get started on my run."

I let my eyes shift back and forth between them, putting my hands on my hips to let them know I'm not in the mood for their nonsense. I understand that Finn feels like an outsider is poaching on his territory and trying to tell him how to do his job, but he needs to cool down. For all we know, Brady is going to run to the tabloids himself and let them know Finn has anger management issues.

"Finn, why don't you head back to the cabin and make sure the guys installing the new alarm system don't screw everything up," I suggest to him softly.

I don't want to push Finn away, but he needs to take a step back for a minute. The longer he stays here, the worse it's going to get between him and Brady. I can already tell Brady isn't the type of person to listen to orders from anyone. There's no way he's going to be the first one to leave. Plus, it will give me a chance to find out what the hell he's really doing here.

Finn whips his head around to stare at me, his eyes wide with hurt and disbelief.

"So it's going to be like that, huh?" he asks me angrily. "Fine. You two have a great run."

Before I can say anything to convince him that I'm not doing this to purposefully hurt him, he's already stalked off and disappeared around the bend.

Brady chuckles and I turn to face him.

"Oh, that's nice. It's good you can see the humor in a situation that isn't funny at all," I angrily tell him.

"Sweetheart, that guy is one argument away from blowing someone's head off with his side arm. Sue me if I think it's a riot that you've put all your trust in someone like *that* and think *I'm* the bad guy."

Until now, I haven't seen or spoken to Brady since right before the concert when I handed him the list he asked for of people who might have it out for me. And actually, I didn't speak to him then either. I was still too keyed up from the fight with Eve to do much more than shove the list in his hands and walk away to warm up.

"Here, the list you requested." I walked up to him right outside my dressing room and smacked the piece of paper into his chest so he had to quickly grab onto it before it fell to the ground.

I ignored the fact that touching his chest felt like touching a brick wall—a very muscular, firm brick wall that radiated heat.

I crossed my arms in front of me as he perused the list, raising one eyebrow at me when he was finished.

"There's only three names on here."

The disbelief and confusion in his voice immediately put me on edge.

"Contrary to what you might think, I'm not hated the world over. Most people actually like me."

He looked like he wanted to say something else, but I cut him off before he could laugh at me or make another snide comment about what he thinks of me.

"I have to get ready. The exit is down the hall to the left. Don't let the door hit you in the ass on your way out," I lob at him sarcastically before turning around, walking into my dressing room, and slamming the door behind me.

The list I gave him only contained a few names: another singer or two who had made a few silly threats to me in the tabloids because I got invited to events they didn't and an interviewer from a magazine who liked to constantly make remarks about how the world would be a better place if I wasn't singing in it. And she was just bitter because she used to work for me, and Finn caught her skimming money from the top.

It's not that I think Brady's the bad guy. Not really. I just don't know him or trust him. I trust Finn with everything and I just sent him away. This guy comes in here like he's hot shit and looks at me like I'm dirt on his shoe. How the hell am I supposed to react to him?

Brady stares at me for a few minutes and when I don't respond to his statement about him being the bad guy, he shrugs it off like he never expected me to disagree. Without saying another word to me, he turns around and takes off jogging on the trail leaving me standing there staring after him.

"You better move your ass if you want to get all five miles in before this trail gets packed with tourists," he shouts over his shoulder as he disappears around the first bend.

I stand there just long enough to curse his name in my

head, then take off running faster than I normally start off so I can catch up to him. Out of spite, and because I'm pissed that my morning routine is thrown off by his presence, I speed past him until I'm a few legs in front of him and slow down so I don't get winded too early.

I can hear his feet pounding on the trail right behind me, and before I can get too cocky about being in front of him, he actually has the nerve to come up on my right and go around me.

"Passing on the right," he says jovially, continuing the fast pace I'm not used to.

My eyes immediately zero in on his ass in those stupid shorts as I watch him pumping his legs to go even faster. The thin material is molded to it, and it's almost impossible to turn my eyes away, but I do so I can once again leave that *ass* behind in the dust.

Pushing my legs as hard as I can, I make up the distance between us.

"Passing on the left."

Two can play at this game.

I stay in front of him just long enough to wonder if he's looking at *my* ass. I'm wearing a pair of tight pink, lightweight running shorts, and even though I'm pretty confident in how great my butt and legs look in them, I don't want him staring.

Regrettably, I slow my pace until he makes it back up to

me and we're jogging side-by-side at a more normal speed.

"I thought for sure you were going to keep that shit up for the entire five miles," he says with a laugh. I notice he's not even breathing hard, and I immediately want to stick my leg out and trip him.

"Figured I should slow it down for you. A man of your age could have a heart attack at any moment, and I'm not really up-to-date on my first aid training."

We jog in silence for a few minutes, the sounds of nature filling the air and making me momentarily forget that my best friend conspired with the enemy.

"You know, I didn't mean to make things strained between you and your body guard," Brady says, reading my mind. "I asked your mother to give me a print-out of your normal routine when you're home. I thought I would case the place ahead of time and make sure there weren't any threats in the area. It took me a little longer than I expected, which is why I was still here when you guys showed up."

I don't reply right away, taking some time to process what he's just told me. He had checked things out before I got here to make sure I'd be safe. It's a sweet thing to do, and I want to tell him I appreciated it, but I can't. I'm a job to him. That's it. He's not doing anything out of the kindness of his heart. He's doing what he was told and what he's being paid to do.

"So, tell me about your mother."

My steps falter a little as I turn my head in his direction. He doesn't look my way, just continues to stare straight ahead at the trail in front of us. I pull my gaze away from his profile and grit my teeth.

"I'm sure you already know everything there is about Eve. Just like you already know everything about me. You probably had a team of people digging into our lives weeks before you even showed up in the conference room the other day."

He doesn't reply and I know I'm right. Being right about something like that doesn't make me feel victorious; it just makes me feel sad. Yet another person to add to the list of those who think they know everything about me.

"I know what the public knows. That she was a secretary for Hummingbird Records, met your father, fell in love, and had you. When your father died, she went through with his life-long dream of making you a star, showing off the talents he recognized in you from an early age," Brady states easily, like he's reading the information from a children's fairytale book.

I can't hide the unattractive snort that comes out when he lists my mother's bio—the one she's painstakingly fabricated and has spread through the media over the years.

"Eve Carlysle: the perfect wife, the perfect mother, and the perfect business owner."

I can't hide the contempt in my voice, and I mentally scold myself. Brady Marshall may seem like an okay guy when he isn't acting like a pompous jerk, but I don't know the first thing about him. Finn is the only person I have ever confided in about what my mother is really like or what she's done to me, and I'm not about to change that now. Brady is a military man, just like Finn, but that's where the similarities end. Just after a few days, I can already tell that Brady is all about the job. He's focused and single-minded, and he will listen to the orders that have been given to him. God only knows what Eve must have said to him about me. I trust Finn with my life, my secrets, and my heart. I know he would never betray me and go back to my mother and tell her anything that I've said in confidence. I don't know the first thing about Brady. For all I know he lives alone in a hovel sharpening his knives and cleaning his guns until someone hires him for another job.

"Care to elaborate?" Brady asks.

"Nope."

If he thinks I'm just going to spill my guts to him after only knowing him for a few days, he's insane.

"You know, I was hired to help you. I can't do that if you aren't honest with me."

Another laugh escapes my lips before I can catch it.

"I'm sorry, but I didn't hire you. If there's something you need to know, ask Eve."

I realize suddenly that he's no longer running beside me, and I stop and turn to find him standing in the middle of the trail with his hands on his hips.

"I did ask Eve. I got the whole run down about you and her and how you've let fame get to your head and you'll probably be difficult to work with. You're definitely a pain in my ass, but I know for a fact you are nothing like she portrays you. And I'm guessing if I asked her why she felt the need to belittle you and make you feel like you were nothing in the middle of your sound check the other day, she wouldn't be honest with me."

My jaw drops and even though we've run roughly two miles and my heart is beating fast, it's about ready to jump out of my chest when I realize he was in the arena when Eve had gone postal on me about changing the set list.

"You heard that?" I whisper as he takes a few steps towards me, closing the distance.

"Every word," he replies softly, bringing his hand up and brushing a few stray pieces of hair out of my face to look me in the eyes. The skin of my forehead where his fingers graze me feels warm, and I hold back a shiver even though it's seventy degrees this morning and I'm sweating from the run. "I also watched your performance. It was good...if you like that sort of music. The crowd loves you and it's easy to see that you were made to do something like that. But you aren't enjoying one single second of your time up on that stage and I want to know why. Why the hell do you do it if you hate it?"

He's so close to me that our feet are almost touching. I can smell his soap and a small hint of sweaty man, and it makes me want to slide my hands under the T-shirt that clings to his chest from sweat. My fingers tingle with the need to glide up the front of him so I can feel the definition of his abs under my palms. I shake the thoughts from my mind and take a step back from him. His close proximity is doing crazy things to me, things I don't understand or have time for. The only thing I can think about right now is that he actually stayed to watch the concert even when I was a total bitch to him out in the hallway beforehand. He had stayed and saw a piece of the real me, even though I've done everything I can to keep her hidden.

"I don't know what you're talking about. I love what I do," I reply in a monotone voice. There's no conviction in what I tell him, and I can immediately see by the way he raises on eye brow and stares me down that he doesn't believe me.

"You're lying. Why are you lying to me?" he asks angrily.

"I don't even KNOW you!" I shout back, trying to rein in my own anger.

I shouldn't be yelling at him. I know that. He's just trying to help. But he needs to know that he has to leave this alone. This has nothing to do with some guy sending me notes. Whether I love what I do or not, it has no bearing on the job he was hired to do. Period. Just because I actually find myself *wanting* to tell him everything doesn't mean I will. His good looks and his strong nature are messing with my mind, making me think that he could be one of the good ones. I've been burned too many times to just throw my trust out there for anyone.

Brady starts to open his mouth, probably to say something cliché like, "You can trust me," when the ringing of his cell phone breaks through the silence in the woods that surround us.

Without taking his eyes off of me, he reaches into the back pocket of his shorts and answers the call without bothering to see who it is.

"Brady."

He closes his eyes and lets out a deep sigh. His face immediately relaxes and loses the look of anger that was all over it a moment before.

"What's up, Gwen?"

A prickle of jealousy shoots through me when he says another woman's name, and I immediately tamp it down.

What the hell is that? What do I care if he gets a phone call from one or a thousand other women? I don't know anything about this guy, remember?

"Yes. No. I don't know. Possibly."

I listen to his one-sided conversation, wondering what this Gwen person is calling him for when he's supposedly in the middle of a job.

Something she says causes his eyes to shoot to mine. I

watch as they grow wide, and he turns away from me a little, cupping his hand over his mouth and the phone and lowering his voice when he replies.

"No. Absolutely not. I am NOT asking her for an autograph. I'm on a job, Gwen."

I cover my mouth to try and stifle a laugh, but he whips his head around when he hears me.

Rolling his eyes and sighing again, he uncovers his mouth and moves the phone away from it a so he can speak to me.

"Sorry. My sister Gwen is a huge fan. She's another giant pain in my ass. She wants to know if you would sign her CD case."

His sister? He has a sister? Why the hell does this make me happy knowing that Gwen isn't just some slut who's calling him at work?

I smile, nodding my head at him. "That's no problem. I'll sign whatever she wants. You should invite her to the cabin one of these nights for dinner, and I can sign things for her then."

Halfway through my sentence, Brady starts shaking his head frantically, but it's too late from the sound of things on his end. Gwen must have heard me. Suddenly, he's holding the phone a few inches away from his ear, and I can hear high-pitched screaming coming through the speaker.

I laugh and he just gives me a look of annoyance, his lips pressing tightly together in a thin line and his eyes narrowing at me.

After a few seconds, the screaming stops and he puts the phone back to his ear.

"No. No, do NOT put her on. Gwen, I'm working I don't have time to—"

His voice instantly goes from loud and irritated to soft and happy. I'm completely taken aback by the sudden change, and I can do nothing but stand there and stare at what's taking place right in front of me. Brady Marshall, bad ass private investigator, just turned into a marshmallow.

"Hi, sweetie! Yes, I'm still at work. How was school? You did? That's so good! I'm so proud of you! Yes, Uncle Brady will buy you something for your good report card. Um, ah, I don't think that's a good idea, pumpkin."

His eyes flash to mine again, and there's a look of panic in them.

"Well, because I'm working. I know I always sing with you, but now isn't a good time."

Oh my gosh, he sings with his niece? This just keeps getting better and better.

"Oh come on, Uncle Brady. I think you should sing with the girl," I say loud enough for my voice to carry through the line to the little girl he's talking to.

I'll get you for this, he mouths silently. I just shrug in response and place my hands on my hips. If he wants to know so much about me, then he better start doing some sharing of his own. Listening to him sing on the phone with his niece is an excellent start.

"No! Not that song. Anything but that song. Emma, please? How about that awesome Nirvana song I taught you last week? No, it does NOT suck. Where are your priorities?"

Brady lets out a huge sigh, rolls his eyes and then turns his back to me.

"Fine. But this is the last time," I hear him say softly to her.

So quietly I have to strain to hear him, I make out the first few words to a song I am quite familiar with.

"It's Friday night and the beat is sick. I'm gonna get my girls and hit the club up quick."

It's absolutely impossible to contain my laughter at this point. Clutching my sides, I laugh harder than I have in a really long time as Brady practically whispers a few more bars of the song before stopping abruptly and telling Emma he loves her before hanging up.

He turns around, stuffing his cell phone back in his pocket and refusing to look at me.

I quiet my laughter and put a serious look on my face.

"Just so I'm clear, was that *Waiting for the Weekend?* You know, one of MY songs that you were just singing?" I ask innocently.

He crosses his arms in front of him and glares at me.

"That's what I thought. Just one more question," I tell him as he rolls his eyes at me. "Has anyone ever told you that you have a *beautiful* singing voice?"

I can't hide the grin that takes over my face, and before I know it, Brady is picking me up by the legs and flinging me over his shoulder so the top half of my body hangs down his back. Once again, I have a clear view of his sculpted ass.

"Oh my gosh, put me down!" I yell in between laughs as he turns towards the trail and heads back the way we came.

"Nope, sorry. Straight to the showers for you so you can wash away every bit of what you just heard," he tells me before smacking his hand on my ass and tightening his arms around my legs.

As I watch the ground fly by while I dangle over Brady's strong shoulder, trying not to think about what his warm hands feel like wrapped around the bare skin of my legs, I wonder if there just might be more to him that I originally thought.

CHAPTER 7
BRADY

"So, what's she like?! Is she as gorgeous in person as she is on TV? Is she totally cool and approachable? I bet she's totally cool. Oh my God this is so awesome! I can't believe you get to spend every day with THE Layla Carlysle!"

Gwen's been gushing and throwing questions at me nonstop since I walked into the office this morning, still sweaty from my morning run with Layla and still focused on how warm her breath felt against my back as it seeped through my T-shirt while she hung over my shoulder.

She hadn't been happy when I tried digging into her mother, and that makes me even more curious about the type of person Layla is. Who just lets someone walk all over them like that, even if it *is* their mother? She has spunk and doesn't mind telling me where to go, but when it comes to Eve, she just shuts down.

"Okay, enough already with the twenty questions. She's a normal human being, not some science experiment you stare at through a cage," I tell Gwen as she bounces up and down on her feet, waiting for me to tell her everything about her favorite singer.

"Well, well, well. Will wonders never cease? Just last week you were calling her a 'no-talent drama queen,'" Gwen reminds me. "And for your information, she is NOT a normal human being, Brady. She is Layla Carlysle. One of the best recording artists and entertainers of the twenty-first century. She is a pop icon." Judging by her foot tapping and the scowl on her face, clearly she's agitated that I don't share her same excitement.

How could I? Everything I read about her in the tabloids is false. Which shouldn't come as a surprise to me since the tabloids also write about movie stars buying land on Mars and a country singer finding a bat child in a cave. It shouldn't have shocked me that she has a sense of humor or that she's more beautiful that humanly possible when she doesn't have all that make-up on her face or shellacked hair. What amazes me, though, is the fact that she's allowed a woman that should have been her number one supporter to verbally abuse her.

The real Layla Carlysle intrigues me as much as I hate to admit it.

"Can we get down to business, please," I beg Gwen as I take a seat at my desk and power up the computer. "Tell me what you've found on Eve Carlysle so far."

Gwen lets out a huge annoyed sigh because I'm not going

to give her the goods on Layla. Finally, she walks over to her own desk and grabs a file folder off of the top of it. Flipping it open, she scans the pages as she makes her way to me.

"Well, there isn't much to be found about Eve. I had to do quite a bit of digging, and even then what I found wasn't very interesting. Parents were blue collar workers, lower middle class. She wanted more out of life and made sure she got it. After high school, she worked hard and put herself through community college. Her first real job out of college was as a secretary for Hummingbird Records, where she met and married Layla's father, Jack," Gwen explains, rounding my chair and putting the file down in front of me so I can flip through it.

"I don't like how little information there is about this woman. I mean, everyone has SOME kind of skeleton in their closet. She has nothing. And when I say nothing, I mean nada, zero, zip. Not even a parking ticket. Which is weird, right?"

I nod my head in agreement. "No one is that clean."

"Exactly. Which makes me think she's got something to hide. As awesome as I am on a computer, I couldn't find squat. I called your friend Garrett for help, but his wife is on some kind of photo assignment and their daughter has been sick so he doesn't have time to help. He gave me your friend Austin's number. Let me tell you, that guy is annoying."

I chuckle as I watch Gwen go back to her desk and sit down.

"What did Austin have to say?"

I pull up my email and shoot off a quit note of thanks to Austin as Gwen regales me with his charm.

"You mean aside from asking me my bra size, what I was doing for dinner tonight, and whether I preferred eggs or pancakes for breakfast tomorrow morning?"

Oh, that boy is so getting his ass kicked the next time I talk to him.

At the closing of the email, I add a threatening little reminder to Austin: My baby sister is off limits.

"Well, when he isn't thinking with his dick, he's actually not too shabby at getting information that I can't. I really don't want to know *how* he got this information. He started to tell me it had something to do with two bottles of wine and a lot of sweet talk, but I cut him off when he mentioned some trick he does with his tongue that always makes women talk. I mean really, Brady. These are the people you worked with in the Navy?"

Same old Austin. He could make a mute talk. He's always been our go-to-guy when the computer had us at a disadvantage. With his good looks and southern boy charm, he could walk us through airport security with a bomb strapped to his chest and no one would pay any attention.

"Sorry, Austin is in a class all his own. What was he able to find out?" I ask, shutting the file folder that has no real useful information in it.

"So get this. According to a few ex-employees from Hummingbird Records, Jack Carlysle married Eve because she was knocked up."

I stare at Gwen for a few seconds trying to do the math.

"That doesn't make sense. They got married over a year and a half before Layla was born."

Gwen nods enthusiastically. "Exactly. According to these employees, Eve faked the pregnancy to get Jack to marry her. He was getting ready to break it off and she needed to do some quick thinking so the money he lavished her with didn't dry up. She never had any doctor's appointments at that time or anything confirming the pregnancy, but Jack, being the upstanding guy he was, took her at her word and made her Mrs. Carlysle. Surprise, surprise. A few months later she *lost* the baby. Once again, no medical records confirming this at all."

I shake my head in confusion. "So if he was getting ready to end things with her, why the hell didn't he just divorce her when she supposedly lost the baby?"

Gwen leans forward in her chair, so excited to tell the rest to me I think she might fall right out of it and onto the floor.

"This is where it really gets interesting. Right around that time, like the same week, Jack added Eve as the co-owner of Hummingbird Records. He made her a shareholder, put her on the board of directors—the works. And what do you know, four months later Eve gets pregnant with Layla," Gwen finishes.

"It's like he bribed her to have a baby," I state in awe.

"That's exactly what it's like," Gwen replies, letting out a deep, gratifying sigh.

I sit back in my chair and run my fingers through my hair.

"Jesus, no wonder Eve hates her. She probably never even wanted kids. Jack only kept her around to pop one out for him."

Gwen looks at me questioningly. "What do you mean Eve hates Layla? Are you serious? How is that possible? Every single interview or news article I've seen of the two of them together, they are like two peas in a pod. They look like the best of friends."

I'm momentarily ashamed at myself for thinking the same thing *and* for thinking Layla was a princess that enjoyed doing things to make her poor mother worry.

"Looks can be deceiving. They are anything BUT the best of friends. Jesus, Gwen. If you could have seen the way this woman speaks to her daughter. It's disgusting," I tell her sadly.

Gwen cocks her head and looks at me in sympathy.

"Kind of like how Dad used to speak to you?" she asks softly.

Even though it's been ten years since I last spoke to him, I can still hear my father's booming voice.

"You're a real piece of work, you know that, son? All you care about is yourself. God forbid you ever think about anyone

else. You're pathetic."

I think back to the day of the sound check and the defeat I saw in Layla, the way she just accepted how her mother spoke to her and the things she forced her to do. It makes me angry, and for the first time since Gwen and Emma, it makes me feel protective. I want to keep her from danger and shame and make sure she knows that doesn't have to put up with all the shit thrown at her. I know exactly what it feels like to be belittled and made to feel like you're worthless. But I got the hell away from that shit as soon as I turned eighteen and I never looked back. I don't have to put up with my father's hatred or general dissatisfaction with the life I've chosen for myself. Layla doesn't have to either, but for some reason, she does. She sticks around and does exactly as Eve says, and by the look on her face the majority of the time, she believes every word that her mother tells her.

I've just met this woman and suddenly I wanted to make sure no one ever speaks to her that way ever again. I want to see her smile more. When she does, I feel a tightening in my gut and an inexplicable need to have her smile at *me,* to shine that brightness on her face in *my* direction. The cockiness she aimed at me on our run this morning and the tiny hint of a spark in her eye when she was singing that song her mother put her foot down about—that's just a small fraction of the real Layla Carlysle. I want more. For the first time in a long time, I feel need stirring inside of me, a desire to get to really know someone. Find out what makes them tick. Find out what makes them writhe underneath me, moaning and scratching their fingernails down my back.

"Hello, earth to Brady. Where the hell did you go just now?" Gwen bellows, breaking me from my thoughts. "Oh my God. You have a crush on her don't you?"

I choke out a laugh at Gwen's observation. *If she only knew what I'd just been thinking, she'd probably smack me upside the head and call me a pervert.*

"A crush? What are we, twelve?" I reply, avoiding the question.

"You do, don't you?! You think she's pretty and you want to kiss her! Oh my God, Layla Carlysle could be my sister-in-law!" Gwen squeals excitedly, clapping her hands together.

I rest my elbows on my desk and put my head in my hands, the makings of a headache coming on strong.

"You really need to get out more, you know that?" I complain, trying my hardest not to imagine what Layla's lips would feel like against mine, what her tongue would feel like swirling through my mouth.

"I know. I spend way too much time with a six-year-old. It's sad when even a proposition from that Austin guy sounds appealing," Gwen says with an exaggerated sigh. "Speaking of getting out more, I recall Layla mentioning something about having me over for dinner. That would be a great way for me to get out of the house. It would also be a great way to watch you two together." She wags her eyebrows.

"Oh hell no. There is no way I'm letting that happen if you're going to act like a fool. And besides, all of this is pointless since she's supposedly dating that Finn guy," I tell her, trying to hide the irritation in my voice.

"Ooooooh, Finn Michaelson! I totally forgot about that. Oh my gosh, he is yummy. That man is sex on a stick. You're totally right. What would she want with you when she's got a fine specimen like that in her bed whenever she wants?" Gwen states nonchalantly.

"Oh give me a fucking break! There is nothing even remotely appealing about Finn. What the hell does she even see in him? He was in the Marines for Christ sakes. Everyone knows they're a bunch of hot-headed Neanderthals. She looks at him like he's some sort of God. Granted, he's got some nice pecks and a good head of hair, but come on!" I ramble angrily.

Gwen stares at me with an open mouth and wide eyes, her arm coming up in front of her and her finger pointing straight at me.

"Sweet mother of God. I was kidding about you crushing on her, but I'm right. Oh my God, you are totally jealous of her bodyguard! Oh this is priceless!" Gwen starts laughing.

"This is a job, nothing else. Just like Mrs. Henderson last

week was a job. I don't mix business with pleasure. Ever," I tell her firmly.

"Mrs. Henderson is ninety-two years old and thought her dog was stealing food out of her fridge. I would hope to God you would never mix that kind of business with pleasure. That's just gross," Gwen says with a grimace.

"It doesn't matter. I'm doing the job I'm being paid to do. Distractions, even the hot, famous singer type, do not have room in my life. End of story," I remind her, smacking my fingers on the keys of my computer angrily.

"Oh, I get it. So they must have changed the job description without letting me know. If I recall correctly, you were hired to look into a stalker, not the personal life of Miss Carlysle," Gwen replies sarcastically.

She has me there. I'm definitely not being paid to find out why Eve is such a raging bitch to her daughter. In just a few short days, I'm starting to get too invested in the job with a woman I barely know. I'm letting my personal feelings and opinions get to me, just like in the Dominican. Just like the hostage negotiation.

"Mr. Franklin, just put the gun down and let your wife and daughter go. Whatever problems you're having, there's no need to put them in danger," Eric, my partner, told the man standing just inside the doorway of the house he shared with his family.

Right now he had a semiautomatic weapon aimed on his wife of five years and their three-year-old daughter, who stood right next to him, with fear in their eyes and tears running down their cheeks.

I'd seen the woman and her daughter before. They frequented the coffee shop I stopped at every morning before my shift. On several occasions, I'd spoken to the woman while we waited in line for coffee and even bought a cookie for her little girl a few times. People always trusted a man in uniform, and it was easy to get them to open up to you, even if you never exchanged names.

Now, standing outside of their home, guns drawn, I knew their names from the intel my captain had given me. The wife's name was Alyssa and the little girl was Lucy. I wished more than anything when I saw her getting coffee two days ago and she mentioned her husband had been behaving awfully towards her—constantly yelling and accusing her of cheating on him— that I would have told her not to go home, to take that precious little girl with the blonde head full of curls and wide blue eyes and go somewhere for a few days.

There were so many things I should be saying to the maniac holding a gun on them right now, things that would reassure him we weren't out to get him so he would put the gun away and we could charge him, but my mind was blank.

All I could think about was the young, beautiful wife clutching her little girl tightly and how just that morning I had thought about her and wished she wasn't married. She was sweet and polite, and her little girl was the spitting image of her and had charmed the pants off of me when she called me "Ociffer." I knew I was too close to the situation and should tell Eric that I needed someone to come in and take my place, but I couldn't make my mouth open or my feet move. I stared at the woman I'd been daydreaming about for weeks, and I knew that if we got her out of this situation, I would make sure no one ever hurt her or her daughter again.

"Mr. Franklin, how about you let Alyssa and Lucy go?" I finally managed to say softly, my eyes pleading with Alyssa to stay calm and not make any sudden movements. "Just let them walk away. Then we can sit down and talk about what's bothering you."

The guy, Joe, flashed his angry eyes in my direction and his lip curled up in a snarl as he shoved the nose of his gun roughly into Alyssa's side. She cried out in pain, and I flinched at the sound of fear in her voice.

"How the fuck do you know my wife and daughter's name? Is this the guy you've been fucking behind my back, Alyssa?" he shouted angrily at her.

Lucy cried even harder as she hugged her mother's leg,

and I wanted more than anything to just shoot a bullet through his brain and end this once and for all.

"No! Joe, I told you, I've never cheated on you. I swear!" Alyssa cried.

"Bullshit! I can see the way this guy is looking at you. You spread your legs for him, I know it."

Eric inched slowly away from me, closer to the situation, and my hands shook with anger. I should be moving with Eric. We were a team and I was supposed to be sticking to him like glue, but I couldn't move. All I could think about was pulling the trigger.

"No one can have you but me, do you understand me?!" Joe screamed as he put his face right up to Alyssa, spittle flying from his mouth with each word.

Before I could react, shots flew out, piercing the quiet night with their explosion of light and sound. I didn't hesitate before jumping into action. I ran past Eric and tackled Joe to the ground, not giving a second thought to the gun in his hand. I only knew I couldn't let him hurt Alyssa and Lucy.

I hadn't hesitated to jump into the action, but I let myself get distracted. I let myself care too much about the subject I was paid to protect. I was paid by the city of Nashville to protect and serve all of its citizens. I let a few small conversations and a silly connection I thought I felt get in the way of doing my job. I forgot about all of my training and what you should never say and emotions you should never give away during a hostage stand-off. After I tackled Joe to the ground and relieved him of his weapon, I stood back up and looked around to find my partner with a bullet through his chest and a mother and daughter with matching ones through their heads. I was so busy trying not to crumble to the ground in grief that I forgot to cuff Joe. He jumped up from the ground, grabbed my side-arm, and shot himself under the chin, blood and brain matter splattering against my police uniform.

The sound of the phone ringing tears me away from my dark memories of that night. I need to focus on what I'm being paid to do. Who gives a rat's ass about the relationship Layla has with Eve? Gwen is right. It has absolutely nothing to do with the stalker case. It has nothing to do with me. If this is the way Layla chooses to live her life, I don't give a flying fuck.

Pulling up the file on the computer where Gwen stored the scanned copies of the letters Layla has been receiving over the last year, I go over them and take some notes, focusing my mind on what's important, not on what doesn't matter.

Layla and the choices she makes do not matter. She's her own person and can do whatever the fuck she wants. I couldn't care less.

CHAPTER 8
Layla

It's been three weeks since Brady and I went on our run. Three weeks since he's actually acted like a decent human being to me. I have no idea what changed between then and now, but the playful, friendly Brady has been replaced with the stand-offish, all-business Brady. I tell myself that I should be happy about that because it's not like I need the extra distraction that friendly Brady gives me. I don't have the time to daydream about kissing the dimples on his cheeks or the warmth I felt as I watched him talking to his niece on the phone.

Then why the hell are you doing it right now?

We're sitting next to one another at the same conference room table where we met. But this time, I'm not on the opposite side of the table wondering who the hell he is and what he's doing in my domain. Now, we're sitting so close that every once in a while his leg brushes up against mine, and I have to fight down the urge to reach over and place my hand on his thigh to see if it's as muscular as it looks.

I'm still wondering who the hell he is, unfortunately. I'm still questioning if I can trust him and if the two sides of I've seen of him so far will be it, or if there's some other personality lurking under the surface waiting to jump out and confuse me even more.

"So you don't read all of your fan mail?" he asks distractedly as he sorts through a pile of stationery, unopened envelopes, and torn-off sheets of paper—all with words of praise, thanks, or backhanded compliments from my fans all over the world.

Aside from barely saying two words to me for the last few weeks, and only replying to me with curt answers, Brady has been here at the office every day poring over all of my mail or following me to all of my meetings and practices, making inquiries and taking notes. He had asked me to come in today because he has a few questions. Well, actually, he had sent an email to Finn asking me to come in today, which of course pissed Finn off. I'm still treading lightly with him after the incident in the woods. He feels slighted, like I chose Brady over him. I would never choose anyone over him. It'll take some groveling and sucking up on my part to reassure him that I would never choose Brady over him, but he'll eventually come around. He always does. I tried my best to smooth things over with him when he received the email.

"Why the hell is he emailing me for? And why does he need to bother you with this shit? If he has questions, he should just ask me," Finn angrily complained as he scanned through his emails on his phone.

"Finn, he's doing his job. You know there is no use fighting this. Eve hired him and we just have to live with it for a little while. He'll see that there's no claim to these stalking allegations Eve has insisted on, and he'll go back to his life and let us get back to our normal routine," I explained, softening my voice and trying not to get frustrated with his constant resentment towards Brady.

I really had no idea where it was coming from. Eve had hired plenty of outside consultants over the years to check that our security was top-notch and to make sure things ran as smoothly as possible. Finn had never been this irritated and outright rude with anyone before.

"You and I both know you are amazing at your job and know what you're doing. Please, don't make this harder than it needs to be."

The pleading in my voice must have gotten to Finn. His features softened; the furrowing of his brow smoothed out and a small smile curled up the corners of his mouth.

"You're right. I'm sorry. I don't mean to make things harder on anyone, especially you. I'm just frustrated."

I walked over to him and slid my arms around his waist and press my cheek to his chest. He wrapped his arms around me and rested his chin on the top of my head.

"Thank you, Finn. He'll be gone before you know it, you'll see."

Thankfully, Finn's kept his attitude in check since that conversation. Brady still isn't gone, though, and it looks like he has no intention of leaving until he finds *something* to validate Eve's claims.

"I don't open any of my mail," I answer, getting back to his question and scooting as far away from him on my chair as I can without falling off the other side. "We have assistants here who open all incoming mail, and they enter all of the sender's information into a database and scan a copy of the original letter. They hand-pick a few a week for me to personally respond to."

Brady nods in response as he picks up a few letters and looks at the return address before placing them in a pile to his left.

"So, did they bring the letters from this Ray guy to your attention when they came in?"

I shake my head, leaning forward and placing my elbows on the table. "No. I get threats and weird letters all the time from people, so when the first few came in, they just filed them away like usual. But after the fifth one, the program we use to keep track of the letters flagged them, letting us there was a pattern with the same sender. That's when they took the letters to Eve. And that's when she called you. I've only seen two of the letters in person."

Brady starts gathering the hundred or so letters from this week into a pile before shoving them into a canvas bag he brought with him. When they are all put away, he stands up and slings the bag over his shoulder.

"I told the admins that from now on I want all mail to come straight to me before they open it. If this guy sends something else, I want to be able to dust it for fingerprints. The old letters have been handled by too many damn people for me to get anything off of them."

He turns his back and starts walking towards the door.

Jesus, he couldn't even crack a smile or say one word to me that isn't about business. *What the hell is his problem?*

"How's your niece? Did she like the signed poster I gave you for her?" I ask, forcing him to stop before he can escape.

Maybe reminding him of that small piece of his life he

120

shared with me will lighten him up a bit so I can see if that man was real.

"Yeah. She said thanks," he replies gruffly, his hand hovering over the door handle.

"I was thinking of going for a run later today before I have that appearance at the new club opening," I throw out there.

Desperate much, Layla?

I'm practically begging him to be alone with me. I just want to see if what happened in the woods was real or just my imagination. He was a real person then, not this robotic business man. He smiled and he laughed and he made jokes. He wanted me to be honest with him and trust him to do this job, but I can't do that if he's going to shut down like this and pretend like he hadn't sung one of my songs to his niece while I stood right there listening or thrown me over his shoulder like a caveman, smacking my ass and making me laugh with stories about his niece the whole drive home. As much as I hate admitting it, I'm attracted to him. There was a spark that day in the woods. I miss that spark—that first initial attraction to someone where all you can think about is what their kisses will taste like and what their hands will feel like on your bare skin. It's been a long time since I've felt those butterflies in my stomach. Hell, who knows if I ever have? We're both consenting adults. If there is a mutual attraction, why not scratch an itch? It's not like it will be a conflict of interest. Sure, Eve hired him, but it's obviously a sham. I'm sure Brady won't find any further proof to her stalker claims, and before I know it, I'll never see this man again.

"Finn's down the hall waiting for you. I'll tell him you need to get a run in."

And with that, he is out the door without another word.

Maybe it *is* be best if I never see him again. Obviously, that spark I felt isn't mutual, and now he probably thinks I'm just pathetic and desperate. I must be if I thought a guy like that would let his guard down long enough to have some fun.

The club is packed so tight, I can barely move. Club Envy is filled with celebrities, reporters, and a bunch of specially selected patrons who can go back out into the world after tonight and tell everyone what a raging success the new club is. I don't want to be here tonight, especially after pounding away my frustrations from my earlier interaction with Brady on a five-mile run. I'm exhausted, mentally and physically. I keep telling myself that any attraction I feel towards the man is foolish and a waste of my time.

All I had wanted to do when I got home was curl up and NOT think about Brady. Unfortunately, that isn't in the cards for me. Eve planned this appearance months ago, and if I even mention the idea of skipping it, my decision will be made into a huge ordeal and a messy argument that I'm not in the mood for.

So instead, I suck it up, put on the hottest dress I have in my closet, and decide to make the most of the night by dancing my ass off with a bunch of good looking men that I'm absolutely *not* imagining are Brady when I close my eyes and our bodies brush against each other on the crowded dance floor. Luckily, the music pumps through the sound system and cancels out the need to make small talk with any of them.

Over the shoulder of my current dance partner, I catch Finn's eye at the bar as he keeps watch over me from a distance while nursing a ginger ale. I roll my eyes and nod my head towards the guy who doesn't understand the concept of loud music and how it isn't conducive to telling someone your whole life story. Finn lifts his chin in response to my unspoken plea to rescue me from Chatty Cathy in a few minutes. Once I'm satisfied that he gets my message, I turn away from Finn and my dance partner, and raise my arms above my head, swaying to the beat of the song. I hope he'll get the hint. If my back is to him, maybe he'll refrain from trying to tell me about his ex-wife. Thankfully, he stops talking, but this just gives him the opportunity to push himself up against me and rest his hands on my hips while he moves his body with mine.

I close my eyes and pretend like he's not there. Oh, who am I kidding? I pretend like it's someone else with their hard body pressed flush with my back, sliding against me and making me burn with need.

The guy's hands momentarily leave my hips and his body moves away. Before I can be grateful that he's finally realized I'm not going to participate in his conversation, he's back, but this time he wraps one arm around my waist from behind and pulls me roughly up against his rock hard chest. In my black, backless halter dress, I can feel his muscles and his warmth through the cotton of his shirt against my bare skin.

Now that's more like it.

I can't tell if it's the same guy or not, but I don't even care as a new song starts, slower and sexier than the last. I recognize it instantly as *Bloodstream* by Stateless. This song always makes me think about sex and this time is no different, especially having a man this close to me. He keeps his arm wrapped tightly around my waist with his fingers splaying across my flat stomach. His other hand grabs my hip and pulls me back as close as possible to his body until my ass is firmly nestled against his erection.

Oh shit. I should move. I should really, really move.

I should not be enjoying this at all, but everything is clouding my judgment tonight, and being irritated at Brady's inability to be a human being isn't helping the situation. This guy's arms around me make me feel secure, and I'm not going to lie, feeling his hardness against me turns me on. It feels good to finally feel *something*.

The thump of the base is pounding through my body, and I push myself even closer to my dance partner who moves his hips slowly and seductively in perfect rhythm to the music. I rest my arm on top the one circling my waist and reach behind me with my other arm, grabbing onto his hip and securely holding him against me as we continue to move together with the sensual tempo of the song. I feel a hand slowly slide across my bare shoulder, and I shudder at the contact of his hand against my skin, realizing he has taken it off of my hip so he can move my hair out of the way. Without conscious thought, I tilt my head to the side to give him access to my neck.

I should have come to my senses long before now, but nothing else matters except feeling his lips on me. I should be embarrassed that I'm acting so out of character. I don't dance like this, I don't get turned on like this, and I don't feel things like this. I should be walking away before a photographer notices me on the dance floor and takes a picture that will be flashed all over the front pages of all the magazines.

Our movements slow until we are barely rocking our hips together, our bodies still pressed as close as we can possibly get, and I can't make my feet move to put distance between us if I tried.

I let out a small whimper at the first feel of his warm, wet lips against my neck. A rush of heat and desire explodes between my legs, and I dig my nails into his hip to keep my knees from buckling when he pulls back slightly and snakes his tongue out to lick my sweat-glistened skin. His lips reattach to my neck, and I feel his teeth graze roughly against the sensitive skin there. I've never imagined that something like this could feel so good, and I never want it to end. I don't care that we're on a dance floor in the middle of hundreds of people or that my mother will most likely have a field day with this when she finds out.

I want more. I want to feel something I've never felt before. I want that explosion of desire and need, and right now it feels like this nameless, faceless man is the only person in the world who can give it to me. I want to forget my problems for just one minute, focus on absolutely nothing but touch and sensation and a thrill of excitement that's been lacking in my life for far too long.

"Do you even care that I could have been your stalker manhandling you out here on the dance floor?"

The sound of Brady's deep voice in my ear is like a bucket of cold water thrown down my back. I jerk around and out of the warmth of his arms, staring at him in shock and embarrassment.

I was rubbing myself up against a guy who obviously wants nothing more than to humiliate me.

"What the hell are you doing here?" I shout angrily over the music, trying to will the reddening of mortification on my cheeks to go away before he notices.

Brady closes the distance I put between us, slides his arm back around me, and pulls me up against the front of him.

He looks down between us, and his nostrils flare as he gets a great view of my breasts which are pushed up against his chest; they practically spill out of the top of my dress with the force of his grab. He quickly brings his eyes back up to mine, and they are cold and hard as they bore into me.

"I came here to make sure you were safe. And it's a damn good thing I did since your bodyguard is too busy with his hand on the ass of some slut up at the bar," he growls.

I break eye contact and glance over to where he's pointing with his thumb. Sure enough, Finn has his back to the dance floor while he chats up a redhead.

Looking back at Brady, I have to force myself to stand my ground as I stare at the anger rolling off of him. His legs are planted in a wide stance, and I can see a vein pulsing on the side of his neck. He really is pissed that Finn isn't paying much attention to me.

"You know, I'm a big girl and I'm pretty sure I can handle dancing at a club without someone babysitting me," I fire back, shoving against his chest until he releases me.

Standing that close to him just reminds me of what it felt like moments ago when I was dancing with him—how lost I was to the feel of his body moving in perfect sync with mine and his arms burning like a brand around my waist as they trapped me against him.

"How much have you had to drink tonight?" he throws back, narrowing his eyes at me in disgust as he looks at my pupils. "Do you even care that you were grinding your ass all over a stranger like a—"

My mouth drops open and a gasp escapes past my lips, the color draining from my face when he pauses with his assessment of me.

"No, please, continue. Grinding my ass all over like a what?"

I know exactly what he's about to say before he thinks better of it. Slut, whore, tramp... I just want to hear him say it.

He refuses to take the bait and continues to stand stock still in the middle of the dance floor, his hands clutched into fists at his side as the anger rolls off of him.

"For your information, I don't drink. Ever. And you may run hot one minute and cold the next, and your moods change so fast you're giving me a constant headache, but last time I checked, you weren't a stranger. And what the hell WAS that anyway?" I demand, throwing my arm out to the side angrily and pointing to the spot where we had been dancing moments ago.

"It was my way of showing you how vulnerable you are. You had no idea who I was. I could have pulled a weapon on you at any point, and you would have been helpless against me," he snaps back, taking another step towards me and invading my personal space once again.

I push down the pang of disappointment that his words bring, reminding me that he couldn't have cared less about being close to me; he just wanted to prove a point.

"Give me a break with this stalker bullshit! You and I both know there is nothing there. You've been here for a week and haven't found anything, so save me the melodrama."

A new song comes over the sound system, and I recognize it as one of my own. I'm not in the mood to listen to people screaming the lyrics, patting me on the back, or jumping up and down to the beat, not when I'm trying to cool down my libido and pretend like Brady's close proximity isn't tying me up in knots.

I shoulder past Brady, quickly shoving my way through all of the sweaty bodies that surround us, until I'm finally off of the dance floor. I can just make out Brady shouting at me, asking me where I'm going, but I ignore him and the crowd swallows me up as I angle my body and squeeze through the mass of partiers to get to the exit for some fresh air.

The bouncer standing by one of the side doors gives me a curt nod and holds open the door for me. I step out into the warm night air and take a deep breath, my ears ringing now that I'm out of the close confines of the club. The music beats are replaced with the distant sounds of traffic from the nearby highway as I hear the door click shut behind me. I close my eyes and tilt my head up to the sky, enjoying my first moment of peace all evening. Before I can fill my lungs completely with fresh air, a hand is clamped roughly around my mouth, and I'm pulled up and off of my feet.

After the shock wears off that someone has just grabbed me while I'm alone on the street, I don't immediately begin to fight. My first thought is that Brady has followed me out here and wants to teach me another lesson.

As the man crosses the street, I realize too late that this isn't Brady. Brady is lean and muscular, not built like a linebacker with arms the size of tree stumps. I frantically begin kicking out my legs in front of me and squirming as hard as I can. My screams are muffled by the large, sweaty hand that pushes harder against my mouth, and my weak attempts at getting free are no match for the giant who towers over me and clutches my back against the front of him. He's dragging me away from the building and across the street. My eyes desperately search around for someone, anyone to come outside and notice me. His arm is banded around both of my arms, forcing them to stay put at my sides so I can't even claw him or pound into him with the fists I've made. I'm still trying to scream around his hand, my voice straining with the effort, but he only squeezes onto my face harder—so hard I can taste blood in my mouth from my teeth cutting into my cheeks. I jerk my head angrily from side to side, trying to dislodge his hand while I continue kicking my feet out as hard as I can. He's holding me off of the ground as he hustles backwards, further and further away from the side door of the club, and my high heeled feet hit nothing but air. One of my shoes flies off and clatters to the ground.

Why did I come out here alone? Even if there wasn't some strange guy sending me letters, I KNOW better than to do something this foolish.

The man suddenly stops walking, setting my feet on the ground but keeping a tight hold on me. He leans his face to one side of my head, and I can feel his sweaty, stale breath against my ear. I shudder in fear and revulsion as he traces his tongue along my earlobe before whispering into my ear.

"You're going to be mine someday very soon, princess. I'm not ready for you just yet, but I will be. And you're going to be ready for me," he states menacingly as the arm wrapped around my arms and waist moves lower, the fingers of his big, meaty hand sliding in between my legs right where my short dress stops.

Oh God, don't let him do this. I don't want his hands on me.

I'm so busy squeezing my eyes shut and trying to block out the way his callused fingers feel on the inside of my thighs as they inch upward, it takes me a moment to realize his grip around my mouth has slipped and he's not holding on so tight. Without giving a second thought to what I'm about to do, I open my mouth wide and clamp down as hard as I can on the knuckle and finger of his right hand. The man lets out a shocked, painful scream as I squeeze my jaw together as hard as I can. His hand between my legs immediately drops, and he shoves me roughly away from him. Only having one shoe on throws me off balance, and I stumble, tripping over a bump in the sidewalk, and fall down hard on my knees. The palms of my hands scrape against the concrete as I use them to brace my fall. Ignoring the pain that shoots up my knees and my arms, I let out the most blood curdling scream I can muster as I awkwardly try to push myself back up to my feet and scramble away at the same time. I continue to scream as I crawl and stumble my way back towards the club, back towards people who will help me.

I see the door of the club that I came out of burst open and slam against the opposite wall, and a feeling of relief washes through me. A feeling that is quickly snuffed out when rough hands clutch a handful of my hair and yank me backwards roughly. My feet slide out from under me, and my butt slams onto the sidewalk so hard that pain shoots up my tailbone and I cry out. I fling my arms behind my head to smack and scratch at the arm that is dragging me away from freedom, my feet slipping and sliding against the ground trying to gain traction.

I tilt my head back to try and finally get a look at who is

doing this to me, but all I see is a fist coming towards my face and then nothing but black.

CHAPTER 9
BRADY

I hear her scream as soon as the bouncer throws the door open. It echoes through the alley, and there is so much pain and fear in it that my heart momentarily stutters in my chest. I take off at a frantic run, shouting over my shoulder for the guy holding the door to call 9-1-1.

I can see her just across the street, crumpled to the ground, blood covering her knees. A large man wearing nondescript clothes and a ski mask over his face yanks her back by her hair, his fist raised above her head. I push myself harder and faster, my legs and arms pumping and my adrenalin spiking as I make it to the other side of the street, but not before I watch the man slam his fist into Layla's face.

Seconds later, I ram my body into the side of his like a fullback during the Super Bowl. We both crash to the ground, my body landing on top of his and pushing him into the dirt. I'm pretty good at hand-to-hand combat, but this guy is three times my size and he fights dirty. I take an uppercut to the chin and a knee to the groin before I can get my bearings and throw my fist into his jaw. With an elbow to my chest that knocks the wind out of me, he shoves me off of him, scrambles up off of the ground, and takes off running in the opposite direction of the club. I quickly push myself up to my knees, whip my gun out from its hiding spot tucked in the back of my jeans, and take aim at his dark silhouette as he weaves in and out of parked cars before disappearing down another side street.

"Son of a bitch!" I shout, smacking my hand down on the ground before turning around to check on Layla, stowing my gun back in its holster as I move.

She's out cold a few feet away from me, sprawled on the ground with dirt and grass stains all over her dress, cinders and blood covering her hands and knees. A lot of blood. Entirely too much for my liking. I need to get her the fuck out of here and fast. The cuts are small from what I can tell, but they are bleeding like a bitch. Sliding my gun back into place, I crawl over to her lifeless form and gingerly smooth her tangled mess of hair off of her face. I wince at the sight of the bruise that's already starting to form on her cheekbone. As sirens in the distance start to get closer, I see groups of people gathering just outside the club door out of the corner of my eye, and I know I need to get her out of here immediately before someone takes a picture.

I cup Layla's uninjured cheek in my hand and gently turn her face towards me.

"Come on, baby, wake up. Let me see those beautiful blue eyes."

My thumb strokes her cheek softly as I continue to coax her awake, scanning her body for other injuries I might have missed.

I swear to Christ if that asshole touched her anywhere else...

I push back my fury as I hear a quiet, painful moan come from her lips.

"That's it, Layla. Come on, it's okay. You're safe now."

Before I can say anything else, the squeal of tires causes me to jerk my head up away from Layla, and I see a black SUV slam to a stop on the street right in front of us. I reach behind me for my gun when the passenger window slides down and Finn yells out to me.

"Come on! Let's go! Get her in the car before the cops get here and this place is a fucking circus. We'll go back to her cabin and call them from there."

I know the right thing to do would be to wait here so we can give our statements and Layla can get medical treatment, but Finn is right. In about five seconds, that club is going to empty when the news starts spreading, and every single person in there is going to be hovering over Layla, taking pictures and asking questions, not caring for one minute that she was just attacked.

Taking one last look at the hordes of people already

gathering on the sidewalk, I curse under my breath, slide one arm under Layla's neck and the other under her knees, and scoop her up into my arms, rushing over to the backseat of Finn's vehicle. Getting inside as quickly as I can, I situate Layla on my lap, cradling her to me as Finn guns the engine and takes off down the street, narrowly missing a parked car.

"WHERE THE FUCK WERE YOU?" I yell at Finn as he weaves in and out of traffic. "You were supposed to be watching her. You are NEVER to let her out of your sight. What the fuck is wrong with you?"

My body is vibrating with rage as I think about what could have happened to the woman lying in my arms. She's sweet, beautiful, smart, and funny, and in just one minute, her life could have been snuffed out. I can't help but take my anger out on the one person in her life that is supposed to protect her.

"I don't know! Fuck! I turned my back for one minute, I swear. I saw you come up behind her on the dance floor so I figured she was fine," Finn rambles nervously before his guilt turns to fury that matches my own. "Where the hell were YOU? You were standing right there next to her! How the hell did she get outside alone?"

Not that I owe this guy any fucking explanation, but I give it to him anyway so he will shut the hell up.

"She stormed off and made her way through the crowd before I could stop her. I got people out of my way as fast as I fucking could. That guy must have been standing there, watching, waiting for her. She wasn't out that door for more than thirty seconds before I got outside."

I ignore my own anger with myself; directing it towards Finn is easier. I should never have said what I did, done what I had to her. I should have kept my cool and remained professional.

Thinking back to earlier in the evening, standing in the shadows watching her dance with all those men all night long filled me with an emotion I'm not used to—jealousy. No one should get to be that close to her, touch her, and hold her. No one except me.

A guttural roar almost slipped out when the last guy put his hands on her hips. Without thinking about what I was doing, I stalked across the dance floor and shoved him away, but not before leaning in close to him and telling him that if he so much as looked at Layla again, I would wipe up the dance floor with his bloody face.

I'm silent in the back seat of the car as I process those last few minutes on the dance floor and how every cell in my body screamed for me to just pull Layla against me and kiss her. Kiss that sweet, smart ass mouth and just forget about all of the reasons why it's a bad idea. Holding her soft, warm body against mine instantly flooded me with need, and I was hard as a rock as soon as she pushed her ass into me. I told her it was all just to prove a point, but that was a lie. I wanted her close to me. I wanted to touch her, taste her.

So I did.

And now I'm completely fucked because one taste of her skin isn't nearly enough.

I feel her squirm in my arms and lower my head to look at her as she slowly starts to wake up. I see flashes of her face illuminated by the street lights outside as we rush through traffic and watch as her eyes slowly blink open and come into focus.

"Ow." She winces and her hand comes up to cup the side of her face with the nasty bruise and small cut on it.

"We're almost home Lay, hold on," Finn tells her, glancing quickly over his shoulder to check on her while he maneuvers the SUV into another lane.

Her chin quivers and I watch the streetlights cast sparkles in her eyes as they fill with tears.

"I'm sorry," she whispers, staring up at me. "That was so stupid. I shouldn't have gone outside alone. I know that. I know better."

A tear escapes from one eye, and I watch it slide down one cheek, mesmerized by the path it takes over her skin. Keeping my palm against her uninjured cheek, I use my thumb to wipe away the wetness.

"Shhh, it's okay. I shouldn't have pissed you off. I'm old enough to know that you never tell a sexy woman you only wanted to dance with her to prove a point," I tell her softly, trying to lighten the mood.

It does the trick. The shame and guilt disappears from her face as she lets out a short, watery laugh.

The car comes to a quick stop, and I pull my gaze away from Layla to look up, noticing we're parked right out front of the biggest, most luxurious home I've ever seen.

Sweet mother of God. This is what they call a cabin? What the hell do they call a mansion? A shack in the woods?

The back door opens and Finn reaches inside trying to pull Layla off of my lap. I shove his hands away, not ready to let go of her just yet, and not trusting Finn to keep her safe, even if it is just to help her walk to the door.

"It's alright, I've got it," I tell him irritably as I slide out of the car, hugging Layla's body to mine and hefting her up higher in my arms as I make my way across the driveway to the front porch.

Finn doesn't say a word, but I can sense the fury pouring out of him as he slams the car door closed behind me, and I can hear him breathing angrily through his nose as he follows, pounding his feet on the stairs behind me.

He brushes past me, his shoulder purposefully bumping into mine as he reaches the front door and punches in the security code to disarm the alarm. The door clicks to let us know the alarm is off, and Finn opens it, holding it wide so I can enter with Layla. My feet come to a stop as Finn hits a few switches to the right of the door, and the living room is bathed in soft, white light.

Layla's house is definitely a cabin of sorts. The walls and ceiling are paneled with natural grain cedar, and the floor is smooth and shiny hardwood, but that's pretty much where the similarities to a *log cabin* end. The living room has vaulted, twenty-foot ceilings with a giant wagon wheel light fixture hanging down in the center, each spoke holding an electric lighted candle. The wall directly across from where I'm standing is nothing but framed windows from floor to ceiling, with a gorgeous view of the fields, valleys, and forest that make up her backyard. Despite its size, the room is homey with dark brown, well-worn leather furniture, throw pillows, and a few unfolded blankets tossed over the backs. The floor-to-ceiling stone fireplace that takes up half of the wall to my left adds to the warmth of the home. Its mantle is filled with pictures of Layla as a child, Layla and Finn, and one of a teenage Layla holding a guitar next to a man I assume is her father.

"Stop gawking and put me down," Layla speaks up from my arms as she catches me staring around the room with my mouth open.

"Sorry," I apologize with a laugh as I walk her over to the leather sectional in front of the fireplace and set her down gently. "I'm not used to hanging out with famous rock stars that live in palaces."

I kneel down next to the couch and take both of her hands in mine, turning them palm up so I can inspect the damage she did when she fell.

"This is not a palace and I'm not a rock star," Layla insists with a grimace as I turn her hands this way and that to try and make sure there isn't any glass imbedded in them.

"Really? So, everyone you know has a 1958 Gibson Les Paul hanging on their wall in a glass case...signed by Jimmy Page?" I'm completely floored and can't even comprehend what I'm looking at. "Obviously, I'm hanging out with the wrong people," I reply with a chuckle as I glance over at the guitar above the fireplace that my eyes immediately zeroed in on when I set her down on the couch.

"The cops and EMTs will be here in about twenty minutes," Finn states, coming up behind me and shoving his phone into his back pocket. "They're finishing up statements at the club." I can hear the guilt in Finn's voice, and part of me wants to turn around and finish our argument from the car and ask him again what the hell he was thinking taking his eyes off of Layla for even one minute.

Layla looks over my shoulder and up at Finn, her face softening with a smile for him. "Hey, it's okay. It's not your fault. I was an idiot. I should never have left the club by myself," she reassures him softly.

I don't share the same sentiment, so I keep my mouth shut and continue checking her hands and knees for glass and to make sure the bleeding has stopped, which it hasn't. I've never seen someone bleed this much from a few little cuts and scrapes.

"What did the guy want? What did he say to you? Did he do anything else to you?"

I watch the color drain from Layla at Finn's rapid-fire questions, and I want to stand up and shove my fist into his face. She swallows roughly a few times, and her eyes blink back more tears as Finn continues his interrogation. If I didn't know any better, I would think he sounded like some crazy fan instead of her friend. Someone who just wants the dirty details and gossip instead of making sure his friend is okay.

"Did you get a good look at him? Recognize his voice?"

I finally stand up and turn to face Finn, our noses practically touching, the tightness in my eyes and my face hopefully warning him that I'm about two seconds away from beating his ass if he doesn't stop.

"I think Layla needs a break. At least until the cops get here. She shouldn't have to go over this more than once," I tell him.

I can see the war of emotions on his face: rage, resentment, jealousy, shame. They're all right there for me to witness as he tries to keep himself in check and not make a scene in front of Layla.

"I'm going to go get you a few wet towels for your cuts and scrapes, see if I can stop the bleeding, and a bag of ice for your cheek," I tell Layla without taking my eyes off of Finn.

Once I'm satisfied he's finished grilling her, I step around him and head for the massive staircase next to the kitchen, hoping it will take me to a bathroom.

As I finish wringing out a couple of small towels a few minutes later, I hear the door slam closed downstairs and a raised voice carrying up the stairs. Grabbing the towels, I go out into the hall and look down over the balcony above the living room to see Eve standing next to the couch glaring down at Layla with her hands on her hips, her posture rigid.

"What the hell were you thinking, you stupid, stupid girl? Have you even seen your face? How in the hell are you supposed to do a photo shoot tomorrow for the cover of InStyle when you look like shit?" Eve berates Layla.

My blood boils when I hear the words coming out of Layla's mother's mouth, and I quickly turn and head for the stairs.

"I swear to God you are WORTHLESS! You see what happens when you don't listen to me? Things get ruined. You ruin everything. Now I'm going to look like an idiot when I have to call the magazine and reschedule the shoot," Eve states as I make my way to the bottom of the stairs.

"Jesus, wash that shit off of your hands and legs for God's

sakes before anyone gets here and sees you looking like this."

I waltz up behind Eve, reach around her, and quietly hand Layla one of the wet towels, giving her a reassuring smile as I do so.

Eve jumps when she realizes she isn't alone in the house with Finn and her daughter and quickly turns around and pastes a fake smile on her face.

"Mr. Marshall! So good to see you again, I didn't realize—"

"No, you didn't realize," I deadpan, cutting her off. "Layla is fine, by the way. I'm sure she appreciates your concern for her well-being. The guy who attacked her only dragged her by her hair and punched her in the face so hard that she passed out. I got a few good punches in, but he took off before I could apprehend him. That's what you were going to ask next, right? If we caught the guy who jumped your daughter right outside of a club packed with people?"

We stand there staring at one another, and the tension is so thick in the room I might be a little uncomfortable with it if I gave two shits what this woman thinks of me.

"Finn, could you go outside and greet the police officers when they get here?" Eve asks, breaking my stare and walking around me towards the kitchen.

She busies herself making a pot of coffee, running water into the carafe, and rummaging through cupboards for mugs and coffee grounds, completely ignoring the fact that I just called her on her bullshit.

Finn spares one more guilt-ridden glance towards Layla before turning and walking out the door. Walking over to where she sits on the couch, I go back to my earlier position of kneeling in front of her on the floor and take the wet towel from her hands. I begin softly patting the cuts and scrapes on her knees to try to get them to stop bleeding, pausing and wincing with her every time she takes in a painful breath when I touch a particularly rough looking spot.

"You shouldn't have done that. You're on her shit list now," Layla says softly, not looking up from what she's doing.

"I couldn't care less what that woman thinks of me," I reply, glancing over my shoulder to make sure Eve can't hear us. "It's disgusting that she cares more about your appearance than what could have happened to you out there."

Layla shrugs and I notice the mirth in her eyes from a few moments ago when I teased her about the size of her home is now completely gone. Her shoulders droop and her head hangs low, the sparkle in her eyes, despite what happened to her earlier, replaced by dullness and resignation.

"I'm used to it. It's no big deal."

I open my mouth to argue with her. To tell her that it IS a big deal and tell her she's worth more than her mother even knows, that she's strong and amazing and nothing Eve says means anything, that EVE doesn't mean anything, but before I can reassure her, the door opens and the cabin is suddenly filled with members of the Nashville police department and three EMTs who all rush to Layla's side, shoving me out of the way to tend to her and ask her questions.

I recognize a few of the men from the force, none of whom I've seen since Eric's funeral because I chose to shut myself off from these people and that life the day I said goodbye to him and began to drown myself in booze. It's awkward and uncomfortable at first as they shake my hand, pat me on the back, and ask me how I've been. I can see Layla's questioning eyes as she watches the exchange between us. I know she probably wonders how they know me and why they look at me with pity in their eyes. If I want to protect her and find out why the hell she was attacked tonight and who was responsible, I need her to trust me. And I know the only way I can go about doing that is to be honest with her about the kind of person I used to be. *Hell, maybe even still am.* She needs to know what she's getting into with me because looking at her right now, with her chin held high and determination on her face as she relives every moment of her attack, I know I'm done for when it comes to this woman. She's gotten under my skin, and I'm not sure if I'll ever be ready to remove her. I can't walk away and I sure as shit can't ignore whatever this is between us. The only way I can figure that out and what happened to her tonight, is to stick to her like glue. And after dancing close to her and holding her in my arms, there's nowhere else I'd rather be right now. I just need to convince her of that.

CHAPTER 10

Ray Bergin holds the phone between his cheek and shoulder, grabbing a bag of frozen peas from the freezer and pressing it against his black eye while he waits for his call to be answered.

The last couple of calls he made on the cell phone number he was given went unanswered, so he decides to call on a number he knows won't be ignored.

"What the hell are you doing calling me on this number?"

Ray rolls his eyes and walks out of the kitchen, flopping down on an old ripped couch in the corner of the living room in his trailer.

"Gee, no hello?" he asks with a laugh as he picks up the remote and flips through the channels until he finds a good soft core porn movie to watch.

"What do you want?" his contact on the other end asks in an angry whisper.

"It seems the cell number you gave me doesn't work. Imagine that?"

An indignant huff sounds through the line. "I must have given you the wrong number. Just don't ever call me here again.

Someone else could have answered and then we would both be fucked."

Ray's blood boils as he listens to the shit coming out of this person's mouth.

"I hate to break it to you, but I'm not the one going behind someone's back who trusts me and living the high life while doing it. I just spent the last twenty-four months in prison and live in a shit hole trailer. I ain't got nothin' to lose, and you got plenty. It would do you good to remember that."

Ray turns up the volume on the two chicks going down on each other and lets his words sink in for a few minutes while he enjoys a little girl-on-girl action.

"Fine, you made your point. Now make another one. Why the hell are you calling me?"

"Just figured I'd check in and make sure the job was done to your satisfaction," Ray replies distractedly as he cocks his head and focuses on the television. He sets the remote down next to him and eases his body lower on the couch so he can put his feet up on the milk crates he uses as a coffee table.

"You went a little overboard, don't you think? I told you to scare her, not beat the shit out of her," the voice replies.

"You should have been a little more specific then," Ray reminds with a laugh.

"I didn't pay you to mess up her face."

"So far you've only paid me for the letters. And what

about *my* face? You didn't tell me that PI asshole was going to be following her around like a puppy dog. That guy came out of nowhere and almost had me. There better be some extra cash in that envelope tomorrow to make up for my pain and suffering, or else I've got a few recorded phone conversations and emails the press might be very interested in listening to."

Ray throws the now-melted bag of peas to the end of the couch and smiles to himself when he hears nervous, rapid breathing on the other end of the line.

"Let's not get ahead of ourselves here. I said I'd pay you and I will. I don't know what the hell Brady Marshall was doing at that club tonight. It's obvious that slut already has him wrapped around her little finger. He's a drunk and one more tragedy away from putting a gun in his mouth. That's the only reason he was hired. It looks good to the public, but he's too busy wallowing in his own misery to figure anything out. Still, you damn well better be covering your tracks. And I think after tomorrow, your services won't be needed anymore."

Ray grinds his teeth in anger. He doesn't let anyone talk to him this way. He's killed people in the past for a lot less, and right now, he's had enough of the pompous, I'm-better-than-you act.

"You and I have known each other for quite some time now. You should know that I don't take orders from anyone, especially someone like you. Now that I've had a chance to get up close and personal to little miss Layla, I don't think I'm anywhere near finished with her yet," Ray says, his cock swelling in his pants—a combination of the movie and thoughts of Layla Carlysle and her hot little body that he had pressed up against him tonight.

"What do you mean you're not finished? I paid you to write a few letters and give her a little scare. That's it."

"Didn't we already go over this? I haven't gotten paid for my services from tonight. We'll see how much of a bonus I get tomorrow. Then I'll decide when and if I'm finished with that pretty little thing."

Ray likes the sound of fear and panic in the voice on the other end. It reminds him that regardless of how much money someone has, it's good to be the person with the upper hand. And he definitely has the upper hand right now.

"I'm bored with this conversation and I've got shit to do. Leave the money in our usual drop-off place by nine tomorrow morning."

Ray hangs up the phone and tosses it in the general direction of the bag of peas, a huge smile on his face as he turns up the volume of the movie as loud it will go, slides his hand down the front of his pants, and palms his erection. Thoughts of Layla Carlysle fill his mind as he remembers the way she fought against him.

She had a hard little body and it made him hot thinking

about her working up a sweat to get it that way. She was also soft in all the right places, especially between her legs.

His cock grows longer and fuller as he slides his hand up and down his shaft, thinking about his fingers sliding between Layla's legs. Her thighs were clenched tight around his hand, trying to deny him access to that sweet place he'd love to sink his dick into, but he still managed to pry his fingers between those smooth thighs and touch all that creamy, hot skin for a few seconds before she bit him.

Ray pumps his fist faster and faster, his balls tightening as he thinks about the heat he felt on his fingers and her wet mouth clamped down on his hand. It hurt like a mother fucker, but Ray got off on the pain. He pictures her wrapping that sweet mouth around his cock and bobbing her head up and down on him while he pulls her hair and pushes himself to the back of her throat until she gags and maybe even bites down on him.

It doesn't take long before he's panting and moaning, cursing Layla's name loudly in the small confines of his trailer as he brings himself to completion.

He slumps back against the couch with a satisfied smile on his face, hoping the next time he has a few minutes alone with Layla Carlysle, she'll fight him even harder. It's always better when they struggle. And Ray can't wait to feel that little hell cat clawing and scratching at him again.

CHAPTER 11
Layla

"You're going to be mine someday very soon, princess. I'm not ready for you just yet, but I will be. And you're going to be ready for me."

The scream rips from my throat as I bolt up in bed, kicking the twisted covers off of my legs. I can't stop screaming and I feel like I can't breathe. The soft, cool sheets suddenly feel like hot, sweaty hands wrapped around my legs, and I just want them off.

The door to my room bursts open and slams against the opposite wall as I continue to whimper and try unsuccessfully to get free, the sheets getting more and more tangled with my legs.

"Get them off! GET THEM OFF!" I scream frantically as I claw at the material.

Brady is across the room in seconds, climbs onto the bed with me, and cradles my face in his hands, forcing me to look into his eyes.

"Shhh, it's okay, Layla. Look at me, it's okay. It was just a dream."

I shake my head vigorously, tears pooling in my eyes as I remember my attacker's words, his breath, and the feel of his hands on me.

"You're safe now, just breathe."

The fight leaves my body, and I close my eyes, sagging forward until my head is resting against his chest.

His bare chest.

"I'm going to untangle you from the sheets, okay?" he asks softly, his hand resting on top of my head.

A chill rolls through my body at Brady's gentle words, and it has nothing to do with my damp, sweaty skin from the dream and everything to do with the man in my bed.

The dream is momentarily forgotten as he moves away from me. With the bright moonlight streaming in through the window, and the nightlight in my bathroom, I have a clear view of him now. His sculpted chest and stomach tightens with the movement of his arms as he starts pulling my legs out of the tangled mess of sheets. The only thing he wears is a pair of drawstring sweat pants that hang low on his waist, the deep V between his abs and his hips clearly visible and undeniably mouthwatering.

"Why are you here?" I ask dumbly as his hand wraps around my ankle and slides one of my legs free so I can finally turn and hang them off the edge of the bed. I ignore the burning on the skin of my leg where he touched me and instead, focus on the fact that I'm barely wearing more than him.

"I heard you screaming from downstairs."

My thin, small, purple tank top doesn't leave much to the imagination so I cross my arms over my braless chest and try to calm my breathing but realize it's pointless because I'm wearing an equally revealing pair of matching boy shorts.

I look up at him in confusion. "What?'

He chuckles and reaches over, running his fingers through my hair. It's still damp from the shower I took before bed to try and scrub the feel of that disgusting man's hands off of me.

"You asked what I was doing here. I heard you screaming. You scared the shit out of me with those lungs on you."

I reach up with one hand and rub my temple, the beginning of a headache forming after the events of tonight and the awful dream.

"No, I mean, what are you doing *here*. In my house. In the middle of the night, like…that," I stutter, my hand waving in his general direction.

Brady looks down at himself and then back up to me, raising one eyebrow.

"Well, I usually sleep in the buff, but when I heard you scream, I didn't have time to throw much else on. Is this bothering you?" he asks with a smirk on his full lips.

Full, kissable lips.

Shut up, Layla.

"As for why I'm here, I didn't feel right leaving when that guy is still out there. I'm going to stick around until he's caught just to be on the safe side."

My arms fall to my sides, and I turn and stare at him in shock, my eyes widening and my mouth dropping open.

"You can't stay here. I mean, it's nice of you to offer and all, but I have a brand new security system. And Finn lives in the cabin right behind me."

And you being this close to me twenty-four seven when all I can think about is licking your stomach is NOT good. Not good at all.

"Sorry, sweetheart, I'm not negotiating this with you. I was hired to do a job, and I'm not going to slack off. What happened tonight should have never happened, and I need to find out why it did. I can't do that if I'm constantly worried about your safety by being elsewhere," he explains.

Would he really think about me and worry about me if he wasn't here? Gaaaah, focus! You CANNOT have this man living with you.

Before I can continue the argument, my eyes zero in on the tattoo I noticed when we went on our run all those weeks ago. Now that he isn't wearing a shirt, I can see the black inked words that flow in cursive script across his upper bicep. Without thinking, I reach out and run my fingers over the words.

"I will never forget," I read aloud in a low whisper.

Brady's jaw clenches as I finish running my fingertips over the words and look up at his face.

"What won't you forget?" I ask him, looking back and forth between his eyes.

He swallows and wets his lips, and I can't help but stare at his mouth when he opens it to speak.

"Friends, family, all the people I've let down," he speaks softly.

I shift my eyes away from his mouth and wonder about his words. This is the most he's opened up to me since that day in the woods and I want more. I want so much more. I don't want him to shut down by asking more questions, though, so I change the subject.

I notice a black and blue mark on his chin that's roughly the same size and shape as the one I currently sport under my eye. I immediately reach out and touch him.

"Was this from tonight?" I ask, my fingers grazing back and forth over the bruise.

Brady sucks in a sharp breath when I touch him again, his eyes roaming over my face, down my neck, and glancing heatedly over the cleavage showing at the top of my tank. I feel my nipples tingle and tighten as I watch him looking at me. He swallows thickly a few times as his gaze slowly makes its way back up to my face. There's nothing more sensual than watching a man struggle to keep himself in check when he's looking at you, nothing more arousing than seeing his eyes darken with desire and his tongue slide out to lick his lips because you know he's thinking about kissing you.

I can feel the heat from his body radiating off of him since we're sitting so close. All I can think about is pushing him back on the bed, straddling his hips, and feeling him between my legs, rubbing against this ache that has blossomed into full blown need.

"It's nothing, just a bruise. I've had worse."

Dropping my hand from his face, I jump up from the bed and stalk to the middle of the room, needing to put some distance between us so I can gather my bearings and think straight.

He can't stay here. I'll never get any sleep or be able to concentrate on anything, but there's no way in hell I can tell *him* that.

"Whatever you're thinking in that pretty little head of yours, you can stop right now. I'm not leaving. Not until that asshole is behind bars," Brady states, standing up from the bed and walking towards me.

"I hate this. I hate feeling helpless. I hate feeling like I have to rely on other people to protect me," I tell him angrily, trying to focus on something other than how good he looks standing half naked in the middle of my bedroom in bare feet like he belongs here.

"You're not helpless," he argues softly.

"Yes I am! He HAD me. I couldn't move my arms. I couldn't get away. I couldn't do anything but let him drag me away and do whatever he wanted to me."

I let the anger flow through me, preferring it much more right now than the desire of moments ago or the fear from this evening.

"You were in shock and scared to death. You can't blame yourself for not being able to take a man down that was three times your size. The important thing is that I got there in time."

Laughter laced with an edge bubbles out of me, and I and roll my eyes.

"You're not always going to be there. What the hell happens the next time?"

He clenches his hands at his sides, and his body tightens even more than it already is.

"There won't be a next time. You can count on that."

His voice is low and deep, and I can tell he means it. I believe that he means it, but he isn't Superman. He can't be everywhere at once, and he can't stop every threat that comes my way.

"But what if you aren't?"

I can see the battle he's waging with himself, and I instinctively move closer to him, wanting to soothe the rage he obviously feels when the thinks about not being there to keep me safe.

"You can't attach yourself to my hip, Brady. I'm a public figure and I have a demanding job that goes along with it. You can't be on stage with me, in my dressing room with me, or next to me for every interview or fan meet-and-greet I do.

"Teach me," I tell him, a sudden idea occurring to me.

He looks at me questioningly, pursing his lips as he rolls the idea around in his head. I can see him getting ready to tell me no, to reassure me that he won't leave my side, but I need this. I need him to understand and to help me.

"I feel powerless enough on a daily basis with my life. Please show me what to do. Teach me how not to be so defenseless. I need to feel like I have control over *something*," I plead with him.

Brady rubs his hand against the back of his neck and sighs and I know I have him.

"You weren't helpless when he had his arms around you," he finally says.

He drops his hand from his and neck reaches out to grab my shoulders, turning me around so that my back is to him.

He steps closer until I can feel his bare chest against my back, his mouth near my ear as he bends down to speak, his hands still holding onto my shoulders.

"He may have had your arms pinned," he tells me, sliding

his hands down my arms and then wrapping them around me, "but you still had a very powerful weapon at your disposal."

My heart rate picks up, and my mouth suddenly feels dry as I try to remain focused on what he's telling me and not how good it feels to have his strong arms holding me against his hard body.

"As soon as the adrenaline kicks in, it will seem like everything is happening in slow motion. If you remember to breathe, stay calm, and focus, it will feel like you have hours to make a decision about what to do instead of just seconds," he says softly, his breath fanning the side of my face as his arms tighten around me just a fraction, holding me in place. "You can't use your hands, and your legs can't reach him, but what part of your body is closest to him right now?"

I don't want to say my ass, which is nestled against Brady's erection, which I can easily feel through the thin material of my shorts, even though it's all I can think about. I close my eyes and take a deep breath, forcing my heart to stop beating out of my chest and think about what I would do if this *wasn't* a gorgeous man I'm slowly beginning to trust with his arms secured around me.

"My head," I tell him quietly.

"Good," he states encouragingly. "With one hard bash of your head against his face, you could break his nose or stun him long enough for his arms to loosen so you can get free. All you need is to connect once or twice to his face or collarbone, and he'll be howling in pain."

His arms drop from around me, and I want to whimper when I no longer feel their warmth cradling me close.

Brady moves from behind, slowly circling around me, making me nervous as he stares me up and down.

"When you fight back, use the strongest parts of your body: your head, your fists, your elbows," he explains, touching his hand to each of those parts on me as he makes a full circle and is back behind me again brushing his body against mine in the process. "If all of those things are incapacitated, use your entire body."

In a flash, his arms are caging me tightly against him, and one of his hands is around my throat. "Don't think. Just act."

I begin struggling as hard as I can, twisting and turning to get out of his grasp, but I'm nowhere near as strong as he is. I can't get free no matter how hard I try, all of this exertion is just tiring me out and forcing my ass to rub against him and feel how much harder he's gotten since this self-defense lesson began. My body freezes in its struggle as I feel how turned on he is.

"Roll your shoulders forward," he says in a husky voice. "Don't try to strain or push away from your attacker."

I do as he instructs, hunching my shoulders.

"Now fall to the ground."

I slide out of his arms and down the length of him until

I'm free, turning my body and jumping up to face him.

"Holy shit, that worked," I whisper, staring at him in awe.

"It works when your attacker is behind you. What about if he comes at you straight on?" Brady asks, bending his knees and putting his hands up in front of him, getting ready to charge.

I swallow nervously, my brain a jumble of emotions as I try to think about the things he's just taught me and if I will ever be able to fully focus when he's standing in front of me looking fierce, his eyes blazing a trail down my body.

I run out of time to get my thoughts in order as he rushes me, wrapping his arms around me and pushing me backwards. My feet stumble over one another, and I lose my balance, falling backwards and taking him with me. One of his arms shoots out behind me to stop me from hitting the carpet. his body slams on top of me instead.

A thrill shoots through my body, feeling him touching me everywhere from chest to toe, and it's like nothing I've ever felt before.

Brady pushes up on one arm to ease some of his weight off of me, his other arm still wrapped securely around my waist.

"If you fall, there's no way he'll be able to keep both of his arms around you. You'll have at least one of yours free. Go for his vulnerable spots," he encourages, his warm breath floating over my parted lips. "Eyes, neck, groin."

As soon as he mentions that last spot, it's all I can focus

on. His groin is resting right on top of mine. Trying to surprise him, I bring my hand up quickly, my fist going for his throat. He catches it in his hand right before I make contact, pushing my arm up and over my head and securing it on the floor. Breathing heavy, my other hand flies up towards his eyes. He catches that hand just as easily, trapping it beside my head just like the other one.

"Good. Really good," he praises softly, his eyes moving to my lips as I lick the dryness off of them.

His breath begins coming out just as roughly as mine as he keeps my arms suspended over my head, his body pushing me into the carpet. Without conscious thought, I spread my legs until they are on either side of his hips, bringing my knees up and cradling him against me.

A moan escapes my mouth when I feel his hardness between my legs, right where I've wanted him all night. Before I even have a chance to be embarrassed at my actions, Brady lets out a low, growling curse and ducks his head down to my mouth.

CHAPTER 12
BRADY

The reasons why this is an incredibly bad idea fly out of my head as soon as my mouth touches hers. Just being in the same room with her is bad enough. Seeing her scared and frantic is a like a knife right through my heart. Watching her angry and determined as she paces in the middle of the bedroom in that tight tank top and shorts that are so small it should have been illegal is intoxicating—better than any buzz I've had in the last year. Holding her in my arms and having her body up against mine is hot and such a turn on I think I may explode from wanting her so much.

But this…being between her legs, feeling the heat of her arousal wrapping around my cock while I attack her mouth is mind blowing.

I can't get enough of her. It's impossible to get close enough, taste fast enough. As soon as my tongue touches hers, I know I'm gone. There will be no coming back from Layla Carlysle. She sucks my tongue into her mouth, wraps her legs around my waist, and in that one instant, it's like she was in my bloodstream and I can feel here everywhere. I want to sink inside of her and never come up for air.

Holding her arms in place above her head, I push my hips forward and slide myself against her, swallowing her moan as I strengthen the kiss, sweeping my tongue slow and deep through her mouth. She takes every part of the kiss and gives back equally, her tongue tangling with mine and moving in the same leisurely motion as my hips. Every time I slide against her, she whimpers into my mouth, and nothing else matters right now but having her continue to make those sounds. I want to hear her moan louder, come with my name on her lips.

I don't want to stop kissing her, but I need more. I need to taste her skin. Pulling my mouth away from hers, I make a trail of kisses across her cheek, down the side of her neck, and pause at her collarbone where I run the tip of my tongue. I let go of her hands and push myself up on one elbow, staring into her hooded eyes as I slide an open palm down the underside of her arm and her side until my fingers meet the bare skin of her stomach. She keeps her arms above her head and tilts her head up, arching her back as I slowly push her tank top up, revealing the creamy smooth skin of her flat stomach until finally her bare breasts are on display. They are full and beautiful, and her hardened nipples are begging for my mouth. I bend over her, holding my mouth an inch away from one of the tight buds, letting my warm breath flow over it and watch as it hardens even more. Layla whimpers

167

softly and her hands fly to the back of my head, clutching my hair between her fingers and urging my mouth to where she needs me. I lean forward the rest of the way, taking her nipple into my mouth and sucking it gently, my tongue circling as I pull her in deeper. I let my other hand gently knead and squeeze her other breast, my thumb rubbing back and forth over her nipple while I continue sucking her into my mouth and listen to her cries of pleasure. I thought just listening to her come would be enough for me, but it's not. I need to feel her when she lets go. I need to touch her heat as she squeezes around me.

I move suddenly, pulling my lips away from her nipple and placing one hand around her neck, tugging her to my mouth and sliding my tongue past her lips once again. I kiss her until we're both mindless with need. I tear my lips away and watch her eyes as I let my hand trail down her body and slide the tips of my fingers under the edge of her shorts. I don't want to do something she doesn't want. As much as I'm dying to touch her, she's been through hell tonight and I don't want her doing this out of some misplaced need to forget about what happened to her.

"Tell me what you want," I whisper against her lips.

She pushes her hips up a fraction so that my fingers slide further into the soft cotton material.

"You," she breathes against my mouth. "Touch me, Brady, please."

I swoop down without hesitation and kiss her lips, my hand sliding the rest of the way inside of her shorts at the same time until I feel nothing but the smooth warmth of her. I immediately plunge two fingers into her wet heat, and now it's my turn to whimper and moan into her mouth. She's soft and tight wrapped around my fingers, and I can only imagine how it would feel to have my cock buried inside of her right now, squeezing me and making me lose my mind.

One of her legs drops from my hip and she rests it on its side against the carpet, opening herself to me so I can push inside of her as deep as my fingers will go. Her body shudders against me as I pump slowly in and out of her, coating my fingers with her arousal. She wraps her arms around me, her hands smacking against my skin and her nails gently scraping down my back. I want to throw my head back in satisfaction and howl like dog.

I move my mouth to her neck, sucking her skin gently into my mouth as my thumb finds her center and circles slowly, around and around, back and forth, until her hips are thrusting against my hand and she's gasping for breath and crying for a release I'm aching to give her. She's so close I can practically feel her vibrating with need. I continue moving my hand against her, taking as much as she'll give me, willing to give her everything I have, including my soul, just to feel her come apart against me.

I move my mouth to her earlobe, taking it between my teeth and biting down gently before whispering in her ear.

"Let go, baby. I want to feel you let go."

My words have the desired effect. She wraps her arms around me tightly and holds her body suspended, racing for the edge and tumbling over. She cries out her release: a mixture of my name, curses, and mumbles of incoherent nothing. It's the most beautiful sound in the world.

I never want to stop touching her, never want to stop feeling her.

"You are so fucking beautiful," I sigh against her ear as she comes back down to earth, my fingers still buried inside of her because I can't bear to move them just yet.

I'm so lost in her I don't even realize one of her arms has moved from around my back. Her small, warm hand suddenly plunges down the front of my pants and wraps around an erection that is two seconds away from exploding after what just happened. I don't want her to feel like she has to reciprocate. Even though it kills me to tell her she doesn't have to do this, I need to. She needs to know feeling her and watching her come was better than any orgasm I've ever or will ever have.

"Layla, you don't—"

She pulls my head down and cuts off my words with a hard, bruising kiss, sliding the tip of her tongue across my bottom lip before pulling back and looking into my eyes.

"It's my turn now," she tells me with a wicked grin, her eyes sparkling and her hand tightening around me.

She slides her hand down to the base and back up quickly, skimming her thumb through the wetness on the tip, making my eyes roll in the back of my head.

Both of her legs wrap back around my waist and she pulls me closer and works me harder and faster. I haven't had a hand job since I was in high school. The women I'm usually with prefer to just hit it and go home. I don't know if it's just the fact that it's Layla doing this to me right now or how on edge I am, but this is the hottest fucking thing I've felt in a long time. She uses just the right amount of pressure and the perfect speed, and I'm thrusting into her hand and biting down on the side of her neck to muffle the cries that are dying to escape from my mouth right now. With my eyes squeezed shut and my face buried against her, I'm conscious of the fact that I still haven't removed my fingers from inside of her, and I slowly pull them almost all of the way out before plunging them back in. Her movements on my cock falter for a second as she groans in pleasure and grows impossibly wetter around me.

"Brady...fuck...I need you...oh God," she moans against my mouth as we race each other to release, both of our hands moving fast and hard against the other.

Her stammered words shoot straight through my body and right to my dick, and I can't move fast enough. She whimpers as

I pull my fingers away from her, and I almost let out my own frustrated groan as her hand drops from around me when I pull back just enough to push my pants down my hips far enough to free my erection. When she realizes what I'm doing, she lifts her hips and begins pushing her shorts down her thighs. I push her hands out of the way, wanting to feel the skin of her legs against my hands as I pull them down for her. I get them off and toss them to the side, lowering my body back down on top of her and positioning myself right at her opening.

"Tell me you're sure. Fuck, Layla, tell me you're sure," I plead as I slide the tip up and down through her wetness.

Her hands come up to my face, and she cups them on both of my cheeks, taking my bottom lip between her teeth and tugging on it gently.

"I'm sure. I am one hundred percent sure I need you inside me, Brady," she whispers.

I let out the breath I don't even realize I've been holding, pressing my mouth to hers and start to push inside of her.

A deafening, ear-piercing shriek of noise blasting through the house halts my movement, and my body freezes in surprise and shock. Neither one of us moves, the seconds ticking by and the racket growing louder as we both struggle to figure out what the hell is going on.

"Fuck! That's your security alarm," I shout over the noise as I push away from Layla and jump to my feet. I pull my pants up as I run over to the side table by the door where I had set my gun when I first entered the room after Layla's nightmare. Lifting it into my hands, I double check the chamber.

I turn around to find Layla sliding back into her shorts, a look of fear on her face. Her skin, previously flushed pink from arousal, is now ashen and her hands shake as she wraps her arms around her waist. I want to calm her nerves and tell her that everything will be okay, but I can't. Just like always, I let myself get distracted and now God knows who is trying to get into the house. I should have walked right back out of this room as soon as I saw she wasn't being harmed earlier. If I would have been downstairs on the couch where I belonged, this wouldn't be happening right now.

"Stay here. Lock the door behind me," I yell to her as I step out into the hall, closing the door behind me.

Rushing down the hall, I get to the balcony overlooking the first floor, creeping up to it and peering over the railing, aiming my gun down into the living room as I scan the area. When I see nothing out of order down there, I slowly make my way down the stairs with my back brushing against the wall, careful not to make any noise. When I step off of the bottom step, I lead with my gun out in front of me as I whip around the corner into the kitchen.

It doesn't take me more than five minutes to do a sweep of the first floor: nothing broken, all the windows and doors still secure, and no one other than Layla and I in the house. I quickly jog over to the front door and punch in the security code Finn reluctantly gave me earlier when he left to go to his own cabin. The alarm stops suddenly and I wince at the ringing in my ears with the abrupt silence.

I start to head towards the kitchen for the cordless phone that hangs on the wall to call the security company when a loud crash and a scream from upstairs pierce the silence.

"LAYLA!"

The shout bellows from my mouth as I take off out of the kitchen, my bare feel smacking on the hardwood floor as I rush to get back to her. I take the stairs two at a time, shouting her name the whole way until I get to the closed, locked bedroom door. Slamming my shoulder as hard as I can into the wood, the door flies open and I see a pile of broken glass on the floor right below her bedroom window, the sheer, white curtain billowing softly in the breeze.

My eyes frantically scan the room until I find Layla huddled in a ball on the floor with her back against the side of the bed, a red brick in her shaking hands.

I rush through the room towards the window, mindful of the broken glass on the floor as I get to the jagged hole and gaze out at the yard below. I scan the trees, the driveway, and the hedges and look as far as my eyes can see under the moonlight. As far as Layla's house is from the road, someone would have had to walk quite a ways to throw something through the window since there aren't any cars in sight and no one currently peeling out of the driveway.

I turn around and make my way over to Layla's side, kneeling down next to her and prying the brick out of her hands. I turn it towards me and there's only one thing written on it in white chalk: the word *WHORE* in big capital letters. Before I can say anything to her, the ringing of a cell phone comes from the table next to her bed. She blindly reaches her hand up to it and answers with a shaky voice without even looking at who is calling.

"Yes, this is Layla Carlysle. The password is hummingbird. Do I need police assistance?" she repeats back to the security company while looking at me questioningly.

I nod my head yes and she tells them to send the police, letting them know she's unharmed and there is currently no one in the house with her that shouldn't be before hanging up and tossing the phone to the side.

There are so many things I want to say to her before the police get here. So many thoughts running through my head that it's all just one big fucked up mess. I didn't want anything to happen with her until she knew everything about me and could make an informed decision about whether or not she wanted to risk getting involved with me. I should have handled things better with her instead of jumping on her the first chance I got. I let it go entirely too far when I was supposed to be protecting her, not losing my mind inside of her. I shouldn't be starting anything with her until this job is finished and it isn't a conflict of interest. I knew there was no way I'd be able to just ignore how much I wanted her, but I could have at least waited until I was off the clock for fuck's sake. It was unprofessional and I was an idiot.

"Look, about what happened between us…"

Layla jumps up from the floor, her eyes glued to her feet as she steps around the broken glass and hurries past me.

"Forget about it. It was a mistake and it shouldn't have happened. I just needed to forget about that guy's hands on me. So…whatever," she says with a shrug.

I stare at her retreating back in shock and anger as she heads towards the adjoining bathroom. Taking only a second before I storm after her, I wrap my hand around her arm and turn her around to face me.

"Let's get something straight here," I say with clenched teeth, staring down into her wide eyes as I try to keep my composure and not scare her half to death with my anger at her ambivalence. "This wasn't a mistake. Not by a long shot. I've wanted to bury myself inside of you since the first moment you and your attitude walked into the room."

Her lips part with a gasp, and I watch as her chest heaves with the breaths she's taking, proving that what just happened between us wasn't some half-assed way for her to forget anything. She liked it, and she wants more.

Letting go of the firm grasp I have on her upper arm, I slide my hand down to her wrist and bring her hand to my erection that's straining against the front of my sweatpants so she can feel just how much I want her.

Her hand closes around me, and I have to momentarily shut my eyes and let out a low groan.

"This is what you do to me, Layla. Every second I'm within a hundred yards of you, I'm rock hard."

She keeps her hand in place and begins to rub me as I move both of my hands to cup her face and tilt her head up so I can look into her eyes, forcing my knees not to buckle with what she's doing to me.

"Don't *ever* say this was a mistake, and don't think for one minute I can't read you like a book and see exactly what you're trying to do: push me away first so you don't get hurt. I'm not going anywhere, especially now that I've felt you come around my fingers and heard you cry out my name."

Closing the distance between us, I claim her mouth with a forceful kiss, letting her know with my lips and tongue just how much I need her. I pull away quickly, long before I'm ready, and wonder how in the hell I'm going to compose myself to go downstairs and talk to the police that will be here any minute.

"We are absolutely going to pick up where we left off, and

the next time you scream my name, it's going to be when I've sunk myself inside of you as deep as I can get."

CHAPTER 13
Layla

With my hands wrapped firmly around a mug of coffee, I take a sip, close my eyes, and lean my back against the counter in my kitchen. Trying to block out the events of last night is useless, especially on only four hours of sleep. And if I'm being honest with myself, I didn't even sleep that long. The majority of that time was spent tossing and turning, thinking about Brady and his parting words to me before the cops showed up.

I've never been around someone who could read me so well, aside from Finn. But Finn doesn't really count. He's just a friend, never a potential lover. We spent a few awkward weeks in high school testing out the dating thing by clumsily holding hands and trying to have a romantic dinner with just the two of us, but we couldn't stop laughing at how weird it was.

The boyfriends I've had didn't care much about knowing who I was on the inside, and I didn't bother trying to change that. Sam…well, Sam was just an asshole who cared more about the bottom line than trying to figure me out. Looking back, I'm glad I kept him at a distance and he didn't have any ammunition to use against me.

I've known Brady for a few short weeks, and he already has me tied up in knots. He already knows about the hatred that flows through my mother, and he can take one look at my face and know what I'm thinking.

"Don't think for one minute I can't read you like a book and see exactly what you're trying to do: push me away first so you don't get hurt."

He was right. Of course he was right. As soon as his body moved away from mine and I realized what I'd done, on the floor of my bedroom no less, I felt more exposed than I ever have. I'd let him in, I'd shown him how vulnerable I was, and that scared the hell out of me. I threw out a flippant remark to push him away before I got burned. Of course I didn't mean a word of what I said. I was with him because I wanted to be. I wanted him. I wanted to feel alive and desired, and I needed him to be the one to do it. Only Brady, with his piercing eyes that could see everything and his killer body that made my mouth water, could turn me to jelly with just one touch of his hand against my skin.

I don't trust easily—a product of my upbringing and shitty life experiences. So why in the hell am I so ready to just hand everything over to this man? I want to confide in him. I want him to comfort me and tell me everything will be okay. I've never wanted or needed anyone to do that for me. I've learned to take care of myself and not lean on anyone. One mind blowing orgasm from him and I'm suddenly ready to throw all of that out the window.

"Morning, Lay," Finn says with a smile as he walks through the backdoor in the kitchen and pours himself a cup of coffee. "You get any sleep last night after the cops left?"

I sigh and shake my head, taking another soothing sip of hot coffee.

"Well, I talked to them this morning and so far they don't have any leads on the brick. They figure it was just some crazy kids out for a few laughs or something." He shrugs like it's no big deal and goes back to adding cream and sugar to his mug. "You have a fan meet-and-greet at Capitol Records this afternoon, right?"

I set my coffee down and turn to face him, wrapping my arms around my waist to ward off the chill that comes over me when I think about standing in my bedroom the previous night scared to death when Brady had me lock myself in my room. I had my ear pressed up against the door, listening for any sound of a scuffle when the brick came crashing through my window and sprayed shards of glass all over the place. I had been petrified. As soon as he'd heard the alarm from his cabin, Finn threw on some clothes and raced between our two yards. He saw how shaken up I was and sat with me through the entire police interview. Now he was thinking it was no big deal?

"Do you honestly think it was just a few kids playing pranks?" I ask, my voice raising an octave or two along with my shock at his disregard.

"Well, yeah. Honestly, what else could it be?" he asks nonchalantly, shrugging his shoulders again and pulling out his cell phone to flip through his messages.

"Oh, I don't know, how about the crazy stalker who's been sending me creepy letters and attacked me yesterday."

I stare at him angrily, my fingernails piercing the skin of my palms as I clench my hands into fists.

"One does not necessarily have to do with the other, Layla. That guy at the club could have been some lowlife bum that was standing around just waiting for a woman to walk by alone and you happened to be the one who did it," Finn argues with a roll of his eyes, talking to me like I'm a child who just doesn't get it.

"Are you seriously trying to tell me that you don't think this is all connected?" I fire back.

"Are you seriously trying to tell me that you suddenly believe all of that bullshit Mr. Navy SEAL has been feeding you?" Finn shouts as he slams his mug down, coffee sloshing over the top and pooling in a puddle on the counter. "I thought you were smarter than that, Layla. I thought we decided that he was just another pawn your mother was using to piss you off.

He's a drunk with a shady past that you know nothing about. He sticks his hand down your pants and now everything he says is gospel. Jesus, if I would have known that was the way to make you listen to me I would have tried a little harder to fuck you ten years ago."

The smack echoes through the room before I even realize what I've done. The sting in my hand tells me I've just slapped my best friend across the face, and the redness on his cheek is further proof that we've both just crossed a very thin line in our friendship.

I'm too furious to be sorry for my actions. I told Finn what had transpired between Brady and I after the police left the night before because I needed my friend to tell me I hadn't made a huge mistake. I needed someone who knew the real me to listen with an open mind and tell me I wasn't just jumping into bed with the first guy that showed me some affection after the clusterfuck that was Sam. He listened and he understood, and he told me to do whatever I felt was right, whatever I needed to be happy.

And now, here he was, throwing all of that back in my face and making me feel like an idiot.

"I'm trying really hard right now to avoid saying something I'm going to regret. I don't know what the hell has gotten into you in the past few weeks, and I'm sorry if you feel like I'm taking someone's side over yours, but you have *no* fucking right to talk to me that way."

Finn cocks his jaw from side to side and runs his hand once down the cheek that I smacked as if rubbing away the sting.

His eyes are cold and there's an ugly twist to his mouth as he turns his head and stares me down. I've never seen him look this angry, and for a second, I want to retreat in fear.

Finn takes a menacing step towards me, and I force myself to stand my ground and not move. He leans his head down towards me and speaks in a low voice.

"I've done nothing but support you, and I've been at your beck and call for most of my life. All I wanted was for you to be careful and to not trust some loser you know nothing about."

I hold my breath as he takes a step back, glancing away from me and at something behind me, over my shoulder.

"I guess the guy with the bigger dick wins. Or is it the guy who *is* the bigger dick? I always get those two mixed up," Finn says sarcastically before turning and walking back out the kitchen door, slamming it roughly behind him as he goes.

I close my eyes and let out the breath I'd been holding as I feel Brady come up behind me and smooth a hand down the back of my head.

"Wow, and I thought I had anger management issues," he says with a small laugh as I turn around to face him.

The half-smile from his attempt at humor dies on my face

when I see what he's holding in his hand by his side: a well-worn, brown leather journal. A book that goes everywhere with me but is only brought out when no one is around. A book that stays hidden in an extra flap sewed behind one of the curtains in my room when I'm home in case my mother decides to go snooping through my things.

"What are you doing with that?" I ask in a horrified whisper as I stare at the book. A book that was a gift from my father on the last birthday I spent with him.

His head turns to what I'm looking at, obviously forgetting that he had it in his hand during the commotion with Finn. He holds the book up between us and raises his eyebrows at me.

"This? The window company came to replace the broken window this morning while you were in the shower. I had to take the curtains down so they weren't in the way and it fell out when I moved them."

He opens the book like he has every right to do so and begins flipping through the pages. I've never let anyone read the things written in that book, even Finn. I'm in such a state of shock that this man is here in front of me, scrutinizing my heart and soul like it's perfectly fine. All I can do is stand with my mouth open and my whole body shaking.

He stops on one page, holding the book wide open, and I know what he's about to do. I can see it on his face and in the way he clears his throat and swallows.

I write things down in that book as a way to escape, a way to get the thoughts and feelings out of my head so I never have to think about them ever again. I don't go back and read what I've written; I don't analyze the words or make changes to anything. I write and I move on. I don't want to go down those roads again. I don't want to relive the things I felt when I wrote them.

Every single page is filled with lyrics to songs. Songs I'll never have the courage to sing in front of anyone because they are too personal. Songs that my mother will never *let* me sing because then everyone would know the truth. I don't want them on display; I don't want him to read them and judge me for the choices I've made.

"Please...don't," I whisper, my voice choked with tears I don't even realize are pooling in my eyes.

He either doesn't hear me or doesn't care. His need to get inside my soul is too great. His deep, resonating voice fills the room with the words that have filled my heart with so much darkness for such a long time.

"Every day is another step closer,
to where I don't want to be.
Another smile, another laugh, another moment
of this fake reality.

Because of you
I see clearer than I ever have.
Because of you
I can't let anyone inside.
Because of you
I learned how to be alone.
Because of you
I am ashamed.

Just for a moment, I was back in time,
to a place where I belong.
Where dreams could lead you everywhere
and wishes could make you strong.
But then I wake up and my eyes are open wide.

Because of you
I see clearer than I ever have.
Because of you
I can't let anyone inside.
Because of you
I learned how to be alone.
Because of you
I am ashamed.

187

Every day I lose

more of who I am.

Afraid to cry, afraid to hurt because

you taught me it was wrong.

Someday there'll be nothing left,

just a shadow of who I was.

Because of you

I see clearer than I ever have.

Because of you

I can't let anyone inside.

Because of you

I learned how to be alone.

Because of you

I am ashamed."

The silence in the room is deafening as Brady finishes up the last line of the song and slowly closes the leather book. I can feel his eyes on me, but I can't do anything except stare in horror at my feet.

I wrote that song when I was in rehab for trying to overdose on sleeping pills. It was my twenty-first birthday and I had just found out that even though I was legal in the eyes of the law, everything I had and everything I was, belonged to my mother.

It was childish and immature, and I regretted my actions as soon as the last pill made its way down my throat. I immediately forced myself to throw up. By the time I had managed to purge some of the pills back up, the rest had already started to do their thing, and I could feel my body shutting down as I sunk to the floor of the bathroom.

Before I passed out, I managed a slurred, confusing call to Finn. After having my stomach pumped and my name splashed across the tabloids, courtesy of my mother ("All publicity is good publicity"), I woke up two days later in an exclusive rehab center in southern California where all of the stars go for some "rest and relaxation."

I wrote those words in the quiet of my room, alone. Words that I knew would never see the light of day because my mother most likely slept her way through the Hummingbird legal team to make sure my contracts were ironclad. I would never have a say in the songs I sang and I would never get to choose the lyrics I produced.

As much as I initially hated the idea that Brady was just here as my mother's lapdog hired to do her bidding, I am painfully reminded by the words of that song that I am the quintessential puppet for my mother. I do what she says when she says it, and I do it with a smile on my face. I take her criticisms and her threats and I let them mold me into the person I am today.

It doesn't matter if I really have a stalker or if his threats against me are real or just contrived by my mother for publicity. It doesn't matter if Brady really wants *me* or he just wants to protect me because that's the type of person he is.

As long as my mother has a say in it, I'll always be the poor, little rich girl who had it all and tried to throw it away. I'm scared to death that Brady will read those words and finally see the real me and realize I'm entirely too damaged for him. But those words aren't really me. They can't be. My mother won't let them be.

"Layla, this is amazing. Did you write all of these?" Brady asks in awe as he flips through a few more pages. I don't even care about stopping him at this point. I know what he's going to say next, probably even before he does.

"I don't understand. Why the hell aren't you singing this shit? This is YOU. This is what people want to hear. They don't care about partying on the weekend or random hook-ups; they want real life. They want the real you."

A cynical laugh bubbles past my lips, and I turn away from him, taking my coffee cup to the sink to rinse it out.

"You're right. You don't understand so don't bother trying."

He comes up behind me, and I see him set the book down on the counter next to the sink out of the corner of my eye.

"Hey, don't do that," he tells me softly.

"Don't do what?" I ask angrily as I shut off the water and whirl around to face him. "Don't be honest?"

"Don't push me away!" he shouts back. "I just found a book filled with songs that make me want to rip out my own heart. Words that are real and deep and fucking amazing and yet here you are, week after week, singing shit songs that have no meaning. I just want to know why?"

He's so close to me that I'm pinned against the counter and it's too much. I need space and I need to breathe. I put my palms on his chest and push him away from me so I can move out from around him to the other side of the kitchen table across the room.

"You don't want to know why. You just want to fix what's broken. You can't fix me, Brady. What you see is what you get. I sing what I have to. End of story."

He advances on me and for the first time ever, I'm glad to hear my front door open and my mother snapping at me from across the room.

"Why aren't you dressed? The meet-and-greet starts in two hours and hair and make-up will be here any minute."

Brady gives me one last burning look, pleading with his eyes for me to tell my mother where to go or to just prove to him that the woman who wrote those songs is real.

I turn my back on him and head upstairs to my room to put on the outfit my mother has chosen for me and have my hair and make-up artfully constructed the way my mother insists.

The woman who wrote those songs may have been real at one point, but she doesn't exist anymore. It was foolish of me to think that with Brady's help I could find her again.

CHAPTER 14

BRADY

When Layla comes back downstairs after getting ready, all traces of the woman I'm slowly getting to know and truly like are gone. Her hair is perfectly styled, her make-up overdone and sparkly, and her clothes are practically painted on, showing enough skin that she might as well be going to this thing bare ass naked. What the hell happened to the fresh-faced, jeans and T-shirt wearing woman who smiles easily and wants to be a fighter? The pop star robot has taken over and that woman is long gone. I'm not even sure she really exists.

The surprised look on Eve's face when she finds out I'm tagging along to the signing is quickly erased, and she graciously asks if I'd like to ride in the car with them. The way she fawns all over me and kisses my ass only proves she is just trying to make sure I won't out her to the world and tell everyone what a raging bitch she really is. Instead, I follow Layla in my own car. I can see Eve turn around in the passenger seat every so often, no doubt lecturing Layla about something. Finn keeps his eyes on the road and continues to drive. As soon as we are a block away from Capitol Records, I can hear the screams through the closed car window. Aside from Layla's concert a few weeks ago, I've never seen so many screaming people in one place.

The tension between Layla and Finn is still so thick, like a wall of tungsten steel that nothing can penetrate. I'm used to seeing them talk and joke with one another, and frankly, it makes me want to punch a wall because all I can think about is the two of them naked in bed, laughing and joking with one another. Right now, I don't know which is worse. The two of them ignoring each other is almost as awkward and uncomfortable as imagining them screwing. Gwen had said there were rumors about the two of them hooking up for years, but in the time I've spent with them, I haven't seen anything indicative of that relationship—unless you count Finn acting like a jealous asshole this morning. I'll definitely be talking to Layla about that later. When she starts sharing my bed, I won't be sharing her. Period.

I hadn't wanted to make it worse for Layla by adding to the tension and riding in the car with them, but now I'm regretting that decision as I finagle my car into a parking spot and look around at the mob scene. Safety in numbers might have been the right way to go. People are lined up on the sidewalk as far as the eye can see. They hold signs that claim they love Layla, a few have marriage proposals on them, and one even asks if they can father her babies. As soon as they see Finn's black SUV pull up to the curb, the shouts and crying that ensues could have broken the sound barrier.

Local police are there to help keep people behind the barricade so Layla can walk through the crowd and inside the store, but it still makes me fucking nervous to see her out in the open like that, where anyone can take a shot at her. Finn and a few of the officers who aren't busy holding fans back usher her quickly inside, but I watch as she graciously pauses a few times to shake hands and smile and laugh with a few people before being rushed through the doors.

It's sheer and utter madness, and I have no idea how she does it. Especially now that I know what's really in her heart and mind after reading through that song journal. I know it was wrong to pry into her life like that, but I couldn't help it. After a short time, I feel like I know her so well, but after reading those words and seeing her reaction, I obviously don't know her at all. She gets up on the stage week after week, shaking her ass, wearing skimpy clothes, and singing about teenage woes when she should be sharing what's in that journal instead. It's like being around two completely different people. The one today with perfect hair and make-up, wearing tight, black leather pants, black fuck-me shoes that are a mile high, and baggy, layered tank tops that show off a lot of sun-kissed skin, that's the Layla designed by Eve—the one the public knows, and the one *I* know she hides behind.

The real Layla, if she actually exists, wears jeans with holes in the knee, old concert T-shirts, and no make-up to cover her beautiful features. She smiles effortlessly, laughs regularly, and she let's go of the diva pretense just long enough to suck me in, making me never want to let her go. That's the Layla who kissed me last night, the one who wrapped her legs around my hips and begged for me to make her come. That's the Layla I thought I would find in the kitchen this morning, but as soon as she saw that I held her journal in my hand, I could almost physically see the wall she put up in her eyes. Her laugh turned cynical and her smile was forced. She hasn't said two words to me since her mother walked in the door and began making her demands. Like a puppy, she hangs her head, puts her tail between her legs, and does as she's told without an argument. I don't understand any of it. I don't understand how a person with so much fire and passion could just let someone walk all over them.

"Hey, Brady!"

A shout over the roar of the crowd breaks me from my thoughts, and I turn to see Adam Koonz, one of the guys from the force I used to work with. We shared a few words earlier the previous night when he came to Layla's house to take her statement about the attack.

I meet him right by the entrance to the record store, and

we walk in together, the quiet of the lobby a much-needed relief from the madness going on outside.

"I just wanted to let you know, we ran some preliminary tests on the brick that came through Layla's window last night," Adam tells me as we stand just inside the door.

I glance over to the table set up on the other side of the room where Layla is already seated and speaking to a few people from Capitol Records while someone primps her hair and freshens her make-up.

"Yeah, I heard. Nothing solid to go on, and you guys are just going with it being a prank from a few teenagers out for a laugh," I reply, turning back around to face him.

Adam furrows his brow and looks at me in confusion.

"No, where did you hear that? We had a handwriting analyst take a look at the writing on the brick and compared it to those letters Layla's been receiving from that Ray guy. They were a match. The DNA test from the scrapings under her fingernails is still at the lab, but I'm going to give them a call later today and see if I can get a rush on it. I have a feeling the scratches she said she gave him might pull up a hit. I guarantee this guy is already in the system. Also, they found some faint traces of blood on the brick. Going by what Layla told us in her statement, she bit that guy pretty hard on the hand when he grabbed her. It's looking good that this all the same guy."

It's my turn to stare at Adam in confusion after he finishes with his explanation. My gaze slides over to Finn, where he stands a few feet from Layla with his arms crossed in front of him, feet spread apart, and a pair of dark sunglasses on so no one can see his eyes.

Why in the hell would he lie to Layla about something like that? Something that could easily be verified.

I thank Adam and shake his hand, giving him my card so he can call me immediately when the results from the DNA test come in. There is no fucking way I want them calling Finn so he can lie about it again.

Walking across the room, I stop right next to Finn and take up the same pose as him, scanning the room and keeping an eye on Layla at the same time.

"So, I just had an interesting conversation with my buddy, Adam, from the police department," I say quietly so no one else can hear me. "You remember Adam, right? He was the one that took Layla's statement after the attack yesterday and the one in charge of running the tests on the brick."

Finn makes no outward sign that he's heard me, but I can see a muscle tick in his jaw, and I know I'm getting to him.

"Funny thing about having friends on the force. They actually tell you the truth."

Finn's nostrils flare and if he didn't have sunglasses on, I'm guessing he would be rolling his eyes at me.

"Is there a point to this? I'm kind of busy here," Finn

states, the irritation clearly evident in his voice.

"I'm just curious why you would lie to Layla. The tests prove the guy who's been writing her those notes is the same one who threw that brick through her window. Do you make it a habit of lying to your so-called best friend?" I question him, my eyes still scanning the room like the conversation we're having is no big deal.

"My relationship with Layla is none of your fucking business," Finn seethes. "I do what I think is right to protect her. You've known her all of a few weeks, so don't come in here acting like you know jack shit."

He turns and walks away from me without another word. The buzzing of my cell phone in my pocket momentarily distracts me from keeping an eye on him.

"Brady," I answer curtly as I stare at Layla.

After a few seconds, her eyes meet mine across the room. There are people talking on both sides of her and someone is speaking in my ear, but I can't take my eyes off of her. She's smiling and nodding to whatever they are saying to her, but the smile doesn't reach her eyes. I want to walk over to the table, scoop her up in my arms, and carry her out of here. I want to strip her out of those stupid clothes, wash the shit off of her face, and just be with the person underneath it all—the person who can write lyrics to a song that breaks my heart and puts it back together all at the same time.

"HELLO! EARTH TO BRADY! Did you hang up on me?"

Gwen's voice bellowing through the phone causes me to blink out of my trance, and I reluctantly look away from Layla before I can't stop myself from following through with the idea of carrying her out of here.

"I'm here. Christ, stop shouting." I sigh into the phone.

"I see someone hasn't had their five cups of coffee yet today," she replies sweetly, and I can almost see the sarcastic smile on her face through the phone.

"Did you call for a reason or just to bust my balls?"

She tsks me a few times and calls me an ungrateful asshole before finally getting to the point of her phone call.

"Well, I sprayed myself down with Lysol and took a preemptive dose of penicillin and called Austin for a favor. When you said that there weren't any hits on the brick that came through Layla's window, I figured we should have our own people do some testing just in case," Gwen explains.

"Yeah, don't worry. I already confirmed with the police department. Finn is a lying sack of shit, and the handwriting was a match to the same guy sending her the letters. We're just waiting for the DNA results."

"Yes, well, when you have a sister as awesome as me, you don't need to wait. Austin hacked into the lab's computer system and got the DNA results," she states.

"Do I even want to know what you had to promise him so he'd do this favor for you?" I ask reluctantly.

"No, you probably don't want to know. He lives like three thousand miles away, so it's not like I'll ever have to make good on that promise. And thank God for that because I don't even know where one purchases pomegranate flavored edible underwear."

Seriously going to kick Austin's ass the next time I see him.

"Get to the point before I throw up in my mouth. What did the DNA results show?"

I can hear the rustling of papers through the phone as Gwen sorts through the pages looking for what she needs.

"Well, the DNA under Layla's fingernails was inconclusive, so we didn't get any hits in CODIS. There just wasn't enough of a sample there. But there WAS a small trace of blood on the brick. They ran it against both you and Layla since you two were the only ones to handle it after it came through the window. Are you sitting down for this?" Gwen asks mysteriously.

"Get to the point, Gwen. In about two minutes, there are going to be hundreds of screaming fans in this room." I watch three security guards head for the doors and prepare to unlock them.

"It turns out the total number of shared DNA segments

between this person and Layla is high and there are quite a few banding patterns."

"In English, please."

Gwen sighs through the phone.

"This means, big brother, that whoever threw that brick through Layla's window is related to her. They share DNA."

My eyes immediately shoot to Eve, standing behind Layla and whispering frantically in her ear. Layla is staring straight ahead at nothing while her mother most likely berates her for something stupid like not smiling big enough or not waving properly.

"It's her mother. It has to be her mother," I tell Gwen angrily as I clench my jaw and force myself not to walk over there and hit a woman. That wouldn't look good in front of all of these people no matter how much she deserves it.

"You're probably right, but even with Austin's hacking abilities, we're still going to have to wait for the conclusive results to come in that will show with one hundred percent certainty who the match is. But going by what you've shared with me, I'm willing to put money on the fact that the bitch is crazy and wants to scare the shit out of her own daughter for some reason. And here I thought our mother had issues."

I thank Gwen and disconnect the call, shoving my phone in my back pocket while trying to come up with a subtle way to tell Eve I'm on to her. What in the hell would she possibly have to gain by doing this to Layla? Publicity? Layla is already a huge star, and her name is in the news if she so much as sneezes.

Just to be a bitch? While that idea has some merit, it still doesn't add up. Why would Eve ever want to risk her reputation if someone found out? Which begs the question, why the fuck did she hire me? She has to know I'm going to eventually put two-and-two together.

Finn's angry words to Layla this morning scream at me. *"He's a drunk with a shady past that you know nothing about."*

He's done his homework. Of course he has. I guess I expected that, considering I was hired to be in the same company of the biggest singing star in the world. They would have to know everything about me to let me within six miles of her. And it's not too hard to Google my name and see it connected to the shooting and plenty of drunken bar fights over the past year.

The security guards unlock the door, and I inch my way closer to Layla's table as hordes of fans come into the lobby screaming and making a beeline for her table, attempting to get in some sort of line without killing each other.

Obviously, I don't have the best reputation around town. I've done what I can to clean up my act, but stories and rumors still follow you around no matter what you do. Out of all of the private investigators in this town, let alone the whole world, why in the hell would they hire me? I know for a fact I am damn good at my job, and I don't stop until I get to the bottom of something, but they don't know that. Going by what you read online, and depending on who you ask, I'm still a drunk with anger management problems that likes to pick fights and leave my brothers in the Navy high and dry because I only care about where I'm going to be drinking another bottle of Jack or what stripper is going to be riding my cock next. I know all of that is a thing of my past now that I have Gwen and Emma in my life, but Eve wouldn't know that.

Why would she ever hire someone as shady as me unless she only did it for show? Maybe there really was an initial threat to Layla, and she couldn't just ignore it or she'd look like an uncaring bitch. She probably thinks that by hiring me, I'll be completely oblivious to what's happening, and she can get away with doing whatever the hell she wants, including keeping up the stalker farce. Hell, maybe she orchestrated this whole thing with the letters and the attack. Is she really low enough to throw a brick through her own daughter's bedroom window though?

I think back to the way Eve berated Layla during her sound check and how she cared more about a photo shoot than her own daughter's well-being, and I know I already have my answer.

I watch with a careful eye as fan after fan steps up to Layla's table. I see a small hint of a spark in her eyes that I've only seen a few times, and it's an amazing thing to witness. She is gracious and friendly to each and every person in line, and she talks to them like they're old friends. She makes eye contact, happily agrees to take as many pictures as the person likes, and signs whatever they hand her without hesitating. She asks them about babies and family members and shares smiles and hugs with each and every one of them.

As I stare in awe at the public figure side of Layla Carlysle, I realize that I'm witnessing something I haven't seen much of the past few weeks: happy Layla. She is genuinely enjoying herself and her fans, and she's grateful to each and every one of them for coming out and supporting her. She doesn't care if she's going to be here for hours; she will spend the same amount of time and give the same amount of attention to each and every person.

The fans adore her. Of course they do. She isn't fake with them. She isn't a diva that never makes eye contact or barely says two words to them before scribbling her name on a CD or poster and shoving it back in their hands. She's real and she's vivacious, and I suddenly want more than anything to make sure she always looks this way: happy and content.

"She's amazing, isn't she?"

I turn to the side when I hear a soft, feminine voice with a thick southern twang speaking close to me. It's a woman in her mid-fifties with long, straight red hair and sparkling green eyes. The freckles that spread over her nose and cheeks makes her look much younger than I'm sure she is; the crow's feet at the edges of her eyes are what gives her away. I recognize this woman. I saw her a few minutes ago at the front of Layla's table. They both screamed in happiness and threw their arms around one another like they were long lost friends. The woman cupped Layla's face in her hands and scrutinized her with her head tilted to the side like a mother would do when checking to see if her child is getting enough sleep or eating well.

"She is," I answer the woman, turning my eyes back to Layla as she signs yet another poster and takes three more pictures. "How do you know her?"

The woman's smile lights up her entire face when she looks over at Layla and answers my question.

"I've pretty much known her all of her life. Her father and I were...good friends. My name is June, by the way."

She turns and holds out her hand to me and I shake it, studying her face while she continues to glance over at Layla every few seconds. I'm trying to gauge how genuine this woman really is since Layla seems to be surrounded by selfish assholes. The way she lovingly stares after Layla while she watches her work makes me quickly realize she is one of the good ones.

"It's nice to meet you, June. I'm—"

"Brady Marshall, ex-Navy SEAL and Nashville police officer, currently hired to keep an eye on our girl over there," June finishes for me.

I looked at her quizzically with raised eyebrows.

"Sorry. The few minutes I had with Layla at her table, I grilled her about the broody hunk standing over here staring at her every few minutes like he wanted to do naughty things to her in front of all these people." June winks at me and smiles.

If I was a chick, I would be blushing like a fucking teenager right now. As it is, I have to look away from June and at a spot on the wall, making sure not to look at Layla or I'll never hear the end of it.

"Anyway, I'm glad she's got someone watching her back. That girl has had too much piled on her shoulders over the years, and she needs someone trustworthy looking out for her," June tells me with a sigh.

"What makes you think I can be trusted?" My eyes instinctively wander over to Layla.

June lets out a small laugh, and I see her shake her head out of the corner of my eye.

"I'm good at reading people, Mr. Marshall. I've owned a bar for almost thirty years, and I see all sorts of people come through that door every single night. I've heard stories that would make your hair turn gray and your toes curl. You look like you might have a few of those stories stored up in that handsome head of yours. And you look at our girl over there like she's the sunshine in the dark, not like she's a meal ticket to a better life."

I don't reply to June's assumptions or her assessment of me. There's no point. Like she said, she's good at reading people.

"Well, I need to head out and get the bar stocked for tonight. If you're not doing anything later, you should make it a point to stop by. I've watched you staring after her since I got here, like you're trying to figure out a puzzle. It's probably not my place to say this, but I love that girl like she's my own daughter, and I want what's best for her. If you want to find another piece to the puzzle, it will be at the Red Door Saloon at nine tonight."

June turns and starts walking away from me before pausing and glancing back over her shoulder at me.

"But if she sees you there and gets her britches all in a bunch, you don't know me and we never spoke."

She winks at me again and then saunters out the door.

I don't know what the hell just happened, but I know one thing for sure. There is no way I'm staying away from the Red Door Saloon tonight.

CHAPTER 15
Layla

Today was exhausting, from start to finish, but there is no way I can miss out on a night at the Red Door Saloon. I practically grew up in this bar. My father brought me here every weekend once I learned how to play the guitar so I could mess around with the band and get a feel for playing with other people and see how I liked it. June is like a second mother to me. Oh, who in the hell am I kidding? She's like the only mother to me. She always made me homemade cherry cokes with real cherry syrup when I came in, and she'd grab me a bag of Cool Ranch Doritos from behind the counter to go with my Coke, even when my dad would tell me it would spoil my dinner.

I've kept in touch with her over the years, and whenever I come home, I always make it a point to stop by and see her. The bar is the epitome of a dive. It's a hole in the wall with peeling paint and sticky floors, and if you order anything aside from Jim, Jack, Jose, or beer, you'll get your ass tossed out on the sidewalk. My favorite part about this place is that it's filled with regulars who have been coming here since the bar opened. They still listen to their music on 45's, and if you ask them if they downloaded your latest song from iTunes they'll reply, "What do you want me to tune?"

It's the one place in the entire world I can go and not be recognized. They don't care who I am as long as I thank the bartender and leave behind a tip. To them, I'm just another tourist stepping off of Broadway to get a feel for the *real* Nashville, and that is perfectly fine with me.

"Baby girl! I was hoping I'd see you here tonight!"

June, my long time friend and the owner of the establishment, shouts across the noise of talking patrons as she makes her way down to the stool I'm perched on at the corner of the bar.

"You know I wouldn't miss a visit to the Red Door, June!" I smile brightly at her. "Thanks for stopping by the signing earlier. Sorry we didn't have a lot of time to talk."

June flings a white bar towel over one shoulder, quickly fixes me a cherry coke, and after setting the drink down in front of me, reaches across the bar to take both of my hands in hers.

"Nonsense, baby girl. I knew you'd be too busy to spend more than a few minutes with an old lady like me. I just wanted to see you in your element. I like watching you do things like that." Her words are genuine as she smiles softly. "So, where's

Finn at this evening? He's usually attached to your hip."

I let out a deep sigh and glance behind me, my eyes finding Finn at a table by himself near the jukebox. We haven't said one word to each other since the smack heard around the world this morning. We've never fought in all the years we've known each other, except for a few stupid little squabbles over nothing that were quickly forgotten within minutes. Regardless of our personal life, he's still my bodyguard, and he has to be with me wherever I go, even if he won't look at me or say a word. He knew without even asking that this is where I would go tonight, and when I got home after the meet-and-greet and changed into more comfortable clothes, he picked up his keys, walked out the door without a word, started up the car, and waited for me to get in. The ride here was long, quiet, and uncomfortable. I'm glad to be inside the noisy bar and not have to feel bad about us not speaking and how strange it feels.

"Finn is back in the corner making himself scarce," I tell her with a smile that I don't really feel as I lift the glass to my lips and chug the carbonated sweet drink that tastes like home. I love June but I don't feel like getting into the whole Finn thing with her at the moment. I just want to do what I came here to do, what I always do: relax and enjoy being in the one place that truly makes me happy.

"I'm sure there's a hell of a story there that you're not telling me, but I'll let it slide for now," June says with a wink, leaning closer to me across the bar so she doesn't have to shout. "It's pretty dead here tonight, nothing new there. How about you get that pretty face of yours up on stage and do your thing so I can gush all over you."

I drain my glass and jump down off of the stool with an excitement in my stomach that I haven't felt since the last time I was here. Nothing ever matches the feeling I get when I'm in this bar. Well, except for having Brady's body and lips against me the other night, but I'm not going to think about that right now. Brady isn't here and therefore I don't have to be distracted.

I walk away from the bar and head towards the small stage set up in the corner of the room. It's not really a stage, just two steps up onto a platform in the corner of the room that's big enough to hold a small piano and a stool in front of the microphone stand. The jukebox is usually the music of choice in this place, playing anything from Willie Nelson to Guns N' Roses, but on occasion when someone comes into the bar who knows how to play and sing, June lets them get up on stage, and the jukebox is unplugged for the night. This is the one and only stage where I can be myself. Where no one knows who I am, no one knows the songs I usually sing, and no one expects anything from me. I can sing what I want, and I can finally breathe.

I make my way up the two small steps and pull the bar stool closer to the mic stand. My eyes scan the crowd until they zero in on Finn. Even though we aren't speaking, and even though what he said punched a hole in my heart that I don't know how to fix right now, I still need him up here with me, and I know he wants the same thing. I can see him in the back of the room staring longingly at the guitar that's propped up against the piano directly behind me. I stare at him while I adjust the microphone so it's level with my mouth, and his eyes meet mine. I offer him a small smile, nodding my head in the direction of the guitar. I'm nowhere near ready to forgive him, but this is what we've been doing together since we were teenagers.

I watch as he tilts his head up to the ceiling and lets out a deep sigh before placing his hands on the table in front of him and pushing himself up off of the chair. He doesn't head towards the stage though. Instead, he turns and walks right out the door of the bar. My breath catches in my throat when I see the door close behind him, and I wonder if we've done so much damage to each other that it will never be salvageable. Before I even have a chance to wrap my thoughts around his actions, Finn is walking back through the door with a familiar case dangling from his hand. I stare in disbelief at the oblong box, covered in hummingbird stickers, as he uses it to maneuver his way through the crowd and up to the stage. He walks right by me without saying a word and flings the case up on top of the piano, flipping the locks open and lifting the lid.

My brain screams for me to do something, say something,

stop him from doing what I know he's about to do, but I can't move. I'm transfixed by the sight of him wrapping his fingers around the neck of *my* guitar, using the muscles in his arms to lift *my* guitar from its case and bring it out into the open in front of so many people. This is MY secret, MY private love and obsession that I don't share with anyone anymore. How dare he waltz up on this stage and reveal the one skeleton in my closet that can do me the most harm?

I watch him with wide, unblinking eyes as he cradles the guitar close to him and perches himself on the stool. When he strums a few notes and the sound reaches my ears, it lights a fire of fury under my ass, and I jump down off of my own stool and move to stand directly in front of him.

"What the hell are you doing?" I hiss angrily at him as he lazily continues to pluck the strings.

"I'm accompanying you on guitar. Isn't that what the whole nod was for?" he asks nonchalantly without looking up.

His careless attitude just pisses me off even more, and I reach out and yank the guitar away from him roughly before he can play it a second longer.

He crosses his arms in front of him and stares me down as I stand there holding my guitar awkwardly, out away from my body like it has a disease and I don't want to get it too close to it for fear that it will rub off on me.

"This is MY guitar. It stays in MY house and no one plays

it but ME," I tell him angrily, sounding like a five-year-old throwing a temper tantrum. I should just stomp my foot and hold my breath while I'm at it. I don't care how juvenile I'm behaving. He knows how important this instrument is to me, and he knows why it stays hidden away in a closet where no one can see it.

"Then play it."

Finn speaks softly, his eyes never leaving mine. The crowd in the bar has disappeared and now it's only the two of us on stage: two friends who know everything about the other and who are slowly using those things to destroy years of love and trust.

"What?" I ask dumbly.

He nods in the direction of my outstretched hand.

"Then. Play. It," he repeats again slowly, enunciating each word. "If that piece of wood means so much to you, prove it."

My hands start to shake and the weight of the guitar is beginning to hurt my arm, so I bring it in close to my body, swallowing roughly and trying not to cry.

"You treat that fucking thing like it's the Holy Grail, but you never show it off. You want more out of your life, but you never do a God damned thing to make it happen," he argues.

"You know why," I whisper to him angrily. "You know why I can't do this. You of all people should understand."

He laughs cynically and shakes his head at me.

"You can't use Eve as an excuse. Not this time. She's not here. It's just you, me, and a handful of people who just want to drink and listen to some good music. Stop being afraid for once in your fucking life. Stop listening to all of the voices in your head telling you why this is a bad idea and just listen to your heart. Bring out that firecracker I saw this morning that stood her ground, told me where to go, and smacked me across the face."

Shame washes through me when he brings up what I did this morning. Shame for letting myself get so worked up over his words and letting my emotions take over.

"Wipe that look off your face right now," Finn reprimands as he unfolds his arms and leans towards me. "I said some things I shouldn't have, and you put me in my place. I deserved it. End of story. Do you want to always be the woman who does what she's told or the woman who does what she loves and to hell with everything else? Because now is your chance to make that decision. Who do you want to be, Layla?"

My heart is pounding and the hands wrapped around the neck of my guitar are sweating as I contemplate his words. I know who I want to be. I've *always* known who I want to be. Could it really be as simple as making a decision and jumping off of the ledge into the unknown?

I turn away from Finn and scan the crowd. They are all laughing and having a good time, slinging back drinks with friends, and listening to the music piped through the sound system. They have no idea that a monumental decision is being made up here on this stage.

"Who do you want to be, Layla?"

I want to be free. For one moment in time, I just want to be free.

I clear my throat, my decision made, and perch on the edge of my stool with my guitar resting in my lap, one foot hooked on the top rung of the stool to balance my guitar and the other one planted on the ground. I hum a few warm-up bars softly to myself while I hear Finn tinkering with the strings of the extra guitar, making sure it's in tune. I see June walk out from behind the bar and over to the jukebox, unplugging the machine and giving me a huge smile and a thumbs up. She glances at the guitar in my hand questioningly, silently asking me if I'm okay, and I nod confidently in her direction. I'm okay. This is okay. I can do this.

In a normal bar when you turn off the music, people will boo and complain and shout profanities. But in June's bar, everyone just goes with the flow. They continue downing their shots of Jack and sipping their drafts of beer, and once in a while, they glance around to see why the music isn't playing. They don't care if a stranger is up on stage, and they don't bat an eye when the music starts back up again, switching from recorded music to live music. They have no idea the woman standing on the stage in front of them is petrified. They are unaware that for the first time in years, she will be playing an instrument given to her by her father and she's putting her heart and soul right smack in the middle of the stage for all to see and judge.

It's absolutely perfect.

I take a deep breath and a grin of excitement takes over my face as I wrap my arms around my guitar and pluck a few random chords to get my fingers warmed up. Finn chooses the first song, just like he always does when we're here, and I smile to myself as he strums the first few notes to Janis Joplin's *Piece of my Heart* and starts us off. This is our song—the first one we ever performed together at June's bar and the first time I ever found out Finn could play the guitar. He is amazingly talented and I never understood why he settled for the military instead of pursuing a career in music. The many times I've asked him about it, he just grunts and replies that I'm the star, not him, and that's the way it should be.

I close my eyes and let the beauty of Finn's playing wash over me. With my eyes still closed, I forget about the fact that I haven't played on stage since my father was alive; I forget about the fact that I've kept this part of myself locked behind closed doors for so long that I almost lost it. I've almost allowed the one part of myself that I actually love to be snuffed out like a candle.

I gently rest my fingers on the strings and familiarize myself with the rough texture of the wire and how natural it feels to have it brushing against the tips of my fingers. I listen to Finn's playing with my head cocked to the side, waiting for the perfect moment to jump in with him, like a child standing on the playground as her friends swing the Double Dutch jump ropes. *Almost, almost, one more time around, there it is: the perfect opening.*

I take a deep breath and join in with Finn's strumming, flawlessly. The vibrations from the guitar work their way up my hands and arms until I can practically feel them wrapping around my heart and shocking it back to life like a defibrillator. Easing into the first line of the song while I play, I use my real, raspy voice instead of the bubble gum pop voice I usually use.

We make our way through the song effortlessly, and I put everything I have into belting out the song and strumming the guitar, letting the words and the music flow through me and take me away. As Finn closes out the song with the last few guitar notes, he barely takes a pause before jumping right in to the next song. By the time we finish a half hour later, I've played and sung covers from Brandi Carlile and Sheryl Crow, to Johnny Cash and Nine Inch Nails. I finally let my eyes scan the crowd after singing the last note of *Something in the Way* by Nirvana and a huge smile takes over my face as I see the patrons in the bar standing on their feet, hooting, hollering, and whistling for me.

For ME. Not Layla Carlysle the pop singer. Layla Carlysle who sings whatever the hell she wants and enjoys every minute of it.

I tip my head forward in thanks but when I look back up, my heart skips a beat, and I feel my face flush with nerves. Standing right in front of me, with a look of awe on his face, clapping and whistling louder than everyone else, is Brady.

I stand there like an idiot, clutching the microphone tightly with one hand and my guitar with the other, while he shakes his head at me in surprise. I come here to sing when I'm home because I can be anonymous. Having Brady here watching me enjoy what I do without having to put on an act sets a swarm of butterflies loose in my stomach, and I have to let go of the microphone and press my hand against it to calm my nerves. It suddenly means more than anything to me that he likes what I just did. I realize I *want* to impress him. I want him to think of me as something other than a pop princess who sings shitty songs that a teenager can write in her sleep. I want him to see that I have talent, even if I rarely exhibit it.

As the crowd continues to shout and demand for more, my eyes don't leave Brady's as he walks the few feet needed to bring him right up to the platform I'm standing on. He's so damn tall that it's strange to be standing above him looking down. It makes me feel powerful all of a sudden, and all I can think about is being above him somewhere else, preferably a bed, where I can be in charge, taking him inside me, and riding us both to the edge.

He crooks his finger at me, and I lean forward until his lips are brushing up against my ear.

"You up on this stage singing your heart out with a voice dripping with sex is the hottest fucking thing I've ever seen. Did you seriously just rock out a Nirvana song? And play a God damned guitar better than Jimi Hendrix?"

I pull away from him just enough so I can look at his face and give him the most seductive smile I can muster, running my tongue slowly across my top lip before biting down on the bottom one. He lets out a heavy breath as his eyes zero in on my lips. I don't know what's got into me tonight, but I feel a boldness flowing through me that isn't usually there when I'm not pretending to be *The Layla Carlysle*. I want to jump down off of the stage, drag him to the back room, and rip his shirt off of his body. I want to push him against the wall, drop down on my knees, and take him in my mouth. I want to do everything to this man, and I don't care about the consequences.

"You keep looking at me like that, and I'm going to haul you off of this stage and bury myself inside of you before we even get outside," Brady groans softly, reading my mind as he finally tears his eyes away from my mouth.

Without answering him, I stand up and lean the guitar

against my stool. I turn around and give Finn a nod of thanks for playing for me, for bringing my guitar, for knowing me better than anyone else, and for pushing me to finally take a stand. He smiles softly at me, and it makes me happy to know that no matter what happens between us, he will always have my back.

Turning back around, I jump down off of the stage, grab Brady's hand, pull him through the bar and out the front door, and wave goodbye to June as I go.

I guide us across the parking lot to Brady's dark blue Ford F150 extended cab and let go of his hand to walk around to the passenger side and climb inside.

Brady gets in behind the wheel and looks over at me with a confused raise of his eyebrows.

"Did I offend you in there or something? Because—"

Leaning across the seat and hooking my hand behind his head, I pull him towards me and crash my mouth against his, cutting off his words and letting my tongue say everything that needs to be said.

Without moving my mouth away from his, I deepen the kiss and slide one knee underneath me on the seat, pushing myself up, and swing my other leg over his lap until I'm straddling him.

He recovers quickly from the shock of me taking over like this and wraps both of his arms completely around me, pulling my body tightly against him.

Both of my hands go to the back of his head, and I clutch handfuls of his hair in my fists as I sink my body down lower on his lap, thankful that I decided to wear a fun, short, flowing black skirt tonight.

As soon as Brady spoke against my ear in the bar, I felt myself getting wet with need. He groans into my mouth as I slide the wet satin of my underwear against his denim covered erection. The smoothness of my underwear combined with the roughness of his jeans creates the most amazing friction that causes a shiver to run through my body.

With his arms still wrapped securely around me, he slides one hand inside the back of my skirt until he's palming my bare ass, pushing and pulling me back and forth over him. His other hand moves up my back until his fingers slide under my hair, wrapping it securely around the back of my neck. I angle my head and push my tongue deeper into his mouth, rocking my hips and grinding myself harder against him.

I've never been the outrageous type of person that just screws someone in a car in a dark parking lot. My handful of sexual encounters have all been in a bed, soft and slow, and lacking something I never knew was missing until right this minute: all consuming passion. There is a fire burning through my body, and I need this right now; I need him and only him.

I bring my hand down from the back of Brady's head and wedge it between us, lifting my hips up just enough so I can jerk open the button of his pants and quickly slide his zipper down.

Brady pulls his mouth away from mine and breathes heavily against my lips as I reach inside his pants and pull his erection free, pressing it against my soaked panties and thrusting my hips, moving against him a few more times until he groans.

"We need to stop before I lose my mind and *can't* stop." His voice is shaky, and I let go of him long enough to shove my panties to the side and bring his cock right back where it was, this time having no barrier between my wet skin and his hard length.

"Son of a bitch." He hisses as I move my hips faster and coat him with my arousal.

"We're not stopping," I whisper against his lips as I gently bite down on the bottom one and tug it into my mouth.

Without giving him a chance to protest, my hand slides down to the base of his cock and I angle him towards me. I lift my hips, line the tip up with my entrance, and push myself down roughly until I'm seated fully on top of him and he's deep inside me.

"Fuck!"

Brady lets out a guttural shout as I hold myself still, letting my body get used to having him inside of me so quickly. He's big and he's full, and I've never felt anything so amazing in my life. There's a tingle shooting through my core, begging for me to do something to ease the ache, so I pull myself up the length of him and quickly push back down, both of us groaning in unison.

Brady squeezes his eyes shut tightly and lets his head fall back to the headrest as I begin quickly moving up and down on him, riding his cock, and loving every minute of what I'm doing to him. I never knew I could be this assertive or in control, and it's a heady feeling— one I never want to end. I want to give him pleasure just as much as I want to achieve it.

He lets go of the back of my neck, and his hand joins the first one, clutching tightly to my ass and guiding my movements, pushing me down harder on him and sliding me up faster until we're both panting and moaning. I smack my hands down on the back of the seat on either side of Brady's head and use them to hold on tightly and ride him harder.

We've long forgotten about kissing at this point. I'm fucking him too hard and too fast for our lips to stay in contact for more than a second, but Brady makes sure to quickly touch my lips to his every single one of those seconds. Staring at his face and watching how tightly he clenches his jaw to keep himself in control is the hottest thing I've ever seen. Unable to help myself, I lean forward to suck and lick the side of his neck, letting my teeth graze his skin. He hums and moans his approval, and I can feel the vibrations against my lips as I move faster and harder, up and down on top of him.

My orgasm is building quickly; I can feel it pulsing just

within my grasp, and it makes me take him in deeper, hold him in place, and grind my hips roughly against that perfect pubic bone of his that hits just the right spot.

My lips continue kissing and sucking at his neck until he speaks softly to me.

"Let me see your face. I want to watch you when you come."

I immediately pull my head back and stare down into his eyes. I force myself to keep my eyes locked on his even though I want to roll them in the back of my head as I push, thrust, and swivel my hips. He's buried inside of me to the hilt, his hands squeezing and kneading my ass as I move.

"That's it, baby." His voice is breathy and soft as he moves one of his hands off of my ass and brings it between us. His thumb finds my clit, and he immediately slides it back and forth over top of it. "Let me feel you come."

His quiet, whispered words and his thumb moving in small, frantic circles makes me tumble quickly over the edge, my orgasm rushing through me so strongly it forces my toes to curl and keeps my body frozen on top of him, only my hips jerking slightly against his hand as I come.

I don't even know if I'm making a sound or if the shouts and exclamations are all in my head because my ears are ringing, and I can't think of anything but the way my body squeezes and pulses around Brady. He grabs onto my hips tightly with both of his hands and slams me up and down on top of him three more times until he thrusts his hips up and holds himself suspended inside of me while he curses through his own release.

"Fuck, Layla! Oh fuck!"

He pulls out and pushes back in roughly one last time before his ass slumps back down on the seat and I collapse on top of him, burying my face into the crook of his neck.

We remain like that for several long minutes, both of us breathing heavy, not saying a word. He's still inside of me, and I can feel myself pulsing around him. It just makes me want him even more.

The ringing of Brady's cell phone cuts through the euphoria, and I push myself up from his chest and off of his lap, wincing as he slides out of me. Brady zips up his pants before lifting up his hips and pulls his cell phone out of his back pocket, wrapping his other arm around my shoulders and pulling me against his side.

His kisses the top of my head before he answers, and I have to smile to myself at the sweet gesture.

"Um, yes. She's right here. Would you like to speak to her?"

I tilt my head back to look up at Brady's face and he mouths, "Your mother."

I roll my eyes and sigh, holding my hand out for the

phone. He gives it to me and I bring it to my ear, regretting that decision as soon as I do it.

CHAPTER 16
BRADY

I roll onto my side and check the clock on the nightstand, realizing it's only one in the morning. I've been lying in the king size bed in Layla's spare bedroom, staring up at the vaulted ceiling for what feels like days, but it's only been about a half hour.

I flop onto my back with a groan, scrubbing my face with my hands.

Normally during a case, I would be restless from thoughts about the job and what I could be doing better, who I need to talk to the next day, and follow-ups that need completed.

Not this time. This time, my thoughts are occupied with a blonde-haired, blue-eyed enigma of a woman. Every time I drive my truck from now on, I'm going to picture her sitting on my lap, taking me inside of her. I'm going to remember the way she felt wrapped around my cock and the noises she made when she was close to coming.

I don't know what the hell got into her tonight and I don't care. I just know that I want to do whatever I can to make *that*

Layla—the confident, sexy, take-charge one—come out to play every single day. Watching her own that stage and the smile that lights up her face makes my dick swell and my chest ache. She doesn't look anything like that when she does a concert. I haven't known her very long, but I've become very well acquainted with the two different Laylas. One only acts confident and happy. The other actually is.

When I first walked into that bar, I had no idea what to expect. I assumed June invited me there to keep an eye on Layla while she drank away her troubles. Fuck, was I wrong. I walked through the door just as she sat down on the stool behind the microphone. I stayed to the back and kept to the shadows so she wouldn't see me. I have no idea why I did that. I could have just walked right up to her and asked her what she was doing, but something told me to hang back and watch what unfolded. It looked like she was having words with Finn at first—angry words. I cheered a little inside because she was giving him hell again after the shit he pulled with her that morning. I saw her grab the guitar from his hands and turn around to face to the audience, looking like a deer caught in the headlights, and it killed me to not know what was going on in that head of hers. As soon as she began playing the guitar and the first couple of words left her mouth, I sagged against the back wall with my eyes bugging out of my fucking head and my mouth gaping open and shut like a fish out of water. I remained that way for the entire thirty minutes that she sang.

After the third song, a cover of *Hurt* by Nine Inch Nails, June walked over to me.

"Ah, you made it. Good to see you again, Mr. Marshall," June said with an easy smile as she patted me on the shoulder and brought me out of my stunned stupor.

"What the fuck is that?" I asked dumbly, my hand gesturing to the stage where Layla currently thanked the crowd and told them she'd be doing a little Sheryl Crow next.

"That, my dear man, is our girl doing what she was made to do."

I had to forcibly remove my eyes from the woman on the stage to turn and look at June.

"If she can sing and play like that, why in the hell does she put on concerts like the ones she does?" I demand.

June let out a huge sigh and shook her head sadly as she stared up at Layla belting out the first line to *Strong Enough*.

"I've asked myself that exact same question for years, son. I used to think she really liked what she did. I mean, it's not exactly what her father had in mind for her, but I figured she found her niche in life and ran with it."

I cocked my head and looked at her quizzically, thoughts

of what I'd read in the tabloids and the research Gwen did on Layla coming to mind.

"What do you mean it's not what her father had in mind for her? He was a record executive mogul who had a talented daughter. Why wouldn't he have wanted to cash in on that?" I asked.

June took a minute to ponder my question before finally answering me.

"I've known Layla her entire life. I've been around for her highs, and I've been around for her lows. I never butt in or gave my two cents because I always just assumed she was doing what made her happy, and that was all I've ever wanted for her. She's not the type of person to complain or do the whole 'woe is me' bull crap, but I figured if things were really bad, she would tell me. She would tell someone," June explained, wringing her hands together nervously. "This is the first time I've seen her in person in over a year since she's been on tour, and I've got to tell you, something is wrong with that girl. I can see it all over her face, and I can practically feel the misery coming off of her." I watched the emotions play across June's face: sadness, worry, and fear. Her eyes got misty and she turned away from me towards the stage. I wanted to reassure June that Layla is okay, but I couldn't.

I glanced up at Layla as she sang about being broken down and not able to stand. She asked the audience, who listened with rapt attention, if they were strong enough to be her man, and I wanted to run up to that stage, grab her by the shoulders, and tell her that I'm strong enough. Pick me.

I knew that was a lie, though, so I turned my attention back to June.

"You've heard about what's been going on with her and the crazy fan, right? Maybe she's just overwhelmed by that right now," I told June, knowing as soon as the words left my mouth that I didn't believe them. Layla was a fighter, even if she didn't believe it. Jesus, the night he attacked her she demanded that I teach her how to fight back. Thinking back over all the concert videos I watched of her before I even took this job, I realized now that what I saw on her face wasn't a diva attitude or the look of someone who was bored with her charmed life. It was the look of someone unhappy and searching for a way out.

"I wondered that myself," June replied. "But that's not what it is. She doesn't look like herself anymore. She doesn't smile easily and that scares the hell out of me. She's a beautiful girl, inside and out, with the biggest heart out of anyone I've ever known. She's closed herself off, and I don't know why. Her father never wanted this life for her. He knew how stressful and demanding it could be, and he always told her that as soon as it became a job, you shouldn't do it anymore. You should only do it if you love it. If it's a passion that burns inside of you, and you feel like you're going to die without it. She doesn't love what she's doing, and it makes no sense to me."

Layla closed out the song to a roar of applause from the bar, and even though I didn't know that much about this June person, I could tell she really cared about Layla. She was genuinely concerned about her well-being, and it occurred to me that Layla really had no one in her life like that right now.

"I think it's because of Eve. She treats her like shit, and Layla just takes it all without batting an eye. I tried questioning her about it, but she got really defensive and just shut down," I explained to June as Layla takes a small bow.

"I always hated that woman. She got her claws into Jack and never let go no matter what he did. He was miserable with Eve, but she didn't care. She just wanted his money," June seethed angrily, her eyes narrowing and her lips pursing.

"I don't mean to be so forward, June, but it's my job. Mind if I ask how well you knew Layla's father?"

Her face immediately reddened and she rubbed the back of her neck with one hand nervously.

"Jack was a good friend. He used to come in here a lot to get away from Eve. He'd bring Layla when she was just a little girl, and I took to both of them right quick. What happened to him was shameful, and I will always regret not telling someone about my suspicions."

June's words set off warning bells in my head but before I could ask her more about what the hell she was talking about, what she meant about having suspicions, one of the waitresses rushed over and grabbed June's arm telling her two of the kegs were empty and new ones needed to be tapped immediately. June walked away with a promise to talk to me again soon.

The conversation with June slips away as I hear the click of the bedroom door handle being turned. I hold my breath as I watch the door slowly open revealing Layla, her long, wavy hair wild around her face and shoulders, her body barely covered in a short, white satin nightie. She steps into the room, and I can't take my eyes away from her full breasts spilling out of the black lace edging of the top. The nightie stops a few inches below her hips, and I lick my lips as my eyes trail down the front of her body and the smooth skin of her legs as I watch them walk towards the bed.

She hesitates shyly at the edge of the bed, and I can see that she's not sure if she's doing the right thing. I don't want her to leave, but I can't find my voice to tell her that, so I reach over and pull the covers back, holding them up above the bed for her.

She looks at my face and smiles before climbing under the covers and sliding over to me, pressing the front of her body flush against my side, draping her arm over my bare stomach, and pressing her cheek to my chest. I tuck the sheet and blanket over the top of her and wrap my arms around her, pulling her closer and kissing the top of her head before finally speaking.

"Can't sleep?"

She shakes her head *no* against my chest, and I reach my hand up to press my fingers under her chin and turn her face up to me.

"Your mother is a crabby bitch. Don't let her get to you."

She laughs softly at my words, and it makes me smile.

"That's the nicest thing anyone has ever said about her," she says with another easy smile. "I should be used to it by now. Everything I do pisses her off. I'm just thankful she wasn't calling to tell me she saw what we did in your truck. That would have been awkward."

Her dry humor is something I'm quickly growing to love about her, and it frustrates me that I don't hear enough of it.

I heard most of the conversation she had with Eve earlier. Layla was sitting close enough and her mother was screaming loud enough for me to make out the gist of it. Eve found out from God knows who that Layla went off on her own and sang a few songs and played music on a guitar at a hole-in-the-wall bar. Songs that weren't "Layla Carlysle" songs and a bar that wasn't "Layla Carlysle" appropriate. Eve criticized and shouted all sorts of venom at Layla about how she was going to ruin her reputation and that she should be ashamed of herself for her behavior.

When Eve said that, Layla looked up at me with the phone pressed to her ear, and we shared a secret smile knowing that out of all of the things that happened that night, her behavior in the bar wasn't even close to being as *shameful* as what we did in the truck.

I wanted to grab the phone from Layla's hand and tell Eve to fuck off before she made Layla feel worse and took away the spark that was still in her eyes, but Layla beat me to the punch.

"I'm sorry, you're breaking up. Must be a bad connection. We'll talk soon."

Layla hung up the phone mid-shout from her mother and tossed it onto the dashboard with a bubbling laugh. I started up the truck and headed towards her house, thankful she hadn't let Eve's words get to her.

Unfortunately, the twenty-minute drive gave her too much time to think, and by the time we pulled into the driveway, her mood had dropped considerably. She jumped down out of the truck without a word, and after I cleared the house and made sure it was safe, she excused herself to take a shower, never coming back out of her room.

"You should tell your mother off more often. I think she needs a healthy dose of reality," I tell Layla softly in the dark, quiet of the bedroom.

"I shouldn't have done that. She's going to make me regret it, just like she always does."

The admission from Layla shocks me, and I don't speak for a minute. Just like June said, Layla isn't very forthcoming when it comes to her life. I found a book of songs she wrote that have never seen the light of day, and I had hoped she would tell me all about them when I discovered it. She's best friends with a man who at times seems like he resents her more than supports her, and she lets a woman who obviously hates her control her life. She sings like an angel and plays the guitar like a rock goddess in bar where no one knows who she is. I want her to trust me, and I want her to tell me why she's made the choices she has.

"You don't have to put up with her bullshit. You know that, right? You're an adult. A very successful and talented adult. You're not a teenage girl who just lost her father and got into something she maybe wasn't ready for. You can quit anytime," I tell her with conviction.

"Did you see all of those people out there today who came to see me?" Layla asks quietly, and I wonder if she's changing the subject or just ignoring what I've said to her. "Forget about the insane stalker I have for just a minute. Did you read any of the other letters I get on a daily basis when you were going through all of my fan mail? Little girls who look up to me, brokenhearted women who say I've put a smile on their face for the first time in ages, kids who've had horrible childhoods that say I give them hope that they can make their dreams come true."

Layla slides her hand up my stomach and perches her chin on top of it so she can continue looking at me while she explains.

"Did you know I volunteer at a children's hospital once a month? I go from room to room and sing to the children who are in there for a few days with pneumonia or the ones who are dying from cancer and know they will never get to go outside and swing on a swing set or play tag with their friends. Those are my fans, Brady. They're real people and they're the reason I continue doing what I do. There are so many musicians out there who let their fans down because they just don't care about them. They don't realize there are people out there all over the world that depend on them, that need them to help forget about their own troubles for just a little while. If getting up on that stage night after night puts a smile on the face of a little girl or encourages her to get up and dance around the room in unadulterated joy, who am I to complain about *my* life?"

I have to swallow back the lump in my throat at her words. I feel like a pussy for getting choked up, but I can't help it. I'm an ass and I never once thought about any of this from her point of view. It's easy for me to tell her to just stop doing something that makes her miserable because I'm not in her shoes. My parents made me miserable, so I joined the Navy and left. I eliminated the thing in my life that was ruining me, and the only person I let down was Gwen. Just disappointing that one person was enough to gut me. The idea that Layla feels like she would let billions of people down is a heavy pill to swallow and one I obviously know nothing about.

"I'm sorry. You probably think I'm a dick for always telling you to just quit," I tell her honestly.

She smiles at me sadly and moves her hand from my chest to cup the side of my face, her thumb sliding back and forth over my cheek bone.

"It would be a hell of a lot easier if I *did* think you were a dick, believe me. This is my life. This is how it has to be; Eve's made sure of that. It's legal and it's binding, and if I go against her, I will let all of those people down. You come in here and you're strong and confident, and I suddenly want to be a different person because I want to make you proud. I want you to look at me like you did tonight at the edge of that stage. You're making me question every single thing I've ever done. Making me want things I never…"

She pauses, stopping herself before she gives away too much, and I just want to tell her to give me everything. I don't care about the consequences. Just give me everything you have.

"What the hell are you doing to me, Brady?" she asks brokenly, her voice choked with tears that she tries her hardest to hold back.

There are so many things I want to say to her now, but I

know everything will come out wrong. I'm not good with words. I'm not good with the hearts and flowers bullshit. The only thing I know to do is show her what she means to me.

With a roll of my body, I push her onto her back and settle myself between her thighs as she quickly opens them for me. Smoothing her hair off of her face, I study her and silently tell her with my eyes everything I don't have the guts to speak out loud.

I've never wanted anyone as much as you.

I'm falling fast for you, and it scares the fucking shit out of me.

I will do whatever it takes to change this life for you, to make it into something you can enjoy and not have to feel guilty about.

"I need you," she whispers softly against my lips, and I shift my hips slightly against her, letting her know that the feeling is mutual and that if I get any harder from wanting her, I'm going to explode.

"I'm right here, baby," I tell her before leaning down and pressing my lips to hers, pushing my tongue past her lips so I can taste her.

Just like the past two times I've kissed her, the hunger quickly ignites, and there's no possibility of us going slow.

I reluctantly pull my lips away from hers, and she lets out a soft moan of protest. I know if I continue kissing her, things will escalate quickly, just like they did in the truck. That was hot as fuck and something we're definitely going to need to repeat soon, but right now, I want more. I need more.

I reach back and fling the covers off of me as I slide down the length of her body until my chin is resting on one of her opened thighs, staring at the black patch of lace that covers her sex. I slowly slide my finger down the center, and my eyes shift up to Layla's face as she whimpers and throws her head back.

Running my finger along the edge of her panties, I slide them to the side and inch forward until my lips are almost touching her and my breath floats over her skin. Holding the black lace to the side, I want to shift my hips into the mattress to ease some of the ache just looking at her has caused.

"Brady, please," she groans from the head of the bed.

I don't hesitate to plunge forward, wrapping my lips around her clit and sucking it into my mouth, overwhelmed with the feel and taste of her on my tongue. She's sweet and musky, and I want to devour her.

Layla's hands smack down on the bed, and she clutches the sheets tightly in her fists as I work her over with my tongue, moving my other hand between her legs so I can use my fingers as well.

Her hips jerk against my mouth, and her cries get louder and louder as I plunge two fingers inside of her and slide my flattened tongue back and forth quickly over her clit. Her climax surges through her so suddenly that a shocked cry flies from her lips, and she grasps the back of my head tightly, holding me in place while she rides it out against my mouth.

I want to keep going, continue sucking her and tasting her until the sun comes up, but she's panting and muttering how much she needs me, clutching onto my shoulders and dragging me forcefully back up her body.

I almost had an orgasm just from feeling her come on my tongue, so there's no way I can even think about trying to slow this down again. In the blink of an eye, my boxer briefs are pushed down around my knees with both of our hands, her black lace thong is ripped from her body, and I'm slamming inside of her, silencing our mutual groans with a kiss.

Her hands smack down to clutch my ass and pull me in deeper, her tongue swirling through my mouth, tasting herself on me, and I can't help but moan.

The sound of pleasure and skin slapping together fills the room as I take her roughly, pushing us both up the bed with the force of my movements. She chants "harder" over and over against my lips, and I wonder if I'll ever be able to take it slow with this woman.

Her legs and arms wrap tightly around my body, and she shouts my name as a second release washes through her, pulsing around my cock and forcing my own orgasm to rush through me like a fucking freight train.

I collapse on top of her, my brain only functioning enough to make sure I don't put all of my weight on top of her and crush her small frame.

In the aftermath, as we both lay there breathing heavily, wrapped up in each other, I think back to the song Layla sang tonight and hope to God I'm strong enough for this woman and can get her out of this impossible situation.

CHAPTER 17

"What the hell were you thinking throwing a brick through her fucking window?"

Ray rolls his eyes as he puts his car in park, lights up a cigarette, and scans through the pictures he just picked up from the one hour photo place.

"I feel like we've had this discussion before. I do what I want, when I want, and I wanted to have a little fun with that hot piece of ass," Ray replies with a chuckle as he runs his finger over a particularly good profile shot of Layla sitting on top of that asshole PI in his truck. Her head is thrown back, her mouth is open, and all of that glorious hair is spilling down her back. It makes him wish he would have walked up to the truck, thrown open the door, and dragged her out by her hair so she could have finished her little impromptu truck-fucking with him.

"This has gone too far. I just wanted her a little scared and some easy publicity," the voice whines in irritation through the phone line.

Ray ignores it and continues flipping through the photos. He's made it a habit of following Layla around everywhere she goes, and it's been a little boring. Imagine his surprise when he woke up from a nap in his car to see her walk right by him, hop into the truck parked across from his car, and fuck that lowlife for all she's worth. He almost regrets spending a big chunk of his payment on a good camera with a telephoto lens, but these pictures prove that the expense is well worth it. Too bad he didn't buy a video camera. He would have enjoyed being able to watch her bounce up and down on that guy's cock again and again, imagining it was him.

"You should be more concerned with the fact that her new bodyguard follows her around everywhere she goes. I don't think that guy is as dumb as he looks. You better watch your step or he's going to find out what a bad, bad person you are," Ray says with a laugh.

"He hates me. I know he already suspects something. Why the hell isn't he doing what he usually does: sucking back booze and screwing random women? He's not the loser I thought he was. He needs to be out of the picture immediately or this is going to blow up in our faces."

Ray takes his favorite photo out of the pile and grabs a black Sharpie marker from the center console. It's regrettable that he's going to give this photo away, but he can always make another copy.

"This isn't going to blow up in MY face," his voice raises in disbelief. "It's going to blow up in YOUR face. You better make nice with the big bad PI, and you better do it fast before he really starts digging into things," Ray states distractedly as he pens a personalized message on the photo, reads it over, and smiles at his creativity.

"Right, right. That's a good idea. Maybe I can throw him off the trail if I just kill him with kindness," the voice replies.

"Or I could just kill him."

Ray barks out a laugh when he hears the gasp of shock through the phone line at his suggestion.

"What?! No! Absolutely not. We're not talking about killing anyone. I told you that in the beginning. No one needs to die. We just need to pull back a little. No more threats, no more going off on your own. This needs to be finished so he packs up and leaves. Layla will go back to doing what she's supposed to, and no one will ever know I had anything to do with this."

Ray sighs as the person rambles on and on, trying to tell him what to do and what not to do. He doesn't like it when people think they can boss him around. He was hired to do a job, and he doesn't care what the fuck this person wants. He's going to finish it how he wants to, and if someone has to die, well then so be it.

He cuts the person off mid-sentence and hangs up the phone without a goodbye, tossing the cell phone into the passenger seat and studying the photo in his hands for a few minutes.

He looks up from the picture when he sees movement out

of the corner of his eye. Layla and the idiot joined at her hip are finally done stretching at the entrance of the trail. They take off into the woods running side by side.

Ray smiles to himself as he tosses the butt of his cigarette out the window, opens the car door, and makes his way over to the F150 parked close to the trail. Luckily, with the nice weather lately, the park is packed early in the morning, and his beat-up Honda doesn't stick out like a sore thumb. He'd found the last available parking space in the crowded lot, crouched down low in his seat, and sat waiting until the coast was clear.

He ambles over to the truck, bends down to tie his shoe next to the front tire, and glances around for any signs of anyone looking his way or paying any attention to him. When he sees no one, he stands up and quickly shoves the photo facedown underneath the windshield wiper blade on the passenger side, right where Layla will see it when she gets back into the truck.

Ray smiles to himself and whistles softly as he makes his way back to his car.

He can feel his dick swell in his pants when he thinks about the look that will be on Layla's face when she sees that picture. Her full lips will part in surprise, and maybe a lone tear will fall from her eye and down her cheek. Soon enough, he'll be so close to her that he'll be able to lick her tears right off of her cheek. He wishes he could stick around for the show, but he'll be with her soon enough. Right now, he's got supplies to purchase and a kidnapping to map out.

CHAPTER 18
Layla

When I woke up this morning, still wrapped in Brady's arms after the best night of sleep I'd had in forever, I decided a morning run was needed to get my adrenaline pumping in some way other than rolling over to face him and pulling him into my body.

When I tried to slide out of his arms, he pulled me back against him, ran his hands down my side, and hitched my leg back over his thigh and slowly entered me from behind. Thirty minutes later, and after I was too worn out to move, he was the one who suggested the run.

Being with Brady is so easy that it scares me. I'm growing attached to him quickly, and for someone like me, that isn't good. I can't get attached to him. He doesn't understand why I do the things I do, and even though he apologized last night for questioning me repeatedly about my choices, I know it still bothers him. If he sticks around after this case is over, it will always bother him. He might try to hide it so as not to upset me, but it would eat away at him. He's not the type of man to sit back and watch someone suffer.

I don't know why I'm even entertaining the idea of him being here after my stalker is caught. We've had sex a few times. That's it. Mind-blowing, brain-numbing sex, but still...only sex. We're not in love and he hasn't promised me anything beyond today. He's here because he has a job to do, and I'm probably an easy way to pass the time. I shouldn't be worried about disappointing him down the road. It probably won't be long now until the police figure out who is behind all of the threats, he'll go to jail, and Brady will go back to his own life.

"So, tell me about your sister. Is she younger or older than you?" I ask, trying to banish thoughts of Brady and I having a future together as we jog past the first mile marker on the trail.

"She's younger by two years," he replies with a smile on his face as he thinks about her. "She's had a rough time of it lately. Married an abusive asshole that my parents loved, and after he busted her face and broke some bones about six months ago, she finally got up the nerve to leave his sorry ass and showed up on my doorstep with her daughter."

I shake my head in both sympathy and anger for this woman and her daughter. Hearing something like this always makes me regret the complaints I have about my own life.

"I'm glad she was able to get away and that she has you to

lean on."

Brady lets out a mocking snort.

"Yeah, well, I was an asshole myself for a long time. She didn't deserve that shit from him *or* me. I have a lot of making up to do with her. Keeping an eye on her and Emma and helping them out is the least I can do."

I wonder what he means about him being an asshole to his sister, but I don't want to push him to tell me something he doesn't want to so I move on to another subject.

We run three more miles, talking easily about both of our childhoods. I tell him about some of the better memories I have of just my dad and me, and he tells me about his three best friends, all Navy SEALS scattered throughout the world. Men he keeps in contact with all of the time and knows he can trust or turn to for help whenever he needs it.

I'm glad he has people like that in his life. I can count on one hand the friends I have who I can rely on like that. Actually, I can count on one finger, but even after what he did for me at June's bar, I'm still not sure if our friendship will ever be the same.

"So, you and Finn. Just friends, right?" Brady asks nonchalantly, staring straight ahead.

I smile to myself when I hear the wariness in his voice.

Could he possibly be jealous of Finn?

"Yes, just friends. We met in elementary school. He was a

252

loner because he lived in the town's only orphanage, and I was pretty much in the same boat because my family had a lot of money and when you come from money it can make people petty and resentful. So we stuck together and defended each other when kids were nasty on the playground," I explain, thinking back to that time and smiling when I picture a ten-year-old Finn shoving some boy who had just called me a rich bitch. "Finn went into the Marines right out of high school, and when he came back injured, he couldn't get hired anywhere. Surprisingly, it was really easy to get my mother to agree to hire him as my bodyguard. It's the one time I didn't have to fight with her."

We round the bend that takes us to the end of the trail and slow down our running until we're walking slowly, stretching our arms as we cool down.

"So, you guys never hooked up? I mean, friends hook up all the time. Sometimes you need to scratch an itch and no one else is around. And he's a good looking guy. And *always* around you. Chicks like Marines and all that 'ooh-rah' shit..." Brady trails off, once again not making eye contact at all, and that makes me smile even wider.

"Brady, are you jealous of Finn?" I ask, turning to face him as he holds onto his foot and pulls one of his legs behind him to stretch out the muscles in his thigh.

"What? Jealous?" he asks with a nervous laugh. "Why

would I be jealous? I mean, you've known him all your life. It would make sense if you guys were together. The media already assumes you are. Every time they spot the two of you in public they take a close-up shot of your left hand looking for an engagement ring."

He's rambling now and it's the cutest thing I've ever heard or witnessed. I can never tell Brady that though. Something tells me he wouldn't take too kindly to being called cute.

"You read tabloid articles about me and Finn?" I ask as I move closer to him, wrapping my arms around his waist as he drops his foot and rests his hands on my shoulders, gently kneading the muscles there.

He rolls his eyes and lets out another awkward laugh before leaning down and kissing my lips quickly before moving back.

"It was just for research. You know, trying to figure you out before I got here."

We break apart and Brady holds onto my hand as we head across the parking lot towards his truck.

"Mmhmm, research, right," I mumble with a laugh.

He ignores my comment, opens the passenger door for me, and helps me climb into my seat. When he gets in on his side and starts up the truck, I stare at his profile.

He finally looks over at me, and I raise my eyebrow

questioningly, waiting for him to just admit it. My silence and the way I'm looking at him finally gets to him, and he lets out a huge sigh of defeat.

"Okay, fine! I'm jealous as fuck. God dammit, I can't believe I just said that," he complains.

I laugh and shake my head in wonder at the fact that he's actually had these thoughts in his head.

"I swear to you there has never been nor will there ever be something between Finn and me. He's *just* a friend. You have nothing to worry about."

Brady seems satisfied with my answer, and I lean over the center console to kiss his cheek. He quickly turns his face though and my lips press against his. I bring my hand up and place it against the day old stubble on his face, liking the way it feels against the palm of my hand. He nibbles teasingly at my lips before gently sliding his tongue past them and tangling it with my own.

I could kiss this man forever and never grow tired of it. His lips are soft but firm, and his tongue sweeps through my mouth slowly and gently as if he's trying to taste every single inch of it. He sucks lightly on my tongue and a whimper escapes my lips. Brady slows down the kiss and gives me one last chaste peck before pulling away and shifting the truck into gear.

"You know, now that I think about it, Finn and I did go on a few dates back in high school to test the waters," I tell him teasingly, trying to pay him back for getting me worked up with that kiss and then pulling away before I was ready.

"You're really enjoying this, aren't you?" Brady asks with a laugh.

I snicker to myself as I look away from his sparkling green eyes, the laughter dying on my lips as I see something stuck to the front of the windshield right in front of me.

"Stop the truck," I tell Brady softly as he begins backing out of the parking space.

"Stop the truck!" I shout in a panic as he slams on the breaks and looks over at me in confusion at my outburst.

I fumble with the handle and fling open the door, standing up on the running board of the truck to lean out and around the windshield to pull what I saw out from under the wiper.

Getting back into the truck and slamming the door closed, I stare in horror at the photo I hold in my hand. It's a picture of Brady and me in this very truck from the night we were at June's. My heart thumps wildly in my chest as I take my eyes off of the intimate moment someone caught on camera to read the words penned in black marker right at the top.

I read them four times before Brady finally snatches the photo out of my hand and growls in anger when he sees what someone has done—what they've said and what it means.

"All that beautiful, blonde hair will be spilling over my thighs soon. I can't wait to wrap my hands around all those silky strands and force your mouth where I want it to go," Brady reads aloud, practically spitting each word from his mouth with the force of his fury.

My stomach clenches in revulsion and fear. My chin quivers as I watch Brady's fists clutch tightly to the photo until he's crumpled it so hard that it's unreadable and his knuckles are stark white.

He reaches across my body and pops open the glove box, shoving the ruined photo inside and slamming it closed before putting the truck back into reverse and peeling out of the parking lot. He doesn't say a word to me as we drive through town. I have my arms wrapped protectively around my body as I hunch against the door of the truck, staring out at the passing landscape and swiping angrily at the tears that have now started to fall.

This disgusting human being took something amazing between Brady and me and turned it dirty; a moment in time where I felt free and alive is now tainted by some faceless person. All this time I've been fooling myself thinking that I wouldn't let this person get to me. Even after he attacked me outside that bar, I thought I could put on a brave face and it would all blow over quickly without ruining a piece of myself in the process.

The rearview mirror on the passenger side of the truck is angled in such a way that I can see myself in it as I rest my head against the window. I stare angrily at all of my *blonde, beautiful hair* that I took down from its high ponytail after the run. It's wild and untamed and even though my mother has always been the one to insist it remain long, I usually don't mind it. I love my hair and the confidence it gives me. I love being able to hide behind it when I need to pretend to be someone else. Now all I see when I look in the mirror is a dirty pair of hands wrapping a handful of it around his fists and forcing me to do something I don't want.

I tear my gaze away from my reflection when I realize Brady just drove right by the road that would take us to my cabin.

"Where are we going?" I ask, breaking the silence in the cab of the truck.

"Someplace safe," he replies rigidly.

An hour later, I stand in front of the small mirror in the bathroom staring at the woman reflected back. She looks nothing like me. But I guess that's what I wanted when I locked myself in here and found a pair of scissors in the medicine cabinet.

"Someplace safe" turned out to be Brady's three bedroom townhouse on the outskirts of town. And he was right. It's definitely safe. He's got more deadbolts on his door than an apartment in Hell's Kitchen in New York City, and his security system is more state-of-the-art than mine. He's turned the walk-in closet in his bedroom into a panic room, complete with a steel door and a keypad for entry and exit, and there is a table set up inside with monitors that show the entryway inside the front door and all around the exterior of the house.

I had barely glanced at his furnishings as he walked me through the home, showing me where everything was, and I regret that now. It's strange being here in his domain and around his things. A man's home is like a window into his soul. It tells you if he's a confirmed bachelor who never wants to grow up or a family man with a big heart who keeps pictures of his loved ones on his mantle and hung on his walls.

His sister and niece weren't home when we got here but I can hear a female voice talking softly to Brady on the other side of the door now and I assume it's Gwen.

"How long has she been in there?"

"I don't know, a fucking long time," Brady whispers *angrily.*

"Don't get lippy with me. Did you even knock on the door to see if she was okay?"

"No. I figured she needed some space."

"You're an idiot. Women don't need space even when we say we do. You should check on her."

"You're standing right there, YOU check on her."

"I can't just knock on the door of the bathroom Layla Carlysle is in! What the hell is wrong with you?"

"Oh my God, she's just a person. A normal, smart, amazing person. You can knock on the door, Gwen."

I'd laugh out loud right now at their whispered argument if I wasn't so numb. Hearing the two of them bicker back and forth makes me wish I had a sibling.

"I knew it! You really DO have a crush on her!"

"Will you shut up? I don't have a crush on her. I'm not twelve," Brady argues.

"Fine, then you're in love with her."

There's a long stretch of silence outside the door, and I realize I'm holding my breath, waiting for Brady's reply.

"You're pesky. And annoying. Like a housefly. Go away," Brady finally says, not responding to Gwen's statement of love.

I let out the breath I was holding, not sure if I'm happy or disappointed that he didn't say something in regards to Gwen's comment, which is completely unfounded anyway. He's not in love with me. That's just silly. We've only known each other for a month, and we live in two completely different worlds.

I don't hear any more of the conversation through the door and realize that they're probably both just standing there waiting for me to emerge. I take a deep breath figuring I might as well get this over with. I walk over to the door and unlock it, turning the handle and opening it slowly. I glance around the door frame into an empty hallway, thankful that Brady and Gwen aren't standing inches from the closed door and staring at it, waiting for it to open.

I make my way down the hallway and notice several framed photos hanging on the wall of Gwen and her daughter Emma, Gwen and Brady, Brady and Emma, and a few of all three of them together. There's one last photo next to all the others of Brady and three other men in their Navy Dress Whites, and I know immediately that these are the men he talked about on our run, the friends he spoke so highly of and admires. I smile to myself despite how I'm feeling, realizing that Brady's home is nothing like a college fraternity house.

I step into the living room and find Gwen seated on the edge of the coffee table and Brady pacing back and forth behind the couch with his hands clasped behind his head.

They both look up when I enter the room, and their jaws drop when I step out of the dark hallway and into the brightly lit room.

"Oh wow," Gwen whispers, a smile slowly turning up the corners of her mouth until she's full-on grinning at me.

"Holy shit," Brady mutters as he stops pacing and his hands drop down to his sides.

I reach one of my hands up to tug self-consciously at the blunt ends of my hair that now rest an inch above my shoulders instead of eight inches past them.

"You look amazing!" Gwen says, standing up quickly from the coffee table and rushing over to stand in front of me. "I'm Gwen, by the way, and I love your music! I'm a huge fan!"

Her gushing and the genuine smile on her face as she stares at my hack job makes me feel a little better about what I've done. I eye the blue and purple streaks in her dark hair, and I immediately wish I had the guts to do something that drastic. I guess this will have to do for now.

"Thank you," I tell her with a smile. "I'm sorry for taking over your bathroom for so long. And I promise I'll clean up the hair all over the place."

Gwen reaches out and rubs my arm gently.

"Nonsense. Brady is the neat freak, so he can worry about it while you and I watch some mindless reality TV before my whirlwind of a daughter gets home from school," Gwen says with a laugh.

At the mention of Brady, my eyes leave hers and wander over to him as he stands perfectly still behind the couch staring at me. Gwen follows my gaze and I see her give her brother a dirty look and not so subtly nod her head in my direction.

"So, Brady. Doesn't Layla look amazing?" Gwen prods.

Brady just nods dumbly without saying a word.

"Don't you have anything to say to her?" Gwen says through her smile and clenched teeth.

After a few awkward seconds, he finally speaks.

"What is it about my bathroom that causes both of the women in my life to lock themselves in there at separate times and chop it all off?" Brady says with a shake of his head, throwing his hands up in the air in puzzlement.

I look back at Gwen and we both stare at each other's hair before we burst out laughing. We're laughing so hard that tears are falling from both of our eyes and Gwen clutches her stomach. At the tail end of our laughing fit, Brady walks up next to me, runs both of his hands down the side of my head, and holds them in place on either side of my face. He stares into my eyes for a few minutes with a soft smile on his face before leaning in and kissing my cheek.

"I thought it was impossible for you to be any more beautiful than you already were," he whispers in my ear while Gwen gives us some privacy and turns on the television.

"Jesus, was I fucking wrong."

I can hear the desire in his voice, and it makes my stomach flip with excitement. This day started out amazing and quickly turned horrifying. I breathe a sigh of relief because it looks like it might end on a more positive note.

CHAPTER 19

BRADY

I snatch up my ringing cell phone and smile when I see who's calling, despite all of the anxiety I'm feeling.

"Garrett, what's up man?"

I hear a baby scream in the background and rustling over the line before he answers.

"Baby shit, lots and lots of baby shit," he replies with a sigh.

"Does that mean married life is good or are you ready to throw in the towel?" I ask with a laugh, receiving a punch in the arm from Gwen who's sitting next to me at my small kitchen table while Layla is showering and the bright morning sun shines through the window.

"Nah, things are good. Things are really good. Parker just got home from a photo shoot in Arizona, and Annie is finally sleeping through the night. It's good having both of my girls under one roof, man."

I can hear the smile and happiness in Garrett's voice. For a minute, a feeling of envy washes over me. Garrett and Parker were able to work through some pretty fucking extreme odds in the last year, and they managed to make it work. They're both happier than I've ever seen them, and it makes me suddenly wish I had that kind of happiness. I never thought marriage and kids would be in the cards for me, not wanting to find someone and then leave her alone every few months while I traipsed across the globe on SEAL missions. Now that I'm retired from the Navy and have a more stable job, not to mention an amazing woman who has worked her way under my skin, I feel more hopeful about the future for the first time in my life.

"So anyway, I got your message last night about looking into Jack Carlysle's car accident," Garrett says as I hear Parker's voice cooing and laughing in the background.

I had left a message for Garrett the night before after Layla fell asleep on the couch with Emma snuggled up next to her. I felt like a pansy-ass for getting all emotional while standing in the room watching them sleep. Gwen and Emma are my whole life, and Layla is quickly moving into that same category. Seeing how well she gets along with Gwen, and then Emma when she got home from school, made my heart feel like it would burst out of my chest.

I tried contacting June at the bar to see if she could expand a little more about the suspicions she said she had involving Jack's death, but I couldn't reach her. I called Garrett in the meantime and had him do some digging.

"It took a while, but I was able to find out something a little weird. You said the guy died when his brakes went out and his car slammed into a tree, right?" Garrett asks.

"Yep, that's what Layla told me, and all the news articles I read and the police report confirmed the same thing."

I hear Garrett flipping through some pages for a few seconds before he responds.

"Here's the strange thing. The day before the accident, Jack Carlysle had an appointment at the same garage he'd gone to for twenty years. Local establishment, same owner since the sixties, reputable place. And guess what he fixed?"

Garrett pauses and a feeling of dread fills my stomach before I answer.

"His brakes," I reply softly.

"Ding, ding, ding! Correct."

I shake my head in confusion and take a moment to make sure I can still hear the sound of the shower running down the hall where Layla is.

"If his brakes were recently fixed, how the fuck did they manage to go?" I ask angrily as Gwen looks at me with raised eyebrows.

"Well, I spoke to the owner, Bill, real nice guy, and I didn't get any kind of vibe from him that he had any ill will towards Jack. He was genuinely upset about the whole thing and swore up and down that when he personally changed the brake pads and fluid, nothing was amiss and everything was in top shape when he finished," Garrett explains.

"So someone got to that car after it was fixed," I conclude. "Why the hell wasn't this brought up with the police? Why didn't Bill tell them there was no way something could have accidentally gone wrong with Jack's brakes?"

Garrett sighs. "Jack's vehicle was the last one Bill worked on that day. The last one he worked on ever, actually. He retired that day and closed the doors to his shop, something he'd been planning for over two years. That night, Bill got on a plane with his wife and flew to Spain. They spent three months all over that countryside and didn't hear of Jack's death until they came home. By that point, the cops had already closed the case as a cut and dry accident. Bill tried to file a report claiming someone must have tampered with the car so the police would reopen the case, but it was a no go. They didn't see any merit in his claims and figured he was just trying to cover his own ass so the family wouldn't sue him."

I spend a few more minutes going over the details of what Garrett found and ask him to email me a copy of the statement Bill filed with the police, along with a copy of the work order form that day.

I hang up the phone just as a knock sounds at the door.

Gwen starts to get up to answer it, but I stop her with a hand on her arm.

"I'll get it. Go check on Layla and make sure she was able to find the towels and anything else she needs. And not a word of what we just found out from Garrett, please. I want to make sure all of this adds up before I put one more thing on her shoulders for her to worry about," I explain.

Gwen nods and heads off down the hall as I go to the door, looking out the peep hole before unlocking the deadbolts and throwing it open.

"Hey, Brady! What's going on?" Finn says with a smile as he tries to walk by me and into the house.

I put my hand up on his chest, stopping him in his tracks, utterly confused by his jovial demeanor.

Finn sighs and we stand there staring at one another in silence for several long minutes. I don't care if Layla *did* call him last night to explain things and have him bring some of her stuff over this morning. I still don't trust him.

He finally shrugs his shoulders at me.

"Look, man, I'm sorry about being such a dick to you. Just look at it from my side of things. Layla and I have been friends for years. She's been through a lot, and I just didn't want her getting hurt again. I had no idea who you were or what your motives were, and I acted like an ass. I'm sorry."

He extends his hand and I want to shake my head to clear it, wondering if I'm still asleep and this is a dream. Why the fuck is he suddenly playing nice with me?

"Come on, don't leave me hanging," Finn says with a laugh, his hand still out in front of him.

"Hey, Finn," Layla says from behind me. I turn away from Finn, thankful for her interruption so I'm not tempted to grab onto his hand, yank him closer, and punch him in the face.

"Hi, Lay. Like what you've done with your hair," he says with a smile as I finally step aside to let him in and close the door behind him. He hands her a small suitcase and the black leather Gibson guitar case that I'd noticed on the stage the other night at June's.

Layla takes them both from him and props them up against the wall in the foyer, all of us awkwardly standing around staring at each other and not talking.

"So, Brady, would you mind if Layla and I had a couple minutes alone to talk? I won't keep her from you long," he asks politely after a few minutes and with another weird smile on his face that I can't tell if it's forced or his real smile since I've never seen it on his face before.

I don't reply because anything I say right now will just make me look like an asshole, so I nod at Layla, and the two of them disappear down the hallway towards the bedroom—the fucking bedroom where they can both sit on a bed and *talk*.

The idea of Layla on bed with anyone other than me makes me feel murderous. Fuck! I need to rein this shit in.

Layla said there was never anything between them, and I

believe her and trust her. I just don't trust that smarmy bastard who suddenly wants to be my friend or some shit. Trying to avoid running down the hall and making an ass of myself by listening to their conversation, I fill my thoughts with Layla and what happened in my bedroom after I woke her up and we put Emma to bed. She locked my bedroom door as soon as we got inside, dropped to her knees, ripped open my jeans, and took me in her mouth without saying a word. I pride myself on being able to last pretty fucking long in the bedroom, but last night, it was downright embarrassing how quickly her lips and tongue brought me to completion.

As I stand here remembering the feel of her hot mouth wrapped around me and wonder when I can kick Finn out so I can get her naked again, there's another knock at the door. It's like Grand fucking Central Station here this morning. Since Finn is the only person who knows where Layla is right now, and I'm not expecting anyone, I quietly move to the door to look through the hole again.

Oh you have GOT to be kidding me.

I step back and open the door with trepidation, staring down into the face of Layla's mother. Unlike Finn, she doesn't wait for an invitation. She just barges right past me and into the living room.

"Sure, come right in," I mutter to myself as I close the door behind her.

She stands in the middle of my living room doing a slow circle, taking in her surroundings. I don't miss the look of revulsion on her face as she wrinkles her nose before turning back to face me and quickly replacing that look with a smile.

"Let me guess, you followed Finn?" I ask her as I stay in the foyer and slide my hands into the back pockets of my jeans.

"Of course I followed Finn. He said he spoke to Layla and he knew where she was and that she was safe. I just needed to see for myself."

She looks around quickly again, and I can tell it's really taking some effort for her to not cringe. My place is small. I know that. But it's clean and it's mine. It's a place to lay my head at night, and it keeps everyone inside of it safe. That's all that matters. She can just take that stick right out of her ass because I'm not a millionaire and I never will be.

"Layla is fine. Shaken up, but she's fine. She's a very strong woman," I tell Eve. Maybe if I say it enough, her mother will actually believe it. She doesn't know the specifics of what happened yesterday. She only knows that Layla received another threatening note. It's none of her business that the note was printed on a picture of the two of us in a very compromising position.

"Well, that's good. That's very good. Actually, I didn't just come over here for Layla," she admits.

Surprise, surprise. The she-devil must want something.

"I wanted to apologize to you."

I quickly glance out of the window in the living room, checking for flying pigs, before I turn back to face Eve.

What the fuck is she apologizing to me for?

"I have to admit, I didn't hire you with the best intentions in mind. I really didn't believe Layla had an actual stalker. I'd heard about your reputation, and I figured you would come in here, not really do much, and then go. I could show the media that I really have Layla's best interests at heart, and it wouldn't turn into a huge circus that could harm anyone publicly. If I were to hire some big-name investigator, it would quickly get out that Layla had been receiving threats like that for years and I never did anything about it."

I can do nothing but stand there staring at the piece of work in front of me. She's actually telling me that she only hired me because she most likely thought I'd be drunk the entire time and not give a rat's ass about my client's safety.

"Let's cut the bullshit, shall we? You've never had Layla's best interests at heart or you wouldn't be forcing her to do something she doesn't love. Why the hell admit this to me now when we're close to catching the stalker? To ease your guilty conscience?" I fire back angrily.

"I know I've made mistakes where Layla is concerned, believe me. And I'm not doing any of this because I feel guilty. I will never apologize for the decisions I've made because they've got me to where I am today. But I would like to apologize to you for underestimating you. You're very good at your job, Mr. Marshall," she tells me with a confident lift of her chin.

Did I wake up in a second fucking dimension this morning? First Finn and now Eve. Why the fuck are they both trying to kiss my ass?

"I see that you really care about Layla, and I just want to make sure you understand that as great of a man as you are, the two of you come from different worlds."

I laugh and roll my eyes at her.

"And here we go. The real reason why you showed up on my doorstep trying to blow smoke up my ass. She's a star and I'm nobody and it would never work between us. Did I get the gist of it?" I ask sarcastically, pulling my hands out of my pockets to cross them over my chest and leaning my shoulder casually against the wall.

"I see I'm not telling you something you don't already realize. I'm not trying to be cruel, Mr. Marshall, but it's the truth. You live two completely different lives. Everyone in the world knows who Layla is. She has enough money to buy a hundred of these little homes and then some," she explains, looking around the small room once again and pulling her purse tighter to her side like I might try to steal it. "I'm doing this for your own good. She's a big deal. She's recognized wherever she goes, and if someone is linked to her, the media will dig and dig and dig into that person's life until they know every single intimate detail about them and their family members. You're lucky that little stunt she pulled at The Red Door Saloon wasn't splashed across the front of every newspaper because right now, the media would know all about you since I heard she dragged you out of there in front of everyone. They'd know about the mistakes you've made, and they'd know about the secrets your sister is hiding. They would know it all."

My arms fall limply to my sides during Eve's little enlightenment, and now I can't stop opening and closing my hands into fists, the muscles in my arms clenching in fury. I want to argue with Eve. I want to tell her that no one will give a rat's ass about me or my family because she's right, I'm nobody. But I can't make the words come out because I know everything she says is true. The first time the media sees me with Layla, they are going to want to know everything about me. They'll find out about every single time I've screwed up in my life and people have gotten hurt. And they'll find out about Gwen. That asshole husband of hers will find out where she is and how he can get to her. If it was just me, I could deal. I could push through that shit until they find another bone to chew on and get bored with me. But I can never let that happen to Gwen. Her and Emma's safety depend on her ex never knowing where she is.

"You're a good man, Mr. Marshall, and I just don't want to see you or your lovely family get hurt," Eve finishes as she walks my way and goes to the front door, pausing next to Layla's suitcase and the guitar case Finn brought with him.

"Where the hell did you get that?" Eve asks with an anxious whisper, pointing at the guitar case.

"Finn dropped it off. Why?"

I step close to Eve and see that she is shaking from head to toe, like she's seen a ghost.

"That's impossible. That thing was destroyed years ago," she mutters softly to herself, still staring at the case.

She reaches her hand out towards it in a daze but snatches it back when Finn and Layla enter the room.

"Mother, what are you doing here?" Layla asks as Eve whips her head around and stares at her daughter in horror.

"What the hell have you done to your hair?" Eve shouts angrily across the room.

I move forward and place myself directly in front of Eve so she can't see Layla without bending to the side.

"I think it's time for you to go now, Eve. I'll make sure to keep you updated on what's going on here, so you can adjust Layla's schedule as needed," I tell her, taking a few steps in her direction and forcing her to move backward towards the door.

She reaches behind her and fumbles for the knob before finally getting it open. "Thank you, Mr. Marshall, for all of your help."

Eve isn't looking at me when she says it. She's staring to

the side at the guitar case, and I see a muscle tick in her jaw. She quickly blinks her eyes back into focus and looks up at me with a smile that is as fake as her entire personality. "We'll be in touch soon."

Closing the door behind her, I take a moment to look over at the guitar case that had Eve so enraptured. It's just a standard Gibson case. It's not like it's plated in gold or something. Why the hell would Eve care about an old guitar case?

CHAPTER 20
Layla

"I just want you to be careful, Lay. That's all I'm saying," Finn said softly as he perched on the edge of Brady's bed next to me.

"I am being careful. For the first time in my life, I'm happy. The future doesn't seem so bleak or hopeless. He makes me want to be a different person, Finn. He makes me want to be me."

Finn looked at me quietly for a few minutes before reaching into his back pocket and pulling out a few pages of folded up paper and hands them to me.

"What's this?" I asked, unfolding the pages and smoothing them out on top of my thighs.

"Just read them."

I looked away from Finn and scanned the pages. I immediately falter when I see Brady's name.

"Finn, where did you get this? I shouldn't be reading this. It's his private life," I told him angrily, thrusting the papers that have copies of newspaper articles and printed information that looked like it came from a government website.

"There's a lot you don't know about this man, Layla. I just want you to go into this with your eyes wide open. He's had a lot of problems in the past. A lot. He fucked up on his last SEAL mission and it got people killed. He fucked up on a domestic disturbance call when he was with the PD and it got people killed," Finn explained. "You just told me not moments ago that he feels guilty for not being there for his sister, so now he's doing whatever he can to keep her safe, and that includes keeping her hidden away from their family and her husband."

I scoffed at his words and angrily crossed my arms in front of me.

"That man beat the hell out of her, Finn. He deserves to be in the dark when it comes to her whereabouts."

Finn placed the pages back on top of my thighs, but I refused to look down at them.

"That's not the point, Lay. The point is he doesn't care about the law or going through the proper channels to get something done. He does whatever it takes because he feels guilty. He's trying to make up for the fact that he wasn't there for his sister by holing her away in his home, thousands of miles from where their family lives. All of that death, all of that loss, it gets to a person. I'm just saying maybe what he feels for you and what he's doing with you has a lot to do with trying to make up for the past."

I stared at Finn in silence for a few minutes, refusing to comment on his theory. There was no way he could be right. Brady wasn't transferring his guilt over to me. It wasn't possible. What we had was real and it meant something to him. I could tell by the way he looked at me, the way he touched me.

"I just don't want to see you get hurt again. I know his type, Lay. SEALS are all the same. He doesn't care about you. He's just trying to make up for his mistakes with you. Getting close to you means you're never out of his sight, and that means he won't fuck this up. He won't have another death on his conscience."

I looked straight ahead at the wall and wouldn't allow myself to look at Finn. He finally got up from the bed with a sigh and headed towards the door.

"I hope I'm wrong about all of this, I really do. But for your sake, please, just ask him about it."

Sitting cross-legged in the middle of Brady's bed, I gently strum my Gibson Hummingbird as it rests on my lap, thinking about the conversation I had with Finn that morning. Brady has been on the phone all day, going outside a few times to talk or whispering so softly I can't hear him. When I asked him what was going on, he just told me he was researching some leads and would tell me what was going on as soon as he had something concrete. Gwen has been just as secretive, tapping away on the laptop at the kitchen table and changing the subject when I ask her if there's anything new.

I know there's something they're not telling me, and it pisses me off that they think they need to keep it from me.

The door to Brady's room clicks opens a few minutes later, and he pauses in the doorway when he sees me, my fingers immediately stilling on the strings. He gently closes the door behind him and walks over to the edge of the bed.

"When did you learn how to play?" he asks as he climbs up onto the bed and faces me, mirroring my position by pulling his legs up in front of him.

I stare at his face for a few minutes, wondering if I have the courage to ask him what he's doing with me. Finn's words have gotten to me, even though I swore I wouldn't let them. Is he really doing whatever this is with me out of misplaced guilt? Does he feel like if he solves this stalker case and I'm safe it will make up for all the bad things that have happened in his life? And what then? He just goes back to his life and I go back to mine?

I look down at my guitar and I can't help but think about my father. I wonder if he felt guilty when he walked out the door nine years ago.

"My father taught me when I was little. We used to go down into the recording studio, just the two of us, every single day after school. It was my absolute favorite time of the day," I quietly admit to Brady as I run the palm of my right hand down the top of the guitar, feeling all of the nicks and scratches from years of use, each one reminding me of happier times.

Placing my the fingers of my left hand on the proper frets, I strum my right hand down the strings, quickly moving my left hand as I play the notes for the song that has been in my head all evening. The fact that I stood on a stage in front of strangers and played when I'd done nothing but hold this guitar in my arms for almost ten years makes me feel almost invincible. The song I play now is an original; it's the first time I've ever played one for anyone, and the fact that I'm fully opening myself up to Brady and not afraid to do so speaks volumes. I've never played a single note of one of my original songs on this guitar, no matter how many words I've written that I know would be perfect for it. Regardless of the confusion I'm feeling about Brady and his feelings for me, I still trust him. I trust him enough to show him this part of me.

Brady doesn't speak as I open my mouth and let the words softly build while I play. It's a song I wrote during one of the darkest times in my life, when I thought ending it all was the only option I had to be free. I close my eyes and let the music flow through me. I strum the guitar slowly, and my words match my playing as I gently sing about the story of my life.

I put everything I have into this song and show him who I really am. I want him to see me, I want him to hear me, and I want him to finally understand me. I'm opening up my heart and soul to him here on this bed, and part of me doesn't care if he's with me because he feels guilty. As long as he's here, I'll take what I can get.

I'm standing on the edge,
close to falling in.
I know I could just let go,
close my eyes and let them win.
If I take that step there'll be nothing left
of who I used to be.

Do I let the darkness swallow me?
Do I let go and finally be free?
This pain leaves a scar that you cannot erase.
Only the darkness can take away my disgrace.

Everyone thinks I have it all together.
They look right through me,
and refuse to see the truth.
That it's all just a great big mess,
and I'm so far from being blessed.

Do I let the darkness swallow me?
Do I let go and finally be free?
This pain leaves a scar that you cannot erase.
Only the darkness can take away my disgrace.

I'm surrounded by so many,
but I've never felt so alone.
It would be so easy,
to say goodbye and make my way home.

Do I let the darkness swallow me?
Do I let go and finally be free?
This pain leaves a scar that you cannot erase.
Only the darkness can take away my disgrace.

I close out the song with a few gentle strums, pressing my palm against the strings over the sound hole, swathing the room in sudden silence. I can hear my heart beating in my ears and the ticking of a clock on Brady's nightstand. I slowly open my eyes and look directly into Brady's as he sits completely still right in front of me.

He doesn't say a word as I slide the guitar off of my lap and stand it upright next to the bed against the nightstand. Just like on the stage at June's, playing my guitar gives me courage and strength I never knew I had. It makes me feel bold and in control, and now that I've played one of my songs for the first time, I have a mass of excess energy and excitement that I need to channel elsewhere.

Getting up on my knees, I crawl over to Brady and straddle his lap, letting my arms rest on his shoulders and my hands dangle loosely behind his head. He hesitates for a few seconds before wrapping his arms around my body and pulling me close, and I ignore the look of guilt that I see on his face for a split second before he turns it into a smile, tipping up one corner of his mouth in the way I love so much.

I love this man. I can't keep pretending like I don't.

"You are amazing, Layla," Brady whispers as he looks at my face and brings his hand up to use the tips of his fingers to brush my bangs off of my forehead, moving his fingers down the side of my face to tuck my hair behind my ear.

He's staring at me so intently. I can feel that he wants to say more, but he's holding himself back. His brow furrows as he looks at me, and I'm so afraid I can barely breathe. I'm afraid of what he's not saying, and I'm afraid of what he *might* say. I want him to tell me he feels the same way I do; I want him to reassure me that guilt has no part in his feelings for me. I want this man to always be a part of my life and to continue giving me the strength and courage I need to survive. I know we need to talk, and there's so much we've left unsaid between us, but I can't do it right now. Right now, I just want to feel. I just want to lose myself in him and not worry about anything else.

I lower my head and kiss him. I pour everything I am into that kiss and hope that he can feel it. I slide my fingers through his hair and hold his face against mine and hope he knows that he's the only man I've ever given this much of myself to.

Without breaking the kiss, Brady moves his legs out from under me and pushes me back on the bed, gently resting his body on top of mine. The few times we've had sex, there's been a kind of desperation to it that I loved, like we can't get enough of each other, and it quickly explodes like a bomb as we crash into one another, giving and taking and pushing us both to our limits.

This time, we slowly undress each other, taking our time to touch and kiss and feel. When he finally rocks into me, it's unhurried and with ease. He moves on top of me slowly, and he never takes his eyes off of my face as we leisurely move against one another. When my orgasm washes through me, it's gentle and delicious and no less powerful than all of the other times, just less frantic. When Brady's own release comes seconds after mine, he holds himself still inside of me, entwining the fingers of one of his hands with mine and holding it between us, against his heart.

He slides out of me without a word and moves behind me, pulling my back up against his front and wrapping his arms tightly around me. I lie there next to him, listening to the sounds of his breathing as they gradually slow until I can tell that he's finally asleep. I can't stop the tear that falls down my cheek, and I bury my face into the pillow so I don't wake him.

I should be happy that what just happened between us wasn't sex, it was making love. I could feel his love for me in every part of my body even if he didn't voice the words.

So why am I not happy? Why do I feel like he was saying goodbye?

I wake up slowly to the sounds of people talking in the living room. Rolling over to reach for Brady, I feel nothing but cold sheets and realize the bed is empty. I push everything I'm feeling as far down as possible and get up out of bed, throwing on a pair of jeans and a T-shirt from my bag and running a brush through my short hair. When I leave the bedroom and walk into the living room, I see Finn, Brady, and Gwen standing around in the kitchen. Brady's eyes quickly leave mine when I look at him questioningly, and I realize with a sinking feeling that the worries I had last night weren't unfounded.

"Layla, good news!" Finn says excitedly as he rounds the kitchen table and walks up to me, pulling me into his arms. "They caught that Ray guy. They picked him up last night after they got an anonymous tip from the APB they put out. We have to get to the station as soon as possible so you can ID him."

I try to catch Brady's eyes over Finn's shoulder, but he's got his arms crossed in front of him, staring down at his shoes. I pull out of Finn's embrace and take a step back, forcing my chin up and putting on a look of bravado that I don't feel. This is a good thing. They caught the guy who's been terrorizing me. He's behind bars and this can finally be over. I can go home and things can go back to normal.

"That's great. I'll just go get my things and—"

"There's no time," Finn says quickly, cutting me off and grabbing my hand as he pulls me towards the door. "They want to book this guy as soon as possible, and they can't do that without you. I'll send someone for your things later."

I let Finn pull me towards the door without a word, casting one last look behind me at Brady. Is he really going to just let me walk out of here without saying anything?

He finally looks up from the floor, but his eyes don't meet mine. They're somewhere over my shoulder.

"If you want, I could follow behind you. You know, if you have any questions about the process or anything…" Brady says quietly, trailing off at the end.

If I want? What about what YOU want? God dammit, say something to me!

"Thanks, but I think we're okay. I can take care of Layla

from here," Finn tells Brady with a cocky smile.

I stand there for as long as I can, willing him to actually look me in the eyes. Have some fucking guts to tell me to my face that this is it, that last night really was his way of saying goodbye. Gwen stands off to the side, looking back and forth between us like someone at a tennis match, waiting for one of us to do something.

I turn away from both of them and start heading out the door Finn holds open, but then I stop in my tracks. Maybe I'm making a big deal out of this when he's probably just acting like a typical guy and doesn't know how to say what he wants. It's not like I actually came out and told him how I felt. I showed him instead. I showed him a part of me that only my father ever saw or understood. I trusted him to see me, to know me.

I want to be strong and I want to be independent, so maybe I should start acting like it. Take what I want for once. Letting go of Finn's hand, I hold up one finger, telling him to wait just a minute, and stalk back over to Brady who is now staring out the window.

"Just because I'm leaving and things are going back to normal, doesn't mean anything has to change between us. You know that, right?" I say softly to his back as he continues to look outside. I see his shoulders tense, though, the only outward sign that he's listening.

"I've spent too much of my life doing things I don't want

and being unhappy. You make me feel like I can do anything, be anyone. You wormed your way into my life and pissed me off a whole bunch, but now I can't imagine spending a day without you. I know I started out as a job for you, but it's more than that now. I know it is."

His shoulders heave with a deep sigh, and he finally turns around to face me, the confidence and smile wilting on my face when I see his eyes. They're cold and hard and they don't meet mine directly.

"Look, sweetheart, we're from two different worlds. You and I both know that. This thing between us, whatever it was, it was just a *thing*—a way to pass the time," he tells me quietly so no one else can hear. "You're safe now, the bad guy is behind bars, and my work here is finished."

I press my hand to my stomach in an effort to keep myself together. Right now, it feels like my whole body is being ripped wide open and my heart and soul are spilling onto the floor at his feet.

"You don't mean that. I *know* you, Brady. Why are you doing this?" I whisper angrily, my shaking voice giving away the torrent of emotions running through me.

"Sweetheart, you don't know a damn thing about me. Just like that fiancé of yours, we were both paid by your mother to do a job. My job is done, so I'll be collecting my paycheck and hittin' the road. You better get going, your chariot awaits," he says with a nod in Finn's direction before turning away from me again, this time pulling his cell phone out of his pocket and punching some buttons like he's sending a text.

Sending a damn text when he just broke my heart.

"You're a coward, you know that? A fucking coward," I tell him angrily and loudly, no longer caring that Gwen and Finn can hear me. Swiping angrily at the tears falling freely down my face, I turn and walk over to Gwen, pausing for a moment in front of her.

"Gwen, thank you so much for everything," I tell the woman with a sad smile. She's the first woman I really thought I could be friends with in long time. She's real and honest, and I had hoped to be able to have her in my life. That won't be possible now. Not when her brother obviously wants nothing more to do with me now that the "job" is finished. He's just going to stand there and let me walk out the door and out of his life, and there's nothing else I can do about it.

Gwen rushes over and wraps her arms around me, squeezing me tight, and I have to struggle to swallow past the lump in my throat and not let myself sob into her shoulder.

"He's being an ass. He loves you. I know he does. Just give him time," she whispers in my ear before pulling away and mirroring my sad smile.

I don't say anything in response to her words, knowing they are just her way of trying to make me feel better. Finn grabs onto my hand again, and we're out the door without a backward glance.

We get into his SUV and pull out of Brady's driveway and head towards town, neither one of us saying a word for several miles.

"I'm sorry, Layla. I really didn't want to be right about him," Finn says after a few minutes.

I turn my head and look out the window, watching the trees fly by in a blur, not sure if it's because Finn is driving so fast or because of the tears pooling in my eyes.

"You know, you're better off without him anyway," Finn continues, not caring that I don't want to be part of this discussion. "I have a feeling your mother has finally seen the light and won't be so hard on you anymore. She mentioned something to me last night about giving you more freedom with your music."

What should have given me a huge burst of elation suddenly just makes me feel despondent. This is what I've always wished for: freedom to sing what I want and be who I want. But what the hell does it even matter if I have no one to share it with?

"Things are going to change. We're both going to finally get what we want," Finn says more to himself than to me, and I turn to look at him, wondering what he's talking about. "People are finally going to know who I am."

Before I can question him and ask him what the hell he means, the vehicle suddenly jerks to the side with enough force to smack the side of my head against my window. The sound of breaking glass, tires squealing, and metal crunching fills the SUV like a booming explosion, and I squeeze my eyes shut as we spin and spin before finally slamming roughly into something else and coming to a halting stop.

I feel a trickle of something warm running down the side of my face, and it gets into my eyes, blurring my vision. I try to move but the seat belt is locked in place and my hands are shaking too much unbuckle it.

"Finn?" I croak as loudly as I can over the hiss of the busted SUV and look to my left to see him slumped in his seat, the seat belt holding him upright with his head down and his chin resting on his chest.

I struggle against the seat belt and reach my arm out to him, grabbing onto his upper arm and shaking him gently. He groans in pain and a feeling of relief washes through me for a minute, blocking out the pain that screams through my body.

"Finn, wake up," I tell him, the effort of speaking forcing me to cough and making me wince in agony. It hurts to cough and it hurts to talk, and I'm guessing it's from how tightly the seat belt is pressed against my chest and how roughly I slammed against it during the collision.

Finn finally raises his head and turns to look at me. His

eyes quickly leave mine as he stares in horror behind me out my window.

"Oh God, Layla. Oh God, I did something bad," he says with a shaky voice.

My door wrenches open and a feeling of relief washes through me when I realize the paramedics must already be here and they made good time since the accident just happened seconds ago. I turn my head slowly to look out the door, and when I see a strange man standing there staring at me with a calculating grin, I open my mouth to scream, recognizing immediately that he isn't there to help us.

He lifts his fist and slams it into my cheek, cutting off my scream before it could even leave my throat, and the world goes black.

CHAPTER 21

BRADY

It's all I can do not to turn and punch a hole in the wall next to me as I watch the door close behind Layla.

I stood here and did nothing, like an idiot. Why the hell didn't I say anything to her?

"You live two completely different lives."

"The media would know all about you. They'd know about the mistakes you've made, and they'd know about the secrets your sister is hiding."

Eve's words come rushing back and guilt overwhelms me.

I should never have even started anything with Layla in the first place. It was a bad idea for so many reasons, not the least of which is the fact that we live two completely polar opposite lives. But just like always, I hadn't given a shit about consequences. I wanted something and I took it, only thinking about myself and not those around me who could be hurt by my actions. I'm a fool for thinking I could have had any kind of relationship with someone as high profile as Layla Carlysle. And what the hell would she want with someone like me in the long run? A washed up Navy SEAL who couldn't hack it with the Nashville PD and owns a floundering PI agency and might be able to pay the electric bill this month, but who knows what will happen down the road? I have nothing to offer her, absolutely nothing.

With a sigh of regret, I turn away from the door and face Gwen's glacier look head on. Her foot is tapping against the floor, her hands are on her hips, and her eyes are shooting daggers at me.

"I know what you're going to say, so don't bother. I don't want to hear it," I tell her as I roughly yank out one of the kitchen chairs and slump down in it, turning the laptop around to face me and opening up my email.

"Oh, you know what I'm going to say, huh? So you know I'm going to tell you that I know for a fact you're in love with Layla and that she is without a doubt, one hundred percent in love with you?"

I grind my teeth and feel my face getting hot from shame and embarrassment.

"You couldn't possibly know that," I tell her, staring at the screen of the computer so I don't have to see the disappointment on her face.

"Oh yes I could. Number one, because you didn't deny it just now. And number two, she told me," Gwen admits.

My head jerks up quickly to face her, my email

momentarily forgotten.

"She *what*? When?"

Gwen shrugs her shoulders and takes a seat next to me. "Well, not in so many words. But she did one better. You see, we women sometimes like to *show* a man how much we love him. Sometimes actions are much better than words. Anyone can say the words, Brady. They can toss them around like they mean something while their actions make you feel small and insignificant. But when they actually show you that they love you? When they open up their heart and soul and show you a side of themselves they've never shared with anyone else—that's love."

My heart starts pounding rapidly in my chest as I think about what Gwen is saying.

"Her music?" I ask her in a whisper.

Gwen smiles at me and nods.

"Did you know the second night she was here and helped me put Emma to bed, she told me about that guitar? You were in the shower and I asked her about it. She hasn't played one single note on that thing for anyone since the day her father died. Not *one*. She said she would just hold it in her arms all these years and wait for inspiration to strike or for it to magically help her live again," Gwen explains as she leans back in her chair and crosses her arms in front of her. "I asked her what made her want to suddenly play on stage at June's, and do you know what she said? She said, 'I just realized that I've found something else to make me feel alive, and he's a lot warmer than an old guitar. I don't need to hide behind it when I have him in front of it.'"

I'm struggling to breathe as I listen to Gwen ramble. Each word she says is like a knife to my heart, making me realize what I've done and what I've lost.

"She also told me about the book of songs she wrote that you found," Gwen continues, not paying attention to the damage her words produce and my mounting anxiety. "She wasn't really mad at you. She was embarrassed. She knows she's talented and she's ashamed that she's done nothing with the songs but let them gather dust in an old notebook. Did you know she's never even shown that book to Finn? He knows she writes, but he's never read one of her songs or heard her play them. She's never played them for anyone."

Except me.

I hang my head down in front of me when Gwen finishes, not sure if I want to scream to the world that Layla loves me or sit in a corner and cry like a baby because...Layla loves me. She sat on that bed and showed me just how much by doing something she'd never done for another living soul.

"It's not too late, you know. You can still get her back," Gwen says softly, resting her hand on top of one of mine on the table.

I jerk my hand out from under hers and stand up so

abruptly that the chair topples over.

"No, I can't get her back. I can't get her back because I don't WANT her back. Can you understand that, Gwen? Can you get that through your head? Stop trying to play fucking match maker here!" I shout.

I want to take the words back as soon as I say them. I shouldn't be yelling at Gwen. I shouldn't be taking my frustrations out on her, but I don't know what else to do. I'm so angry at the fucking world right now for putting Layla in my life just to snatch her away again. A little tease to get me thinking about white picket fences and happily-ever-afters, then a harsh smack of reality in the face to bring me back to the real world.

The phone on the kitchen wall rings, and Gwen stomps off angrily to answer it, leaving me alone to stew in my misery.

"What? What the fuck are you talking about?" Gwen screeches into the phone. I step over the toppled chair and quickly walk into the kitchen, more than a little surprised at her outburst. Gwen rarely swears and when she does, it's never with a doozey like this one.

"That's impossible, check again. He's there. He has to be there," Gwen argues.

I stand there staring at her and when she gasps, puts her hand over her mouth, and looks up at me with wide eyes brimming with tears. I snatch the phone out of her hand.

"Who is this? What the hell is going on?" I ask angrily.

"Brady, hey, it's Adam. I'm sorry, I didn't mean to upset your sister. I was calling to tell you guys that we finally found that guy who's been stalking Layla, and Gwen kind of freaked out."

Gwen has her back to me now so I can't gauge by her face if she's okay or what the hell just happened.

"Yeah, we already know, Adam, thanks for calling though. Is the guy cooperating at least?" I ask with a sigh.

"We don't have him yet. That's what I was calling to tell you," Adam says.

My blood runs cold and Gwen finally turns around to face me, and I'm sure the look of horror on her face mirrors my own.

"What the hell do you mean you don't have him yet? Finn said you guys caught him and put him in custody, and he just picked up Layla to ID the guy."

Adam hesitates and that little pause through the phone lines speaks volumes.

"Brady, I have no idea what you're talking about. I've been on duty since two in the morning, and I'm telling you he was never brought in. We literally JUST got the DNA results thirty seconds before I called you, man."

I can barely hold the phone to my ear my hands are shaking so badly. Gwen is full on crying now, and I have to look away from her or I'm going to lose my shit.

"Can you fax me a copy of the DNA results, Adam?" I ask

him, trying to keep my composure while I'm on the phone with him. There's no point letting him know I feel like I've lost my fucking mind. "And also, I need you to put out a BOLO for a 2012 black Chevy Tahoe, license plate number seven, five, four, Delta, Charlie, Victor."

I maniacally pace back and forth in front of the fax machine, willing it to come to life and spit out the information I need.

"You're making me nervous, Brady," Gwen complains as she walks up behind me.

"I can't fucking help it. Why the hell isn't anyone answering their God dammed phones?" I reply angrily as I hit *end* on my phone and toss it onto the table. I tried calling Layla, Finn, and Eve about a hundred times each, and no one was answering. I want to get in my car and chase after Layla, but Adam told me to stay put for now and they would call me when they found Finn's vehicle.

Why the hell would he lie to us about Ray being in custody? To get Layla alone? But that makes no sense. She would have easily gone anywhere with him. He didn't need to lie to her. She trusts him.

The fax machine suddenly starts *whirring* and spitting out

pages. I pull them out before the ink is even dry and scan them. Before Adam hung up the phone, he said there was something weird on the test results they got. He didn't give me any more of an explanation, just that I'd know what he meant when I saw them.

"The first sample got a hit in CODIS matching a man by the name of Billy Marsh. A.K.A. Eric Dobbs, A.K.A. John Smith, A.K.A. Ray Bergin," I read out loud to Gwen. "Billy Marsh has been in and out of prison since he was eighteen years old for domestic violence, assault with a deadly weapon, sexual harassment, rape, robbery, and drug possession."

Gwen slumps down in a chair closest to her and folds her hands on the table in front of her.

"Oh my God," she whispers as I keep going, trying to ignore the voice screaming in my head telling me that Layla should never, ever be within a foot of this guy again.

"It looks like they ran Layla and Finn's DNA just to make sure the samples they had weren't confused with what they found at the scene," I explain as I blindly walk over to the table, the words in front of me swirling together.

"Right, I have a copy of the work order on the computer," Gwen replies, punching a few keys into the system and pulling up the report. "The lab was supposed to bump them up against the sample taken under Layla's fingernails and the blood found on the brick that came through her window."

I continue reading the report in silence, not believing what I'm seeing.

There's no way. No fucking possible way...

A harsh knock at the door has me dropping the papers on the floor and racing across the room hoping that what I just read isn't true and that it's Layla on the other side of the door, perfectly unharmed, so I can wrap her in my arms and beg her to never leave again. I throw the door open hard enough for it to smack against the opposite wall, my hope sinking when I see Eve standing on my doorstep.

"Where the hell is my daughter? She was supposed to be at the recording studio a half hour ago, and now she isn't answering my calls," Eve says angrily. Just like yesterday, she pushes her way right past me and into my house like she owns the place. "I left her ten voice mails from the studio. You did this, didn't you? You convinced her to go off on her own and ignore me."

Eve stands in the middle of my living room in her perfectly pressed business suit and not one hair out of place on her head. Her arms are crossed in front of her, and she's staring at me like I'm the scum of the earth. I almost believe I am until I remember what I just read on that DNA report.

"Layla isn't here. Finn picked her up an hour ago," I tell Eve as calmly as I can when all I want to do is fly across the room and choke the life out of this woman for being so conniving and such a liar.

"Nonsense, Finn would have told me if he was planning on picking her up and bringing her to the studio," she states, pulling her Blackberry out of her handbag and scrolling through the messages.

I take a few deep breaths to try and calm my anger but it's no use. My blood is boiling and I feel like I'm two seconds away from ripping the doors off of their hinges and punching holes in all the walls. I want to scream and bust every fucking thing in this place right now.

"Really? Finn would have told you the truth? Just like you've been telling the truth all these years?" I question her with my jaw clenched, biting down so hard on my teeth that it feels like I'm going to crack all of them.

"What the hell are you talking about?" Eve asks distractedly, still paying more attention to her phone than what I'm saying. Her cavalier attitude is all it takes for me to crack. I storm across the room, grab the phone from her hand, and heave it so hard into the wall that it shatters into a million pieces and leaves a nice size dent behind in the drywall.

"What the hell is your problem?" Eve demands. "That was a brand new phone!"

I see that Gwen picked up the papers that I tossed to the ground in my haste to make it to the door. Her face is filled with shock and anger, her nostrils flaring as she walks up next to Eve and shoves the pages at her roughly.

Eve grapples with them so that they don't fall to the floor and flips through the pages.

"DNA results? What are these for?"

I finally walk across the room towards her, making sure to stay out of arm's reach so I'm not tempted to do something I'll regret.

"Those were the lab reports that were run after the attack on Layla. They were supposed to just bump them up against Finn and Layla to make sure they didn't confuse the real perpetrator with the two of them. But someone at the lab screwed up. They ran Layla and Finn against each other."

I've never seen someone's face pale as quickly as Eve's. She goes from having her cheeks red with anger to her entire face looking chalky and sweaty within seconds. She looks like she might throw up right in the middle of my living room.

"So I assume you know exactly what they found when they accidentally ran that test, don't you, Eve?" I ask, standing there waiting for her to find her voice.

Her mouth opens and closes but no sound comes out. Her hand goes up to her throat, and I can see it's trembling uncontrollably. She starts shaking her head back and forth in denial as she stares at the piece of paper in her hand, reading the results and realizing that her world is going to slowly unravel now.

"All this time, you knew. You knew and you didn't say a fucking word. Does *anyone* know about this?"

Eve continues shaking her head back and forth, and I'm so angry that she's not giving me an explanation that I find it impossible to control my temper. I grab tightly to her upper arms and shake her so hard I can hear her teeth rattle.

"SAY SOMETHING GOD DAMMIT!"

Eve just stares off into space, not even acknowledging me. I'm so scared and furious that I don't care if I hurt her. I don't care if I snap her neck. I continue shaking her and shouting at her until Gwen finally wraps her hand around my arm and squeezes it just hard enough to pull me out of my murderous rage. I drop my arms from Eve and take a few steps back, my breath coming out in gasps.

"He took her, Eve. He took her and he lied to us about where he was going. Does Finn know about this?" Gwen asks softly, turning Eve to face her to try and reach her through sympathy and a little kindness.

It's more than this woman deserves, but I keep quiet and let Gwen work her magic.

"Eve, please. Does Finn know about this?" Gwen asks again.

Eve finally stops her manic head shaking and looks at Gwen, her lips and chin trembling with panic. "Oh God! He knows. He's known since he was in Afghanistan and there were complications with his injuries. When he came home, he was so angry. He broke into my house and threatened to go to the tabloids. He demanded that I hire him or else he would tell everyone. Layla was already huge by then. I couldn't let anything ruin it. I had to do something. I had already done so many bad things by then, what was one more?"

Eve continues to ramble, spilling her guts about everything. She tells us about Finn and Jack and Ray/Billy. She confesses all of her sins right there in the middle of my living room. She admits to things that will break Layla's heart into a million pieces and makes me fear even more for her safety. I can't just sit here waiting for the police to get their heads out of their asses and find Layla. I can't do it. I may not be active, but I'm still a fucking Navy SEAL, and I'll be damned if I lose one more person in my life.

I walk away from Gwen as she tries to comfort a woman who doesn't deserve her kindness while Eve breaks down on my couch, sobbing hysterically and rocking back and forth.

Scrolling through the contacts on my phone, I call the first person I can think of who is always up for a little off-the-books search and rescue mission. The phone is answered mid-ring.

"Hey there, dick bag! Tell me you need me for something. I'm going crazy sitting here on my ass waiting for Uncle Sam to call."

I'd smile at my friend's words if I didn't feel an immense

amount of panic suffocating me right now.

"Austin, I need you, man. How soon can you get here?" I ask.

"Already got my go-bag in my hand, and I'm walking out the door. I had a side job two hours from you. I can be there in an hour. Fuck speed limits."

I thank Austin and hang up the phone, grateful once again that I have friends who will always have my back.

I just hope to God that wherever Layla is, she knows that no matter what, I will come for her.

CHAPTER 22
Layla

I blink my eyes into focus and stare up at a ceiling covered in water spots and mold wondering who booked such a shitty hotel room for my tour. Turning my head to the right, a burst of pain shoots across my forehead and behind the back of my eyes with the movement, and I realize that I'm not in a hotel room but what looks like the basement storage room at Hummingbird Records. I've only been in here once, and it was years ago when my dad was still alive and he brought me down here to unpack the case for the guitar he'd given me. Twisting to my side on the cold, cement floor, I push myself up so I can try and clear the cobwebs from my head. I lean my back against the concrete walls and glance around at all the old boxes of vinyl records, out-of-date recording equipment, and framed posters of musicians and bands Hummingbird has represented in the last thirty some odd years.

My head feels like it's going to explode, and I try to think back and remember what the hell happened and why I'm in this basement. I press my palm against my temple, pulling it quickly away when I feel something sticky there and see spots of bright red blood.

Blood, screeching tires, breaking glass, crunching metal...

"Finn, wake up."

Everything comes rushing back to me all at once: Brady's brush off, Finn rambling nonsense as we drove, the accident and...oh God, that man, the one who opened my door and stood there with a huge, disturbing smile on his face. It has to be *him*—the man who wrote all those notes, who attacked me and threw a brick through my window, who watched Brady and me together in his truck. I don't know how and I don't know why, but he was there at the accident. Did he cause it? Was he the one who ran into us or was he just following Finn and me and by some freak twist of fate happened to be in the right place at the right time? And where the hell is Finn? I don't remember anything after my door opened and I saw that man standing there.

Using the wall as support, I press one of my hands against it and push myself up so I can stand, every muscle in my body aching from the impact of the accident. I gingerly walk around a few boxes, trying not to jar my throbbing head too much. I have to get out of here and find Finn. As I make my way across the room, I hear the door at the top of the stairs open, and I move faster, wincing as each footstep makes my head feel like someone is taking a hammer to it.

"HEY! Hello? Is someone there? I need help!" I yell as I make it to the bottom of the stairs and look up. "Finn? Oh, thank God! What the hell happened? Why did you leave me down here? Are you okay?" I ramble as he gets to the bottom step and walks right by me.

"Did you see that Ray guy after the accident? That was him, wasn't it? Did he escape from the police department? Are we hiding here or something?"

Finn still doesn't answer me or turn around. He just walks over to one of the support poles in the middle of the room, crouches down, and starts securing rope to the bottom of it.

"Finn, what the hell is going on?" I demand, as I stare at his back while his arms work furiously tying knots and wrapping the rope around the pole.

"Yes, Finn. Do tell her what's going on," a male voice says as I jump in surprise and turn around when I hear a sinister voice in the room with us.

I watch in shock as the man from the accident strides down the stairs cracking his knuckles, a pair of handcuffs dangling from the front pocket of his pants and clinking together as he descends.

I scramble backward, knocking over boxes of records and tripping over a broken microphone from the sixties and an equalizer from the eighties. I continue falling over all of these things until my back slams into Finn's chest, and he wraps his hands around my upper arms and squeezes tight, holding me in place.

"Finn, what are you doing?" I question angrily, trying to struggle out of his grip.

"Oh, Finn, I think it's time to clue the lady in on a few things, don't you?" the man says as he finally comes to a stop right in front of me, taking the tip of his finger and sliding it up my neck and chin.

I bite down so hard on my lip that I taste blood as the man stands there staring at me with a smile on his face. He's over six feet tall, and I have to crane my neck to look up at his face. It's a face that immediately makes me think of nightmares and scary movies. He's got a scar that runs from right below his eye to his bottom lip, and I can tell that he was most likely on the receiving end of a knife fight. The stubble on his face makes him look dirty, and the dark color of his eyes as he stares down at me reminds me of a black, bottomless pit. The tattoos that run up and down his arms are of flesh-eating monsters, devils with flames shooting out of their heads, and other sinister markings that make my skin crawl. The fingers that he uses to touch me are inked with what look like hand-made prison designs, and I cringe in disgust as he uses a dirty, broken fingernail to scrape the trail of blood off of the side of my face.

"I really don't like this new look you're going for with the hair. You look like a whore," he tells me seriously as he runs his dirty fingers through the short locks.

I jerk my head away from his hand, and he grabs my chin roughly, forcing me to turn my head back and look at him. My fear is quickly being replaced by anger. Anger that this man thinks he has any kind of claim over me. He's kept me in fear long enough.

I growl at him. "Like I give a shit what you think."

My boldness is quickly silenced with a backhand across the face. I cry out in pain and my eyes immediately start to water, the hands holding me in place clenching tighter and tighter to my arms as I struggle as hard as I can against them.

"Billy, man, not so rough," Finn scolds.

My confusion mounts as I listen to Finn talk to this man like he knows him.

"Finn, let me go, please," I beg him softly. "Why are you doing this?"

He still doesn't speak to me, and after a few seconds, I stop struggling and immediately let my body relax against him, remembering each and every thing Brady taught me that night in my bedroom.

"You're so clueless about everything, Layla. All this time, all these years, and you never figured it out. How is that fucking possible?" Finn finally speaks, the contempt for me dripping from his voice right by my ear. "All of this should have been *mine*. The fame, the fortune… *I* should have been the star, not you. I came first, I was the one with the talent, but she threw me away like yesterday's trash."

What the hell is he talking about? Nothing he says makes sense. Why is he doing this to me? I have to get out of here. I have to get away from these two men who have obviously lost their minds.

While Finn is distracted telling me all the ways he hates me, my body goes limp and his hands loosen on my arms. I close my eyes and throw my head back, smashing it into Finn's nose as hard as I can. While he screams in pain, I collapse to my knees on the floor, whirl around, and slam my fist between his legs. He lets out another painful shout and drops to his knees right in front of me, holding his hands over his crotch while blood pours down his face from his broken nose.

I quickly crawl away from him, but in my haste to get out of his grip, I forgot about the other man in the room. His hand quickly grabs a handful of my hair and yanks me up off of the floor while Finn continues to whimper and moan.

"Get up, you weak fuck," the man spits at Finn as I flail my arms and try to hit my target. I get a few smacks and punches in before he grabs onto one of my arms and wrenches it behind me so hard and fast that I hear a snap in one of the bones and a white hot, blinding pain shoots up my arm.

A blood curdling scream flies out of my mouth, and he

suddenly shoves me away from him. I trip over my feet and throw out my uninjured arm to try and brace my fall as I smack my hip to the hard floor.

The pain in my hip is no match for the excruciating agony radiating through the upper half of my body, and it's quickly forgotten as I cradle my arm against my chest.

"We haven't formally met. My real name is Billy, but you probably know me best as Ray," the man says as he stands above me.

Using my feet, I push against the floor and slide myself away from him, but he follows me until my back hits the pole in the middle of the room and I have to stop. Billy crouches down in front of me while Finn finally regains his composure and stands up behind him, staring at me with hatred burning in his eyes and blood dripping off of his chin.

"I used to fuck your mother, you know," Billy says casually with a smile. "Back in the day, before she got all high and mighty. She liked to slum it and come to my trailer late at night, asking me for favors, and in return I got a piece of that sweet ass. She wrote me off after she sank her claws into your father, but I knew she'd be back. And sure enough, she darkened my doorstep one night asking me to do a little mechanical work on your father's car. A little poke to the brake line so the fluid would slowly leak out and POOF! No more Daddy."

A sob bursts from my mouth and echoes around the room

as I listen to this man admit that he killed my father. And that my mother had him do it.

"No! No, no, no," I mumble over and over as I shake my head back and forth in denial and cry for the man who would have done anything for me.

"Yes, yes, yes, princess! Isn't it good to finally hear the truth?" Billy asks with a laugh. "The truth shall set you free! And since we're on a roll, Finn, how about you clue her in on some more truths that will blow her mind."

Finn wipes blood off of his mouth with the back of his hand and limps over next to Billy. If I could muster up the strength, I would laugh in his face right now, pleased with myself at how much damage I did to him.

"I'm sorry, Layla! Oh God, I'm so sorry. I didn't want it to go this far, I didn't. You have to believe me," Finn pleads, his mood doing a complete one-eighty as he squats down next to me and reaches out to gently touch the bruise that I can feel forming on my cheek from the hit.

Billy scoffs and rolls his eyes. "Jesus Christ, you are such a fucking pussy. GET UP!"

Finn looks at me sadly and quickly stands back up next to Billy.

"Tell her how you really feel, Finn. Tell her all the things you've told me this last year. Get it all out of your system," Billy encourages.

I watch as the kindness in Finn's eyes is once again replaced by anger.

"You were always the golden child. The little princess who got everything handed to her because you had a perfect father, not some nameless, faceless asshole who knocked your mother up and then fled. I found out the truth when I was in another country, shot to hell and bleeding out in a two-bit operating room in a tent in the middle of the dessert," Finn says calmly.

I don't like the monotone timbre his voice has taken on. It's like someone flipped a switch in his brain and he's turned into a completely different person. I need to get Finn back. The real Finn. The one who has been by my side all these years, the one I know is still in there somewhere. I don't know what truth he's talking about, and I don't care. I just need to make him remember what we mean to each other.

"Finn, please. I love you, you know that. You're my best friend and I would do anything for you. It's not too late, we can fix this. We can fix everything," I plead with him.

Billy moves in a flash, stopping my appeal to Finn's good side as the steel toe of his boot connects with the side of my thigh. Once again, my screams of pain fill the room as I fall to the side, gingerly holding my broken arm to my chest and clutching onto my thigh with my good hand. My forehead rests against the cool, hard ground as I sob into the floor and wonder why the hell this is happening to me. It has to be a dream. This can't be real. I need to wake up.

WAKE UP DAMMIT!

"Shut the hell up!" Billy yells at me, and I flinch at his raised voice. He quickly squats down to my level, and just like a moment ago, he grabs onto my hair again and yanks my face up so he can hold it inches from his own, the stench of alcohol on his breath hitting me in the face and making me gag. "Haven't you figured it out yet? Haven't you realized why Finn hates you? Because he does, you know. He hates you. Isn't that right, Finn? Tell her why you hate this bitch!"

It hurts to cry but I can't stop the tears from falling as I look away from Billy and into the eyes of the man I've known almost my whole life. We took care of each other and we did everything for each other. My heart is breaking all over again wondering if he really does hate me, that all these years have been a lie, that his friendship was a farce the whole time.

"No, I don't hate her! I don't! I'm just mad. It wasn't supposed to be like this. I just wanted what should have been mine," Finn cries.

"Is all of this about you not playing guitar?" I ask him with a sob. "Finn, you know I have always supported you and your choices. I have always wanted what was best for you. If you wanted to do it professionally I would have helped you. I would have done everything I could to make it happen for you."

Billy laughs and Finn growls in anger. "I didn't want your charity! I wanted your life! It should have been mine. All of it should have been mine!"

I gasp at his words, not understanding how all this time he never said anything. He never once made his feelings or his desires known.

"I would have given it to you! Do you understand that, Finn?" I shout back at him. "I never wanted any of it! I love you and I would have gladly handed it all to you if I knew it was what you wanted."

Finn's anger falters at that point, and I can see the war that's going on his head as he stares at me. He wants to be pissed at me for having everything he's always wanted, but he knows I'm right. He knows I would have done anything for him. All he had to do was ask.

Billy frantically looks back and forth between Finn and me, tosses me to the side again, and suddenly jumps up, turning around and throwing a fist into Finn's face. I cry out as I watch a spray of blood fly from Finn's mouth and splatter on the floor.

Finn rounds on Billy and clenches his fists tightly to his side, his body shaking with the need to hit back.

"Does that make you angry? Huh, Finn? Are you good and pissed off now? TELL HER THE TRUTH!" Billy screams.

"I don't care about the truth, Finn," I rush to tell him, trying to get him to focus on me and what we mean to each other instead of what this monster is trying to do to us. "It doesn't matter. You're my best friend and we've always done everything for each other. Remember when you were twelve and you had pneumonia? I made you Campbell's chicken soup every day and we played Mad Libs until our sides ached from laughing and you forgot about how sick you were. And remember when I was fourteen and you dared me to jump my bike over the stream behind my house and I crashed and cried like a girl? There was so much blood everywhere and you carried me ten blocks to the hospital, apologizing the whole way and telling me you'd never let me get hurt again?"

The tears blur my vision as I remember back on our years together and how it was always us against the world. Right when I think I'm finally getting to him though, the softness in his eyes from remembering immediately turns to fury.

"Of course I remember carrying you to the hospital. I also remember listening to the doctor tell you that you were bleeding so much because you had this weird, rare blood disorder called hemophilia. Something passed on by your mother," Finn spits out angrily at me.

Billy stares at Finn and nods his head enthusiastically. "There you go, boy. Finally, the grand finale."

"Yes, I remember," I mutter in confusion, ignoring Billy's excitement. "They couldn't get the bleeding to stop from the gash in my leg so they ran tests. You made a joke that you'd have to put me in a bubble so I'd never bleed again," I whisper, wondering why he's bringing this up now.

"When I was in Afghanistan and bleeding out on the table, they couldn't understand why my blood wouldn't clot, so they ran some tests. Do you have any idea how rare it is for someone to have hemophilia, Layla? Do you have any idea how rare it is for two *best friends*, who live in the same town, have the same eye color, and the same two dimples in our cheeks to have hemophilia?"

My brain hears everything Finn is saying to me right now, but my heart refuses to process the words. It refuses to acknowledge that what he's saying makes sense.

"I should have had your life. I COULD HAVE had your life. It should have been MINE! I was the first born. Our mother should have made ME the star. She should have put ME on the pedestal. When I came home from the war, armed with the news the doctors had given me and a hunch about who I was, I demanded that she tell me the truth. Instead of being happy about it, she paid me to keep my mouth shut."

I gasp at his words, running them through my mind over and over as he stares at me with murderous rage in his eyes.

Our mother, our mother, our mother.

"No. It's not possible," I mumble, even though I know he speaks the truth.

Our mother, our mother, our mother.

"Look at that! I think she sees the light, Finn!" Billy exclaims from behind him. "Layla, meet your brother, Finn. I'm so glad I get to be a part of this heart felt family reunion."

"All these years I've been wanting to get back at dear old Eve for using me only when she needed something. Imagine my surprise last year when Finn here found my contact information in some of Eve's things," Billy explains as he paces back and forth in front of me. "Finn hatched up a genius plan where I would get to stalk the beautiful Layla Carlysle, and he would come in and be the hero, saving the day, and have his face plastered all over magazines and television. The grateful public would want to know everything about him of course, and they would soon learn that, oh my gosh, he can play the guitar?!"

Billy stops pacing and pulls the handcuffs out of his pocket, swinging them around his finger as he continues.

"And of course, once the news broke, people would start digging into Finn's life and wait, what's this? His mother is really Eve Carlysle? She had a bastard child right before she married Jack and tossed him into an orphanage? Oh the horror! And wait, there's more!" Billy says with a sinister laugh. "A grown-up Finn comes home from the war, after fighting for his country and almost losing his life, and he knows the truth! Oh my! But Eve, she pays him off to keep him quiet. Offered him a job close to her so she could keep an eye on him. Oh no. How tragic. Poor Finn."

I crumble to the ground, unable to hold myself up any longer, crying so hard I'm surprised I have any tears left.

Turning my head against the floor so I can look up, my gaze goes back and forth between the two men staring down at me.

"So Finn would get his fame and fortune and you would get revenge on Eve when everyone found out the truth," I croak with a raspy voice, my throat aching from all the tears.

"Little Miss Perfect would be blackballed in the music world. It really was a perfect plan," Billy states. "Until that bitch felt the need to hire a PI who started sticking his nose in things."

Billy bends over and slaps the cuffs on my good arm, pulling on it roughly until it's extended out from my body, securing the other end to the support pole. I moan in pain, not even attempting to struggle against him.

"I tried to warn you, Layla. I tried to tell you that guy was bad news, but you didn't listen," Finn states softly. "I bugged his place when I dropped off your stuff the other night. He knew about your dad. He knew all about Jack's death, and he didn't tell you. He kept it from you because he doesn't give a shit about you."

Finn is back to sounding like he cares about me, and my head is spinning from the back and forth he's doing. One minute he's pissed and the next he's on my side. I don't know which Finn is the real one. I don't know what is happening to him.

My eyes close and I rest my cheek on my arm handcuffed to the pole, wanting to just give up. I don't care about anything anymore. There isn't one person in my life who hasn't betrayed me. I am alone and I'm going to die in this basement alone. Billy and Finn have divulged all of their secrets. Secrets they won't want anyone to know about. No matter what confusion is going on in Finn's head right now, there's no way he's going to want the truth of what he's done to get out.

"Finn here was getting a little nervous about the whole stalking thing," Billy tells me after making sure the handcuffs are secure. "After a few of our phone calls, I had to wonder if he had the balls to follow through with our plan. He thought I was taking it too far with you. I had to convince him that I knew what I was doing and it would all work out in his favor in the end. I had to promise him that you wouldn't *really* be harmed. A little white lie never hurt anyone."

Billy grabs onto the neck of my T-shirt and rips it right down the middle until my black lace bra and bare stomach are exposed. He cups my breasts in his hands and squeezes them roughly until I cry out.

"Billy, STOP! What the fuck are you doing?" Finn shouts, grabbing onto his shoulder and trying to pull him away from me.

Billy takes one hand off of me, reaches into his back pocket and pulls out a gun, turning his head and pushing the barrel into Finn's chest.

"I'm doing what I planned on doing all along. Making Layla mine," Billy says quietly, cocking the gun and holding it steady right at Finn as he backs away with his hands in the air.

His other hand that still kneads my breast distractedly slides down the front of my body until it reaches the snap of my jeans. He yanks them open roughly, and regardless of the pain, I start to struggle against his hands.

Billy stands up and holds onto the gun with both hands.

"Be a pal and take her pants off for me," Billy tells Finn as he nods in my direction.

Finn looks at me with terror in his eyes but doesn't move.

A loud blast of the gun explodes through the room and Finn screams, dropping to the ground and clutching his thigh. Blood pours between his fingers as he tries to hold his hand over the wound in his leg.

"I said, take her pants off," Billy states calmly as he stares down at Finn and cocks the gun again, loading another bullet into the chamber before pressing the nose of the barrel into the top of Finn's head.

Finn uses one hand to pull himself over to me and refuses to look me in the eye as he does what Billy says.

"Finn, no. No, no, no, please, don't do this," I sob hysterically as he quickly removes my jeans with one hand, and I fight him as best I can, the pain in my leg from being kicked and the jostling as I try to struggle bringing so much agony to my arm that I start to see spots.

"I'm sorry, Lay. I'm so sorry," Finn whispers as tears fall down his face. He stares at my feet and doesn't meet my eyes.

Billy lifts his arm above Finn's head and brings it down fast, the butt of the gun cracking his skull. Finn slumps to the side, unconscious and even though he was shot and going back and forth between hating me and feeling sorry for what he'd done, at least a part of me feels like he might still be on my side. He might still be able to stop all of this from going any further.

"That's better. His voice was grating on my nerves," Billy says, sliding the gun into the back of his pants and shoving Finn further away with the heel of his boot.

He advances on me with desire burning in his eyes as he stares up and down my body and licks his lips.

"Just kill me!" I shout at him through my tears. "Just fucking kill me!"

I'd rather die than have his hands on me again. I'd rather close my eyes and never open them again than have him on top of me, taking something that isn't his. This will ruin me. This will be much worse than dying or having my best friend betray me or my mother take away the one person in my life who ever loved me. This will be something I'll never be able to stop seeing, stop feeling, or stop experiencing from now until the day I really do die. No amount of happiness will be able to erase from my mind what's about to happen.

"Oh, you don't really mean that," Billy says with a laugh as he stands next to me and continues to look up and down my half-naked body. "You know, I usually like it when they struggle, but you're kind of useless in that department," Billy says as he takes his boot and presses it down hard on my injured thigh.

I close my eyes tight and clench my lips together, refusing to scream or let him know how much it hurts.

"Fuck you!" I spit out angrily, finally opening my eyes and staring at him with hatred.

He sighs and shakes his head at me.

"We really need to do something about that mouth of yours. I think this will be better for both of us if you just shut the fuck up," he tells me before bringing his fist down against the side of my head.

CHAPTER 23

BRADY

"I should have known better than to tell you to stay put," Adam tells me with a small laugh.

Austin had made it to my place in record time. I jumped in his car, turned on my portable police scanner, and quickly discovered the address the police department was searching.

Looking around the small mobile home, I curl my lip in disgust when I see the dirty dishes piled in the sink, the stains on the walls and carpet, and enough fast food wrappers to feed a small country littering every single surface.

"This is the third address we've found for Billy Marsh. The other two were apartments, and they were empty. The landlord for both places told us the guy hasn't been there in months and if we see him to let him know he's been evicted," Adam explains as he turns and tells the fingerprint analyst to start in the back of the trailer and make his way forward. "There wasn't anything in the other two places linking this guy to Layla, Finn, or Eve, so we're hoping we'll find something in here. Otherwise, we're back to square one."

Adam gives me a pat on the back, then walks away to talk to a detective who just came through the door after interviewing neighbors.

After Eve had confessed everything to Gwen and me, I immediately called Adam to fill him in. He knows Eve hired Ray/Billy to kill Jack, and he knows she kept the secret of Finn and Layla being siblings all these years. Adam had sent a patrol car to my house to pick Eve up and take her into the station. Surprisingly, after Eve unburdened herself of all her transgressions, she accepted responsibility for all of the things she's done wrong and went with them willingly. She knows her life is pretty much over and there's nothing she could do about it but cooperate.

Adam comes back over to me and flips open his note pad.

"We found Finn's vehicle. It was in a pretty bad hit and run accident just south of downtown on a side street that doesn't get much traffic. The front end is completely smashed, and it was hit so hard that it was pushed into a telephone pole," Adam explains as he reads the notes in his hand.

"Oh Jesus. Is Layla okay? Was she in there?" I ask frantically, hoping to God that she wasn't hurt too bad.

Adam looks up from his pad and shakes his head.

"The vehicle was empty, Brady. There was some blood on the driver's side and passenger side. The lab is running the samples right now just to make sure, but…"

Adam trails off and I'm glad he doesn't continue. I know what he's about to say, and I don't need to hear him say it out loud.

Layla was in the car when it crashed, she's bleeding, and now who knows where the fuck she is. I know from when she was attacked outside the club that her blood doesn't clot very well, so if she's hurt bad enough and doesn't receive treatment, her life will be on the line. I should have never let her walk out that door. I should have told her the truth when she stormed over to me with all that passion and conviction in her voice. I should have turned around and told her I loved her instead of pushing her away and making her feel like she didn't matter.

"Hey, Brady," Austin calls to me from the hallway. "There's something back here you need to take a look at."

Stepping over trash and dirty clothes, I head down the hall behind Austin, following him into a small, cramped bedroom with Adam right on my heels.

"Oh my God," I mutter as I look around the room.

"Holy fuck," Adam whispers, echoing my shock.

Every single available surface is covered with pictures and news articles of Layla and Hummingbird Records. There's a picture of her on stage at practically every venue she's been to and pictures of her from magazine articles, photo shoots, and entirely too many candid photos taken from a distance with a telephoto lens. Layla having lunch with Finn at an outdoor café;

Layla grocery shopping at Puckett's; Layla sitting on her front porch holding onto the guitar she'd just played for me; a copy of the picture of the two of us in the truck that had been left on my front windshield.

There are articles pinned to the wall about each new recording artist that Hummingbird signed, copies of their financial reports, and print-outs of Eve's personal brokerage and savings accounts. Her net worth and that of Hummingbird Records is plastered all over one wall and up on part of the ceiling.

"Jesus, this guy is a sick fuck," Austin says as he bends down and looks at the picture of Layla and me. I want to tear that thing off of the wall and rip it to shreds so no one else can see it, no one else can be a part of that private moment between the two of us, but I know I can't. It's evidence and it needs to stay right where it is.

"Eve swore she hadn't talked to this guy since that night she asked him to do something about Jack, right?" Austin asks. "If she's telling the truth and she didn't hire this guy to stalk Layla as some sort of twisted publicity stunt, who the hell did?"

I run my fingers through my hair in frustration and turn around in a circle, my eyes running over every single thing in the room.

"Finn. It has to be Finn. He lied about Billy being in custody to get her out of the house," I reply.

"Okay, so he was pissed about the fact that they were siblings and she got all the limelight when he got diddly squat, but that doesn't explain how the hell he even knew who this guy was or why he would do something as stupid as put her in his path," Austin replies.

"How would you feel if one day you found out you had a rich megastar for a sister, and the mother who did everything she could to make sure your sister rose to stardom completely denied your existence?" I ask him.

"Yeah, that's pretty messed up, and it would probably make me mad, but mad enough to form a connection with a dangerous, convicted felon who would probably stab you in the back, literally and figuratively, to get what he wants? This Billy guy is ten shades of fucked up from what his rap sheet says. Why the hell would Finn want to tangle with him?"

Glancing over at the wall that holds the only window in the room, my brow furrows as I step closer to a large blueprint that hangs on the wall to the left of it.

"Is that the layout of Hummingbird?" Austin asks, coming up behind me.

"Yeah, it is. Why the fuck would he need this?"

Austin and I study the page, but it's just a standard blueprint. There's nothing written on it and no notes to clue us in as to why this guy has this in his home.

"Can you say obsessed much? Maybe he's planning on

taking all of Eve's money, taking what he thinks should be his since she basically used him and then tossed him aside," Austin thinks aloud.

"That would explain why he has all of her financial information, but what the hell would he need this for and where does Finn fit in?" I ask, pointing to the blue-tinted engineering design that shows every emergency exit, every cubicle, every meeting room, and every storage space.

We stare at it for a few more minutes, my impatience growing with each breath I take. Every second we waste is another one where Layla is missing.

"Is Finn his kid? Eve messed around with the guy nine years ago. Who knows how long it was going on before that? Maybe the two of them hatched a plan. Father and son taking what's rightfully theirs," Adam states.

"Eve denied that when I asked her. She said that she knows for a fact Finn isn't Billy's son, and when I accused her of lying, she told me to go ahead and rerun the DNA. The father was a one-night stand. She hadn't seen Billy for at least a year before Finn was conceived," I explain.

"Well, there goes that idea," Austin complains, angrily flicking his finger against the blueprint. The tack holding it to the wall comes loose, and the page flutters to the floor. It lands facedown, and I quickly pick it up when I see handwriting on the back in the lower left-hand corner.

332

"Soundproof basement. Access door next to conference room B. Building will be closed on Sunday, will make sure the delivery door on the south side of the building is left unlocked. I'll make sure she's there," I read aloud. "This is Finn's handwriting."

I feel sick to my stomach as I read the words that Layla's own brother wrote on the back of the page.

"Son of a bitch. He delivered her up like a lamb to the slaughter," Austin curses.

Crumpling up the page in my hand, I throw it against the wall and stalk from the room, rage flowing through me as I shove people out of my way. Slamming open the door of the trailer, I pull my gun from my side holster and check the clip, making sure I have more than enough bullets to shoot through Finn's heart when I get to that lying sack of shit.

"Brady! Hold up!" Austin yells as he jogs up to me and grabs my arm.

I fling it off and quickly turn to face him, my fear for Layla's safety exploding out of me.

"Don't fucking tell me to hold up! I've been climbing the walls this whole fucking day hoping and praying that she's still alive," I shout at him.

"Dude, I know. I know you're freaked the fuck out, but you need to be smart about this. You can't go in there alone, half-cocked or you'll get yourself killed," he argues.

I shove both of my hands against his chest and push him away from me. He stumbles a few times before regaining his footing.

"Do you think I give a fuck what happens to me if Layla is gone? DO YOU?" I scream.

Austin quickly advances on me and gets in my face as a few neighbors and a handful of Nashville's finest stand around outside the trailer watching me lose my shit.

"Don't be a fucking asshole, man! I'm here to help you, you stubborn son of a bitch! What do you think you're going to do? Go in there with that Nancy-ass weapon and light the place up like fucking Rambo?" Austin shouts back.

We stand there staring at one another, both of our chests heaving in anger and our fists clenched to our sides until the fight finally leaves me and I realize I'm standing outside having a shouting match with one of my best friends instead of formulating a plan to get Layla back.

"Stop calling my Beretta 9mm Nancy. It can shoot circles around your pitiful excuse for a weapon," I finally tell him.

Austin throws his head back in a laugh and punches me in the arm.

"You only wish, asshole. Now, are we going to go get your girl back or what? Because something tells me you've gone to the dark side with Garrett, and now I'm going to have the two of you boring me with details about your amazing women and all the hot sex you're having," Austin says with another laugh as we walk towards his car and get in.

"Guys, hold up!"

We hear Adam's voice through the open window as he runs across the yard with papers in his hand.

"I just called in for backup. They're going to meet you at Hummingbird. But you need to see this before you go," he says, sticking his hand through the driver's side window.

Austin takes the pages from his hand and gives them to me before starting up the car.

"Thanks, man. It's going to take us about twenty minutes to get there, so let me know if anything changes," I tell Adam before Austin guns the engine, throwing rocks and dirt out behind his car as he speeds out of the driveway.

"What is it?" Austin asks as he weaves in and out of traffic while I read what Adam gave me and hold on tight to the door handle.

"It looks like emails between Billy and Finn dating back to a few months ago.

August 14, 2012

From: bmarsh@gmail.com

To: Finnegan26@gmail.com

The plan is in motion. Letters have been sent.

September 9, 2012

From: Finnegan26@gmail.com

To: bmarsh@gmail.com

No more letters. It's getting to be too much, and I think Eve is actually going to do something about it.

September 23, 2012

From: bmarsh@gmail.com

To: Finnegan26@gmail.com

Don't think. It's not something you're good at. I'll decide when it's too much.

October 1, 2012

From: Finnegan26@gmail.com

To: bmarsh@gmail.com

What in the hell are you doing? You weren't supposed to attack her. That wasn't part the plan. We need to stop this right now.

October 5, 2012

From: Finnegan26@gmail.com

To: bmarsh@gmail.com

I'm so tired of watching all of these fans kiss her ass. Everyone loves her when they should love me instead. We need a new plan. I don't think what we're doing is a good idea. It will never work.

October 8, 2012

From: bmarsh@gmail.com

To: Finnegan26@gmail.com

No, we don't need a new plan. Everything is moving along just like we want it to. Stop being such a pathetic excuse for a man and get me those blueprints.

October 12, 2012

From: bmarsh@gmail.com

To: Finnegan26@gmail.com

Two weeks from today will be the day. We will bring Hummingbird Records burning to the ground with a sweet little present tied to a pole in the basement. Eve will finally get what's coming to her when she no longer has a business to run, and you'll finally get what you deserve when she no longer has a main attraction to flaunt.

October 21, 2012

From: Finnegan26@gmail.com

To: bmarsh@gmail.com

I can't do this. I can't bring you Layla. I know that's what we agreed, but I can't do it. I can't do that to her. We can still go through with the plan of burning the place down, but I'm not bringing Layla. I made sure to cancel the insurance policy, so Eve will get nothing and you win.

October 24, 2012

From: bmarsh@gmail.com

To: Finnegan26@gmail.com

Bring her to me today, or you'll be the one tied to the basement as it goes up in flames.

CHAPTER 24
Layla

In the dark, cold room, I blink my eyes to focus, but all I can think about is the pain. It hurts to breathe and every inch of my body feels bruised and battered. Probably because it is.

Oh God! Why is this happening to me?

I try to move, to get up off of the hard floor, but my broken body isn't cooperating. I need to find a way out of here or I won't survive this. I know with every part of my being that if I don't leave this room, I'm going to die here. Alone.

The tears run down my face, and I can't even move my arms to brush them away; something is holding them in place.

I slowly turn my head to the side, trying not to throw up from the pain that rushes through me with that one simple movement. I'm tied down to something, but I can't make out what it is. The only light in the room comes from a street lamp right outside, which throws a thin ray of light through the small window close to the ceiling.

With all of the strength I can muster, I try to pull one of

my arms free from whatever is holding me in place, the bindings cutting into my wrists and pain instantly shooting up my arm that's most likely broken in several places.

My scream echoes through the empty room and my throat aches from all of the screaming I've already done…yesterday? The day before? I'm losing track of time.

Oh God, this is the arm I play with. This is the arm that cradles the guitar to my side and the fingers that strum the notes that take me away to another place. Notes and melodies that bring me back to life and allow me be who I really am.

"Shhh, don't scream. It's okay, it will all be over soon."

I think I hear a voice by my ear, but I know it's just in my head. It's a voice that used to always soothe me, but now it just makes me want to weep. This voice doesn't tell me how much it loves me anymore or how much my friendship means; it tells me how much it hates, how much it resents, and how much it wants me to suffer. All of my good memories of this voice have been replaced by the bad that happened here in this room.

I know I'm going to pass out again soon. My vision is swimming. Spots flash before my eyes as I struggle to remain conscious. I'm cold, so cold. I've lost a lot of blood. Blood I can't afford to lose because of my condition. I can taste it in my mouth, feel it on the side of my face, and see it dripping onto the floor next to my head in a puddle. My body shivers and my teeth chatter so hard I think they might crack.

Flashbacks of the past few months run through my mind like someone flipping the pages of a book, and my heart shatters at the memories. I should have seen what was happening. I should have listened to Brady from the beginning when he tried to warn me about Finn, but everything about him scared me. The force of what I felt for Brady shouldn't have been so strong so quickly. He had my heart and my soul from the very first touch, the very first moment. But he didn't want it. He didn't want any of it. I trusted too quickly, gave my heart away too easily.

Trusting someone is what got me into this mess. I trusted the wrong person, and now I'm going to pay for it with my life. Someone who should have been there for me and protected me…it was all a lie from the very beginning. Finn never cared about me. Deep down I knew it, I'd always known it. Every time I finished a performance and got off the stage with the crowd screaming and cheering for me, Finn would try to look happy, but looking back, I see now that his happiness was forced. He was jealous. He had always been jealous. I just never wanted to believe the hatred ran that deep.

I let the darkness wash over me, knowing it's the only way the pain will go away. Ray, Billy, whatever the hell his name is got down on his knees between my legs after he punched me earlier, and as I floated in and out of consciousness, there wasn't any fight left in me to stop him from tying me to the pole with the rope Finn secured or unbuckling his pants. The only thing holding me together right now is the fact that something stopped him from ruining me any further. Something caused him to scramble off of me quickly, and I remember watching him through the tiny slits in my eyes. His hands were in the air, and he was arguing with someone. I don't know who it was, and I don't care since they didn't bother to save me. Billy isn't here anymore but I am. I'm still here and I'm not going anywhere.

I can smell smoke now. It's all around me, burning my nose and clawing at my throat. I'm handcuffed and tied to a pole in the basement of a room that I'm pretty sure is burning.

Closing my eyes, I think back over the last nine years and wonder about all of the things I should have done differently, the choices I made that have led me to where I am now. If I had never let my mother control me, never succumbed to the undeniable connection I had to Finn…if we hadn't experienced that initial pull towards each other that I now know was something more than friendship—it was blood—maybe things wouldn't be ending this way.

I hear shouts and the pounding of footsteps in the distance, but I can't force my eyes open no matter how hard I try. Billy and Finn are probably just coming back to finish the job, not satisfied with how much they have already broken me, how much they have already taken from me.

Maybe if I had realized sooner, listened earlier, put away my pride and the belief that deep down everyone has some good in them, I wouldn't be where I am now—fighting for my life and wondering if the person I love cares enough to save me from this hell.

With my eyes closed, ready to just be done with all of this, I see a burst of light behind my eyelids as someone flips on the light switch and I hear Brady's voice. But I know it's not real. It can't be real. I'm hearing it because I *want* to hear it. I want him to love me back, and I want him to be here making all of this go away.

"Put the gun down, Finn! NOW!"

The dream is so real I swear I hear Brady screaming. It makes me smile, knowing that my last thoughts are of him, even if he doesn't love me. His strong, deep voice washes over me and warms every inch of my cold body.

"NO! It's over! It's all fucking over! I've ruined everything!" Finn shouts back.

"Don't do this, Finn. You killed Billy, you did something good to make up for all of the bad. Put the gun down so we can get out of here," Brady argues.

My eyes slowly open and I gingerly turn my head to the side, the cold, unblinking eyes of Billy looking right at me a few feet away with a bloody bullet hole right in the middle of his forehead.

"Come on, man. The building is about to blow. We all need to get the fuck out of here right now."

Another man's voice echoes through the room, and it's not one I recognize. I can't tell if this is a dream anymore. They said Billy was dead and he is. I'm looking right at him, but I don't know if what I'm seeing is real. I don't know if what I'm hearing is really happening. It's all so confusing and I just want to go to sleep.

"I can't leave! Don't you understand? I deserve this! I deserve to die here!" Finn shouts.

His words make me sad for some reason. No matter what he did, no one deserves to die here all alone.

"Don't make me shoot you, man. Put the gun down. I need to get Layla out of here, Finn. Look at her. She's barely holding on," Brady pleads with a shaky voice.

I suddenly feel a hand on my face, and I want to tell whoever it is not to touch me. It hurts. Everything hurts.

"I'm sorry, Layla. I'm so sorry. I just wanted what you had. I didn't mean for this to happen. I was so mad at you for getting everything and you didn't even want it. I should have never made that phone call to Billy. I should have known he wouldn't let it be that simple," Finn tells me with a sob as I feel his hands smoothing the hair off of my face.

"Get away from her, Finn, right now!" Brady screams, his voice closer than it was before.

"I'm so messed up in the head, Layla. I'm messed up and I fucked up. You need to know that I changed my mind. I wasn't going to bring you here today. But Billy knew it and he followed me and he slammed into my SUV and made me bring you here. I'm so sorry. I'm so sorry, Lay. It will be over soon. Don't worry, it will all be over soon," Finn coos softly next to my ear.

I hear the cock of a gun and shut my mind off, knowing that this is the end.

"GOD DAMMIT, FINN! NO!"

Explosions from several different guns go off all at once and the noise ricochets off of the walls and all around me. I don't feel like I've been shot but who knows. I'm already in so much pain I probably wouldn't even notice if a bullet pierced my skin anyway. I let myself drift away in the darkness, happy for the first time since all of this started.

I'm dying. I can feel it. My head is fuzzy from the blood loss. A couple of punches to the head wouldn't be much for some people, but it's everything to someone with my condition. My blood doesn't clot like a normal person; it just pours and pours out of me until there's nothing left. My lungs are filling up with smoke, and it hurts too much to cough to get it out. Nothing flows past my lips but a few gasps and whimpers. I let the smoke travel down my throat and enter my body hoping the fog circling around my lungs, my heart, and all through me helps to numb the pain. It's probably crazy that my heart is happy when my life ebbs and flows out of me and I can feel my heart slowing down. But at least I have that one little thing left to hold onto as I float away. I'm happy because even if it was a dream, even if Brady was never here, at least for a moment I got to pretend that he was. For just a moment, I felt cared for and loved. He found me and he tried to save me, even if he didn't succeed. With my eyes closed, I can almost smell his body wash through the stench of smoke; I can almost feel the warmth of his body as he holds me close and calls me baby. I always love it when he calls me baby.

"Layla, open your eyes, baby. Don't leave me, please." I imagine his soft voice pleading with me as he easily lifts me into his arms and takes me away from my own personal hell.

"Stay with me. Please! Stay with me!"

I smile as I imagine the things that he might say to me if he was really here, but my imagination isn't exactly accurate. His voice sounds sad and completely wrecked. That's not how he really sounds, so I know it's all just a wonderful dream. Brady doesn't cry. He's strong and he's amazing and he turned me into a fighter. I want to tell him that I tried. I tried to make him proud, and I tried to fight today, but it was too much. It was all too much.

"It's okay, Layla. You did good. You did so good, baby, and I'm so proud of you."

I sigh contentedly, knowing that's all I ever wanted—to make him proud and show him that I'm worth it. I will always remember his voice and his smile and his laugh. No matter what,

I will remember. I love him. I love him. *I love you.*

"I love you too, baby. Do you hear me? I love you. Stay with me." I imagine him begging again, his voice ripped apart with sobs as I float away grabbing on to my love for him and taking it with me.

CHAPTER 25
BRADY

Three months later.

Flipping on the light switch as I walk into the office, sorting through a pile of mail, I smile to myself when the room is bathed in florescent lighting. I've managed to take on steady work in the last few months which means Gwen has been able to pay the electric bill on time. It's a little thing, but right now the little things are all that's keeping me together. I could have cashed the final check that the board of directors for Hummingbird Records sent to me and I wouldn't have needed to take on every single job thrown at me the last three months, but I refused. I couldn't take the money. Even though I said the words, cashing that check would mean that Layla really *had* been just a job. Her life was worth more than some stupid check the company sent me as their way of saying "thank you" and persuading me not to sue them.

"It's about time you got here. The phone has been ringing off the hook, as usual," Gwen complains as she sets the receiver back in its cradle. "That's the fifth call I've gotten from Dateline. You really need to do one of these interviews they keep begging for so people stop calling."

I throw the pile of mail on Gwen's desk and walk over to my own, flopping down in my chair.

"I'm not doing any interviews, Gwen. We talked about this," I argue with her.

Everyone already knows what happened down in that basement, and my name has been linked to the news story. Because the tragedy involved a national music sensation, the story hit worldwide. Luckily, since I've avoided the interviews so far, no one knows about Gwen. I've still been able to keep her whereabouts a secret for now, and I need to keep it that way. The most anyone knows is that I have a woman with short, dark hair with blue and purple streaks working for me. They don't know she used to be a blonde and is the wife of one of the most renowned plastic surgeons in Manhattan or that he used her for a punching bag. They don't know that every time someone knocks at the door, we hope to God it isn't him. It's the reason I lied to Layla, the reason I ruined everything that could have been between us. To go back on that now would make everything I did pointless. It would mean that I hurt Layla for nothing. She'd suffered enough. That day in the basement of Hummingbird Records, her pain finally ended. She was at peace, and I wasn't going to talk to some stupid television show and fuck all of that up.

"Brady, I can't hide from him forever. Sooner or later, he's going to find out where I am. Mother isn't stupid. She knows I'm here with you," Gwen says softly.

"What the hell do you mean she knows you're here? How does she know? Did she say something?" I fire at her angrily.

"No, of course not, calm down. You know how she is. I only talk to her from your secure phone line, but she always says little things like, 'The next time you talk to your brother, tell him I said hello.'"

Resting my head in my hands on top of my desk, the worry that has consumed me since the day Gwen and Emma knocked on my door overwhelms me. I need to keep them safe. He can't find out where they are. I won't let him take them away from me or hurt them ever again.

I feel Gwen's hand on my back, and I lift my head up to see her standing next to me looking stronger than I've ever seen her look.

"It's time for me to do this the right way, Brady. I need to file for divorce. I can't really start living my life until I'm free from him, and you can't start living yours until you can stop worrying about me all the time," she says softly.

I open my mouth to argue with her but she quickly stops me.

"I know why you said what you did to Layla the last day

you saw her. I'm not stupid either. You've paid your dues, big Brother. You've more than made up for any wrong you think you might have done to me. I know you love Emma and me, and I know you would do whatever it takes to keep us safe, but you can't hide from your own life to do that. Do you plan on spending the rest of your life turning down love out of some twisted sense of duty?" she asks.

Yes. Because the only person I will ever love is gone. None of that matters any more.

My chest physically hurts when I think about her. I have to rub away the pain that feels like heartburn only ten times worse when I think about our last moments together and the smile on her face when she told me she loved me, when she told me she tried to be strong like I taught her.

Even though I pushed her away, even though I was the one who put that first crack in her heart that day and the rest of the events that followed shattered it, she still loved me. She still lay dying in that basement hoping that I would come for her, believing in me.

Gwen leaves me alone to my thoughts as she grabs her purse from her desk drawer and leaves to go get some coffee.

I know everything she's said is right. I can't keep her and Emma hidden away here forever. Even though that asshole hurt Gwen, he never laid a hand on Emma. He doted on that child, and he has to be going crazy not knowing where she is. It's not like I give a fuck if he's hurting, but Emma deserves to see her father. She still asks about him almost every day. It's not right. None of this is right. Working my ass off day and night so I don't have to think about how much I miss the touch of her lips, the smell of her skin, and the sound of her voice isn't right. Forcing myself to go days without sleep because when I close my eyes all I see is Layla's broken body in my arms and all I hear are the sounds of her gasping for breath is not right.

I miss her so fucking much I feel like if I didn't have Gwen and Emma here with me, I would curl up in a ball and let myself wither away. Just let myself fade into nothing so I don't have to feel this pain anymore.

Reaching into one of my desk drawers, I pull out the file with her name on it. I trace the name *Layla Carlysle* with the tips of my fingers and wish it was her face I was touching instead of a cold piece of cardboard. I flip open the file and stare at the document right on top.

When I was released from the hospital that day, my lungs clear from all the smoke inhalation after running through the burning building, I found her room and sat by her bedside even though there was no reason for me to be there. Her broken body still under the covers, hospital equipment and discarded wrappers from gauze, syringes, and oxygen tubes scattered all over the room, everything was in the same spot from when they were working on her. No one had cleaned up the mess after they finished.

They assured me she was no longer in pain. They promised me that they did everything they could. I sat there staring at her for twelve hours, willing her to open her eyes and look at me, to make it all stop being real, but she never did. She never moved and she never woke up, and I was finally asked to leave so they could move her. It took the strength of both Gwen and Austin to drag me from that room, to tear me away from her so I could go home, get some rest, and shower the soot and Layla's blood off of me. This never should have happened to her. She should have never walked out my door with Finn, and I should never have made her feel like she wasn't worth it. She was everything to me. She was my heart and my soul and my reason for living and now she was gone.

I read through the document in the file three times as I remember the day I left the hospital and Layla behind. I went back to my house and tore the place apart because of the unfairness of it all. It wasn't right that she was there in my arms one minute and gone the next. It wasn't right that I couldn't have her when I needed her so much. I ripped curtains from windows, broke picture frames that hung on walls, and shattered half of the dishes in the kitchen, and no matter what they did, Austin and Gwen couldn't stop me. The only thing that did was the object resting against the nightstand in my room. All of the rage and sadness drained out of me when I saw Layla's guitar next to my bed. I thought about the soft, raspy timbre of her voice when she sat in the middle of my bed and sang me that song—one of her originals that she'd never sung for anyone before me.

I picked up the guitar and held it in my arms like she did. I awkwardly strummed my fingers over the strings before the memories of her overwhelmed me, and I angrily tossed the guitar across the room, watching it bang against the wall and fall to its side.

I was ashamed of myself and immediately regretted my actions. This was Layla's most prized possession, and I just took out my grief on something she cherished. I crawled over to the guitar and gingerly picked it up, noticing something white hanging down behind the strings in the sound hole. The knock against the wall must have jarred something loose. Gently setting the guitar on its back on the floor in front of me, I carefully pried apart the strings and reached in with two of my fingers to pull a folded up piece of paper out from the inside of the instrument.

When I saw what it was, I closed my eyes and cried like a fucking baby in the middle of my room until Gwen finally came in to check on me. When she asked me what was wrong, besides the obvious, I soundlessly handed the letter over to her and listened to her gasp as she read it. The look on Eve's face that day when she saw the guitar case by my front door suddenly made sense. She knew what was in that guitar. She'd known it all these years but in her foolishness, she assumed the guitar was lost in Jack's accident. She never knew Layla had kept it hidden from her all this time.

My sweet hummingbird,

Soon, you and I will have a much better life than the one we have now. You won't have to walk around in fear of saying or doing the wrong thing, and you'll finally be able to live your dreams. I'm taking you away from here, my beautiful girl. We'll build a log cabin in the woods, just like you've always wanted. You can play this guitar out under the stars, and you can finally be happy. If for whatever reason, something happens to me before I can make this a reality for you, this letter serves as legal and binding proof that sole ownership of Hummingbird Records transfers over to you immediately. Your mother's stake in the company was never legally binding; it only existed on paper, and only for the length of our marriage, so she would let me keep you. You are the sole owner of your life and the decisions you make about your future. No one can tell you what to sing, what to play, or who to be. It's all up to you, hummingbird. If I'm not around and you ever forget for one moment how much I love you, just take out this letter and you'll always be reminded. Sing what you want to sing, write what you want to write, and play what you want to play. Be amazing and be free. Let the music take you where you want to go.

Love,

Dad

My fingers trace Jack's handwriting as I read through the letter one last time. It was signed and notarized by Jack Carlysle's private attorney who coincidentally passed away from a heart attack the week before Jack died. By making a few copies, I was finally able to set Layla free. Sitting here in my office, I look around at the emptiness and realize that I'm not ready to be free of her. I don't know *how* to be free of her. I don't know how to move on without her in my life, and I don't think I'll ever learn. Shutting the file and shoving it back in my drawer, I jump up from my desk and run towards the door, opening it quickly and running right into Gwen.

"Jesus, it's about time. I was wondering how long it would take you sitting there feeling sorry for yourself before you finally got your head out of your ass," she says with a roll of her eyes.

"I thought you went for coffee?" I ask her, staring down at her empty hands.

"Nope. I knew what you would do as soon as I walked out the door. You read that letter every time I'm not in the room. I was standing out here with my fingers crossed hoping this time it would finally sink in," she explains.

"Hoping *what* would sink in?" I ask her dumbly.

"Duh. That you can't live without her. And that Emma and I will be okay. You've done more than enough, Brady," she replies softly, reaching into her purse and pulling out her cell phone.

I stand there staring at my sister with a look of shock on my face as she dials the phone.

"Don't worry, I've got it all under control," she tells me as she puts the phone to her ear. "Good thing I'm the smart sibling in this relationship and kept in touch with June."

I continue to stare at her in wonder, but she keeps right on talking without waiting for a reply.

"I've been talking to her every couple of days to see how things are going and I swear to God, it took everything in me not to punch you in the face for staying away, making *both* of you completely miserable. June's going to be so happy that we won't have to talk about what an idiot you are anymore. Hi, June, it's Gwen," she says into the phone, no longer talking to me.

I stand there not saying a word as I listen to Gwen making plans and arrangements for me, laughing and joking with June about how I'm finally finished being pig headed. I'd scoff at her, but she's right. I've been an asshole. I've made so many mistakes that I don't even know where to begin making amends. Thank God I have Gwen.

I'll do whatever she tells me because I want this to work. It *has* to work. I can't go on living like this anymore.

"Pack your bags, Brother. You're going on tour," Gwen tells me with a huge smile a few minutes later as she hangs up the phone.

CHAPTER 26
Layla

It's been three months, three weeks, and six days since my world turned upside down. I don't remember much of my time in the basement of Hummingbird Records, and I guess that's a good thing for now. The doctors and my shrink have all told me that it's my brain's way of trying to protect me and that, in time, I will most likely start to slowly remember everything when I'm ready. From the bits and pieces I do remember, and what I've been told by the police, the lawyers, the media, and my entire management team, I know enough to keep me wide awake most nights.

When I woke up in the hospital two days after Hummingbird Records burned to the ground, I had a concussion, a fractured cheek bone, a dislocated shoulder, a small fracture in my clavicle, bleeding in the muscle tissue of my thigh from the kick I sustained, and a depressed skull fracture. Due to my blood disorder, that skull fracture quickly turned into bleeding on my brain that required emergency surgery. I woke up to a room full of people: my band, my agent, my lawyer, and June; I had never felt more alone in my life. My eyes searched the room for the one person I had hoped would be there, but I never found him. Later that night while I lay in bed thinking about everything I'd lost, June quietly walked in the room, climbed into bed with me, and held me while I cried. Everything changed that day. My heart was broken by each and every person in my life, and I wasn't sure if it would ever fully heal.

For a few short hours, I had a brother. A brother who I always thought of as my best friend, the one person I trusted and thought I could always lean on. He let jealousy and hatred cloud his judgment and allowed a man obsessed with revenge to corrupt him even further. In the end, from what I've been told, he tried to make up for his sins by killing the man who hurt me and then taking his own life right next to me. I'm thankful that is part of that day I can't remember. I don't know if I ever want that memory to surface. He turned on me and tainted every good memory I ever had of him, and that's not something I can ever forget. But he was still my friend. He was still my brother, and he died trying to make amends with me.

Apparently, my mother had admitted to hiring Billy to tamper with the brakes on my father's car. She claims my father was the love of her life, and she's regretted the decision every single day since then, but who knows. Just like her son, she was filled with jealousy. She knew my father never really loved her.

She was never the love of his life. That role belonged to June. Something that still amazes me when I think about it, but deep down I think I always knew. My father and June were high school and college sweethearts. After graduation, June went on a backpacking trip across Europe. Time and distance got the better of them and they broke up. A few years later, my father started Hummingbird Records and met my mother. Not long into their relationship, June came back to town and opened up The Red Door Saloon, and my father found it impossible to stay away from her. Right when he was getting ready to break it off with my mother and spend the rest of his life loving June, my mother told him she was pregnant with me.

She had always known about June, always known my father's heart belonged to someone else, and after a while she just couldn't take it anymore. She wanted him out of her life, but she didn't want to lose the money and social status, so she hired Billy, her one-time lover.

Under Tennessee law, her actions would have gotten her charged with solicitation of first degree murder, which is a class B felony and punishable by no less than eight and no more than thirty years in prison. Fortunately for her, the statute of limitations for class B felonies in Tennessee is eight years. She was one year past the expiration date when she confessed, so she never went to prison. I haven't spoken to her once since I got out of the hospital. She had called when I was still out of it and spoke to one of the nurses to check on me, but I'm sure it was only for show. She may have admitted to all her wrong-doings, and she may have apologized, but deep down, she'll always be the same cold, calculating person she's always been. I don't care how much she tries to make it up to me, I will never forgive her for taking my father away from me.

I never really had a mother, just someone who was in my life that took on the name but never the role. I've always looked at June as a second mother, and who knows, maybe in another life, she could have been my real mother. She has always loved me, always looked out for me, and she loved my father. I couldn't really ask for anything else. She's been by my side through every step of my recovery, and she's been helping me heal my head and my heart one day at a time.

I haven't seen Brady since the day he told me I was just a job and pushed me away. I have a few wonderful memories of him telling me he loved me, but I have no idea if those memories are real or just part of my brain mixing things up from that day. June told me during one of my many crying fits over the last couple of months that he was out of his mind with worry trying to find me that day. She told me he stayed by my bedside until I went into surgery, and Gwen and his friend Austin had to forcibly remove him from the hospital because he put up such a fight about leaving. None of that makes any sense though. Aside from the letter that came in the mail a few days after I got out of the hospital, I haven't heard a word from him. If he was so broken up about what happened to me, why wasn't he there? Why didn't he stay?

I push thoughts of Brady from my mind and try to concentrate on what I'm about to do. Thinking about the man who is still taking up residence in my heart will make me want to curl up in the corner and cry, and that wouldn't be good. I'm here to say goodbye to one chapter of my life and hello to a new one.

I close my eyes and take a deep breath, trying to calm the butterflies fluttering around in my stomach. I'm nervous, but it's a good kind of nervous. The kind that excites me and makes me want to push through it until I come out on the other side, proud of myself and what I've accomplished. Pulling the note from my father out of my back pocket, I read through it for the hundredth time without any tears for once. I smile as I fold it back up and stick it inside the sound hole of my nineteen-sixty Gibson Hummingbird guitar and tighten the strap that holds the instrument around my neck.

Tonight is the first stop of my farewell tour. It's not a long tour, just a small handful of cities. I don't have the energy to travel the globe, and thankfully, after what I've been through, my fans have understood.

I'm beginning this tour of saying goodbye at the place that started it all: The Red Door Saloon. For the first time in my life,

I'm doing things my way, singing the songs I want to sing and playing the music I want to play. I'm taking my father's advice and letting the music take me where I want to go. I want to be a songwriter, not a performer. I don't have the heart for performing anymore.

June did a few renovations in the last few months, and the bar finally has an actual stage instead of just a platform in the corner. Now there's room for a guitar player, a piano, a set of drums, *and* a singer, and I couldn't be happier to be christening the stage for her tonight.

Standing off to the side of the stage behind the curtain, I watch as June walks to the middle of the stage and taps the microphone a few times.

"Ladies and gentlemen, put your hands together for Nashville's very own, Layla Carlysle!"

The small crowd of around two hundred and fifty people, the most The Red Door Saloon has ever seen in its lifetime, all stand up from their seats, clapping, shouting, and whistling as I take a deep breath and walk out on stage.

I take a few moments to thank everyone for coming and introduce them to my band before adjusting the guitar around my neck and strumming a few chords to warm my fingers up.

My arm and shoulder are still a little sore, and my physical therapist advised waiting another week before starting the tour, but I can't do that. It's now or never. If I want to truly heal, this is something that I *have* to do, right now, before each day that I'm away from Brady makes me forget what it is I'm fighting for and why I'm happy to be alive.

I open my set with one of the first songs I ever wrote when I was a child, back when I had my whole life ahead of me and nothing to fear but the unknown. It's a song about growing up and moving on and not being afraid. I sing with my heart and I can tell that the crowd senses the difference. They clap along with the rhythm of the drums, and they sway to the beat of the music. I'm not just going through the motions performing like a robot. I'm performing like I love it. And I do.

I sing eight original songs tonight and I mix in a few covers to get the crowd up on their feet and singing along with me. I smile easily and talk to the fans happily in between songs, but even though there's a feeling of freedom and peacefulness that flows through me tonight, there's still something missing. There's still someone who isn't here that should be. My heart is full of pride in myself and love for what I'm doing, but there's a huge chunk that remains empty: a piece of myself that has broken off and lives in someone else now, someone who saved me but then walked away.

"This last song is something I wrote not too long ago. It's called *Your Breath on Me*," I tell the crowd with a smile as they whistle and cheer some more, and I place my hands where they need to go on the frets. Maybe singing this song isn't the best choice to close with since it cuts my heart open all over again, not the brightest idea when I'm trying to heal, but I'm pushing through and I'm doing it. I'm not going to let my fears control me anymore.

I close my eyes and begin the song, singing from the heart and pushing my voice as far as it will go, hoping just like I have every time I've practiced it the last few weeks that maybe he'll hear me.

When you're wrapped around me,
my soul feels alive.
Maybe this is a fairytale,
and not meant for my life.
I need you to hold me in your arms,
and chase my fears away.

Your breath on me
makes me sigh your name out loud,
gives me warmth when I feel cold
Your breath on me
makes me ache to touch your skin
gives me strength to live again.

When the morning sun comes in,
I'm not afraid of what the day will bring.

Your fingertips that touch my face,
and your eyes that know the truth,
show me that I'll be okay,
as long as I have you.

Your breath on me
makes me sigh your name out loud,
gives me warmth when I feel cold
Your breath on me
makes me ache to touch your skin
gives me strength to live again.

This dream of mine has finally come true.
I'm living every day just how I intended to.
But there is something missing, and I just can't let it go,
that piece of the puzzle, that I need to feel whole.

Your breath on me
makes me sigh your name out loud,
gives me warmth when I feel cold
Your breath on me
makes me ache to touch your skin
gives me strength to live again.

Gives me strength to live…
Gives me strength to live…
without you.

I slowly open my eyes when I hear the roar of the crowd, and I smile despite the ache in my heart that singing this song always brings. I take a small bow and clear the emotion from my throat so I can push the man this song is about from my mind and accept the crowd's praise without breaking down.

An hour later, after the bar has closed and everyone has gone home, I sit alone on the stage with my legs hanging down off of the edge. The only lights on in the place are the ones directly above me; the rest of the bar is swathed in darkness, and I can barely make out the tables and chairs that fill it. I quietly strum my guitar and hum softly to myself, thinking about all the ways my life has changed in the last few months.

"Hey, Layla. The band is all packed up and ready to leave when you are."

My hand stills on the guitar and I turn to face Dylan, my new bodyguard as of two months ago. He's twenty-eight years old and probably could have made more money as a male model than a bodyguard, but he loves his job and he's good at it. He came highly recommended to my management team. I have a feeling Brady was the one who suggested him. When I questioned Dylan about it, he explained it was better if I didn't know. I ignored the feelings of disappointment knowing Brady would rather send someone he knows to keep me safe instead of doing it himself. Dylan has stuck to me like glue since his first day, even though in the beginning I was a total bitch to him because he wasn't Brady. He's extremely professional and does everything by the book, but every once in a while he'll let his guard down and show me a fun, playful side of himself that puts me at ease.

"Thanks, Dylan. I'm just going to enjoy the peace and quiet for a few more minutes before I have to get on the bus with a bunch of rowdy boys," I tell him with a smile as I move the guitar off of my lap and set it down on the stage next to me.

Dylan crouches down next to me and searches my face for any signs that I'm not okay. He knows better than to come right out and ask me anymore after the last time he did it and I told him I would shove my foot up his ass if I heard that question from one more person.

"You need me to stick around in here?" he asks softly.

I stare at his handsome face, and I wonder why I feel absolutely nothing when I look at him. My heart doesn't speed up from his gorgeous brown eyes, and my stomach doesn't flutter with butterflies when I watch him lick his lips as he waits for me to answer him. He's never come right out and said that he wants me, but sometimes a woman just knows. Sometimes, all it takes is a look, and right now he's giving me that look. It would be so easy to just close my eyes, lean forward, and let him help me forget. Let him kiss me and touch me and help me fill in the gaping hole in my heart with new memories. I feel myself leaning towards him as I stare at his lips, willing myself to feel something, *anything*. I pause, an inch away from his mouth and pull back quickly with a sigh.

"I'm sorry, that was stupid," I mutter as I stare down at my hands in my lap.

I see him rub his hands over his face out of the corner of my eye and I'm filled with guilt. Dylan is a good man, an honest man, and he's slowly becoming my friend, and here I sit, thinking about using him just to help me stop remembering someone else. It's not fair to him.

"It wasn't stupid. This was a big night for you, and you've got a lot of shit going on in your head right now. I'm not going anywhere," he explains as he stands up. "When you finally get that jerk out of your system, I'll be here. In the meantime, I'm going back out to the tour bus to make sure the band hasn't mooned anyone or snuck any groupies on."

We share a laugh and I watch as hops down off of the stage and turns to look at me one last time. As I sit here staring at him, thinking about the huge mistake I almost made, I hear the buttons of the jukebox being pushed and the click and slide of a record falling into place. Within seconds, the soft sounds of piano music fill the empty room.

370

My heart stutters in my chest, and I hold my breath, not really believing that this is happening, that this song is playing right now. It's a song that will always be synonymous to *him*. It's a melody that will always remind me of dancing close to him, our bodies pressed up against each other as we swayed to the erotic beats in the club what seems like a lifetime ago.

"I have a confession to make," Dylan says, breaking me out of my thoughts. "There's no way I would have taken advantage of you like that. Not when I know your heart belongs to someone else. I just wanted to make sure HE WASN'T GOING TO PUSSY OUT ON THIS WHOLE THING TONIGHT," he explains, shouting the last part of that statement so his voice would carry through the bar.

Dylan winks at me and I watch him in bewilderment as he walks to the side door and pushes it open, disappearing into the parking lot.

After the door slams closed, I slowly slide down off of the stage and stand still right in front of it, barely breathing, feeling every emotion this song brings out of me as the beat of the drums and the soulful voice belts out the hypnotic words. As the man sings about words being like knives and cutting you open, Brady walks out of the shadows with his hands in the front pocket of his jeans like something out of a dream. His hair has gotten a little longer, and his face looks tired and sad, but otherwise, he's exactly as I remember him: tall and commanding as he strolls towards me, the long-sleeved T-shirt he wears molded to his sculpted chest and arms. I can't believe it's only been a few months since I last touched him. As he closes the distance between us and the subtle, masculine scent of him surrounds me, my mouth waters and it suddenly feels like years since I was this close to him.

The music continues to play and the words flow through me as he stops directly in front of me. He doesn't smile, he just stares. He searches every inch of my face like he forgot what it looks like and he's busy memorizing every feature. His eyes pause when they get to my lips and I nervously wet them with my tongue. He lets out a shuddering breath and pulls his hands out of his front pockets, holding one out in front of me, palm up.

"Dance with me."

It's a statement, not a question, and I don't even hesitate before sliding my hand into his and letting him pull me against him. His body is just as I remember it: rock hard in certain spots and soft and warm in others. He wraps his arms around me and pulls me closer and within in seconds of being enveloped in his arms, I feel like I'm safe. I feel like I'm home.

My nose and lips are right against the skin of his neck, and I can't help but breathe him in. I've missed this so much. I've missed the clean smell of his skin and the strength of his arms. We aren't really dancing, more like gently rocking to the music, but I don't care. I don't care about anything but the fact that he's here with me right now. It's easy to forget about all of the bad memories when the one shining light in your life is back and brighter than ever. It's easy to forgive the hurts and disappointments when the only thing you've ached for is standing right there in front of you.

Brady pulls his head back and looks down at me, giving me that half smile that I love so much, and I stare at the dimple on his cheek as we continue to rock back and forth together. I force myself out of the daze I've been in since I heard the first notes of this song echo through the room and finally find my voice.

"I can't believe you're here," I whisper softly.

"I can't believe you sang your own songs tonight," he replies back, the smooth timbre of his voice forcing shivers down my spine. "They were amazing. *You're* amazing."

I look away from him for a second in embarrassment, not because he heard all of those songs, but because he heard *the* song. The last song. As much as I dreamed about him hearing it, it's an overwhelming feeling to know that it actually happened.

"It was about you," I admit softly to him when I look back into his eyes, not specifying which song I'm referring to but seeing from the look on his face that he knows.

"Oh thank God," he says with a sigh. "I really didn't want to have to kick someone's ass tonight. Especially Dylan. That asshole promised me he would never dream about touching you.

373

I was only going to give him one more second before I came out here and fucked up his pretty face."

I laugh and shake my head at him, not even caring that he just admitted he was behind Dylan being hired. My elation at his words quickly sobers.

Once again, I find myself putting my heart out there on the line for him. But right now, staring up at his handsome face, I don't care if it's been trampled on or if he threw it away once before. I will give it to him time and time again because it's his. It's been his since the first moment I saw him, but I still need more from him.

"Why are you here?" I ask him softly as our rocking stops and we just stand together, his arms tight around my waist and my hands resting on his chest.

"Well, Gwen said I needed to do something huge to get you to listen to me once I got my head out of my ass. She actually suggested I get up on stage and sing a song for you. I thought something a little more low key was more my style. Did it work?" he asks uncertainly.

"I'm listening, aren't I?" I tell him with an encouraging smile.

He tentatively reaches his hand up and brushes my bangs that are now almost the same length as the rest of my hair off of my forehead. I close my eyes and lean into his touch, starving for it after all this time.

"I'm sorry," he tells me quietly as I move my cheek back and forth against the palm of his hand.

I can see the sadness in his eyes as he searches my face for a sign of forgiveness, but I can't give it to him. Not just yet. I stay quiet and let him go on as the song ends and begins softly playing again from the beginning like a soundtrack to a movie.

"What we had wasn't just a thing. What we had was *everything.* I lied to you, Layla. If I could take back everything I said to you that day, I would. I would take it all back and tell you that I love you more than my own life. I would tell you that I was stupid and scared and trying to keep the people in my life safe by pushing away the one person who meant the world to me," he admits, leaning his body closer to mine so I can feel every inch of him. "Running down into the basement that day and seeing you on the floor, tied to that pole, bleeding and struggling to breathe, almost broke me in two. I could barely do what I'd been trained for because all I could think about was how much you were hurting and how I could have prevented it if I'd just been honest. But walking out of that hospital and leaving you behind, thinking that I couldn't have you and keep my family safe, almost killed me. I can't live without you. I don't *want* to live without you."

With his hand softly framing my face, he leans forward until his forehead is resting against mine.

"I don't care if we come from two different worlds or two

different planets. I love you, Layla. If you let me, I will spend the rest of my life showing you just how much, every single day. Please tell me it's not too late. Tell me I didn't fuck everything up with you," he begs.

Reaching both of my hands up to cup his face, I pull it up so I can look into his eyes.

"Because of you, I am stronger than I've ever been. Because of you, I can finally live my own life and make my own choices. You sent me that note and you gave my father back to me. You gave my *life* back to me. Because of you being here right now, coming here tonight, even though it took you long enough," I tease him with a smile, "I know that I never want to be without you again."

Brady lets out the breath he was holding and quickly closes the distance between us, his lips finally against mine after so long. I breathe him in and I savor the taste of his mouth and tongue, and in an instant, it's like we were never apart. All of the hurt and pain and sadness is gone, and there's only Brady loving me and holding onto me, never letting me go.

Just like always, our kisses never remain innocent; they never stay gentle. We've been apart too long and our hearts are too wide open right now to do anything other than devour each other. Brady lifts me up and sets me on the stage as I wrap my thighs around his hips and pull him closer, instantly feeling how much he needs me when he pushes himself between my legs.

The song starts over for a third time, and now the words affect me differently. I'm burning with need for Brady, and I can't get close enough, touch fast enough. We break the kiss long enough for me to quickly slide my hands up his stomach and chest, taking his shirt off as I toss it to the side, then our mouths immediately fuse back together. Brady's hands slide around my ass and pull me closer to the edge of the stage and closer to him.

"Fuck, I need you so much, but I don't want to hurt you," he speaks against my lips, glancing down at my shoulder and my arm and all of the places where I was hurt. I run my hands down to the button of his jeans and unsnap it.

"I'm fine, you won't hurt me. Please," I beg him as I get his pants unbuttoned and slide my hand inside and wrap it around his hard length.

Brady buries his face against the side of my neck and groans as I slide my hand up and down him, loving the feel of how smooth he is against my palm. After a few seconds, he curses and moves away from my hand before quickly sinking down to his knees between my legs. He pushes my skirt up to my hips and slides my panties to the side, and before I can even blink, he places his mouth on me. I let out a cry of pleasure as his tongue slides back and forth, over and inside me, bringing me so much pleasure that I want to cry at how much I've missed this, how much I've missed him. His fingers join his mouth and they glide through me and inside me as his tongue flicks against me in rapid circles. He quickly brings me to the edge with his skilled mouth and fingers. I clutch onto the back of his head and hold him in place as he tastes me and pushes me and soon has me spiraling out of control as I come against his mouth and shout his name from my lips.

While my orgasm is still pulsing through me, he stands up and in one swift, hard movement buries himself inside of me and we both gasp and clutch onto one another.

"Jesus, you feel so good. I've missed you so much. I've missed your taste and I've missed how good you feel wrapped around me," he tells me softly against my ear as he slowly slides in and out of me.

"I love you, I love you," I repeat over and over, in the same rhythm of his thrusts, as I wrap my arms around his shoulders and pull him close. He rocks his hips against me and echoes my words until we're both chanting them together, not willing to stop letting the other know what we feel.

It doesn't take long for Brady to ignite the fire in me, and once again, I'm hurdling through another orgasm and taking him with me. He pulses inside of me as we pant and mumble more words of love through our release until we finally stop moving and sink against one another, holding each other up as best as our exhausted bodies will allow.

My legs are still firmly wrapped around his hips, and my fingers lazily slide through his hair as he pulls back slightly and looks into my eyes.

"You're wrong you know. About what you said before. I'm not the one who made you stronger. You always had it inside of you. It was always because of *you.*"

EPILOGUE

BRADY

"No! Absolutely not. You are NOT using the bathroom of *our* bus to have sex with one of your groupies," Layla argues with one of her band mates as she puts her hands on her hips and stomps her foot.

I laugh from my spot on the couch of the Luxury Marathon Coach that Layla ordered specifically for the two of us so we wouldn't have to travel the next few months with her band. She wanted us to have privacy and who was I to argue? I wasn't about to leave her side for one minute, even while she finished out her farewell tour, so living a few months on a bus that is bigger than my house is fine by me, especially when I get to go to sleep every night with the feel of Layla's body pressed up against mine.

Layla shoots me a dirty look over her shoulder for my laugh, and I drop my head to my laptop and finish typing up a report to send to Gwen while the argument on the bus continues and I work to keep my smile contained.

I have a lot to smile about lately. Things are going good

with Gwen. She filed for divorce and so far, her ex doesn't seem to be causing much of a fuss. He's not contesting the divorce, and he hasn't even tried to contact her since he was served. Even though I feel better knowing we don't have to keep looking over our shoulders, I still don't trust the guy. Since I plan on being by Layla's side through this entire tour, Layla suggested that Dylan stay behind to keep an eye on Gwen. Not only was I elated that I wouldn't have to worry about Gwen and Emma while I was gone, I wouldn't have to worry about that asshole trying to make a move on my woman. Two birds, one stone, and all that shit. Gwen and I knew Dylan back in high school and finding out he was in the bodyguard business was an added bonus. He and Gwen used to date back then, now that I think about it. This might be a recipe for disaster when she sees him, but that's not my problem. At least she'll be safe.

It's been three weeks since I went to the Red Door Saloon and got my girl back. Her tour is going great, and while her fans are sad that she won't be performing for them anymore, they understand her need to move on, and I couldn't be more proud of her.

Even though Finn tried to cancel the insurance policy on Hummingbird Records, he didn't have the power to succeed. All of the money came directly to Layla, and once she's finished touring, she's going to build again and run the business the way her father did: by being fair, open-minded, and listening to her clients' wishes. Every time I look at her, I'm amazed at how strong she is after all she's been through. She has her moments, though, and every once in a while I can see the grief and sadness overtake her features, and I know that I need to remove her from whatever situation she's in, close the door, and just hold her in my arms and let her cry. Some days are more of a struggle then others, particularly when something reminds her of Finn. He was her whole world for a long time, and she constantly battles with her emotions, not knowing whether to hate him or feel sorry for him. She's going to be okay though, my girl's a fighter. And I'm going to be here every step of the way to take care of her.

I look up at Layla when I hear the door to the coach slam closed and she sighs, turning around and removing the computer from my lap before climbing onto me and taking its place, straddling my thighs and wrapping her arms around my shoulders.

"Boys are gross," she states with a roll of her eyes.

I laugh and reach up to brush her bangs out of her eyes.

"I'm a boy. Am I gross?"

She shakes her head at me and smiles. "No, you're not gross. You're hot. And we should get naked now."

Layla starts unbuttoning my shirt while I laugh, and when she's halfway down, my cell phone rings. With a groan, I pull it out of my pocket and growl my hello while Layla tries to distract me by nipping her teeth into the side of my neck.

"Austin, what the hell do you want?" I ask, goose bumps rising on my arms as Layla swirls her tongue around my ear lobe.

"I just got your voice mail. Um, are you sure you want me to fill in for you at the office? I don't think your sister is going to like that very much," he asks unsure.

"Yes, I'm sure I want you to fill in for me at the office. Gwen's got some personal things going on in her life, and there's no way I want her handling any cases on her own while I'm gone," I explain to him as I slide my fingers through Layla's hair and hold her head in place while she nibbles and sucks on my neck.

"Alright, but don't say I didn't warn you. That chick will be pissed off when she sees me walk through that door," Austin replies with a laugh.

Layla grinds her hips against me, and I have to clench my teeth so I don't moan into the phone.

"Austin, I have to go. Just remember one thing: no sleeping with my sister," I warn him before ending the call and tossing the phone onto the bench next to me.

Layla pulls her mouth away from my neck and stares down into my eyes.

"So, where we headed tonight?" I ask as I slide my hands up her thighs and cup her ass.

"Texas. Then Colorado tomorrow, and after that, Nevada. Are you sick of being on a tour bus yet?" she asks as she cocks her head and smiles.

"Baby, because of you, I get to travel with the most beautiful girl in the world and go to sleep every night knowing that she loves me," I reply, leaning in and placing a soft kiss on her lips. "I'll never get sick of being here, as long as you're with me."

For the first time in my life, I know what true happiness is: she's right here in my arms, and I'm never letting her go.

The End

Turn the page for an excerpt from Playing with Fire, #3!

PLAYING WITH FIRE, #3

Coming Soon!

Untitled, Playing with Fire, #3

by T.E. Sivec

"Okay, so, you've got your 9mm, your .22, your .38 Special, and your .357. You probably can't handle anything more than that, so take your pick."

Crossing my arms in front of me, I take a step back and watch Gwen as she looks through the display glass at the firing range for a gun she'll like. After what happened yesterday, I'm not taking any chances with her safety. Brady will probably kill me because I'm teaching his baby sister how to use a gun, but too fucking bad.

We've been standing in the lobby of the gun shop which is attached to the firing range for thirty minutes, and I've gone over each gun in detail ten times. If she doesn't pick a gun soon, I'm going to stomp my foot and throw a temper tantrum, the likes of which even a woman with a kid has never seen.

"I want a pink one, Austin," Gwen finally says, looking up

from the case and straight at me.

"What?"

She huffs out an irritated breath and mirrors my pose with her arms crossed in front of her.

"I said, I want a pink one. Where are the pink ones?" I bite my lip so I don't say something completely irrational like, "Are you fucking kidding me with this pink shit? Just pick a fucking gun already!" I take a deep breath and a step closer to her.

"This is a gun shop. A place where people come to pick out deadly weapons and then go out back to practice firing at deadly people. Pink does not equal deadly."

Gwen takes a step closer to me as well until she's right up in front of me with her hands on her hips and that vanilla cake smell that always follows her around is tickling my nose and making me want to lick her.

"I. Want. A. Pink. Gun," she says softly, enunciating each word with a fierce gleam in her eyes.

She's so tiny I could scoop her up with one arm and probably carry her in my pocket, but standing here right now, so determined with her hands on her hips and an attitude on her face, she looks ten feet tall. She's also got a great rack that's being pushed out of her tight t-shirt. If I don't stop staring, she's going to find a fucking pink gun and shoot me in the balls with it.

"How about we just pick out a nice, shiny, black one for today, and when we're done, I'll order you a pink gun. I'll even order you a pink holster with sparkles on it," I beg her.

Normally, I could spend all day in the gun shop talking weapons with the owner and testing out new items. Using the word *pink* and *sparkles* in the same sentence at a fucking gun shop makes me want to puke in my mouth a little.

"Ooooooh, sparkles! Mommy, you should get a gun with sparkles!"

We both turn and look at Emma, Gwen's six-year-old, standing a few feet away from us, brushing the hair of some slutty Barbie in her hand.

"Good idea, baby! Can I get a pink gun with sparkles too?" Gwen asks.

"Jesus H...YES! We can bedazzle any fucking thing in this store you want, just pick one!" I growl angrily at her.

"You owe me a dollar, Austin," Emma pipes up from right next to me.

I look down and she's got her hand out, palm up, waiting for her payment.

Ever since I started hanging out with a single mom, I've had to try and watch my language. Being a Navy SEAL made it damn near impossible, so instead, I gave Emma a mason jar and told her I'd give her a dollar every time I swore. I do believe this one here puts that mason jar up to one hundred and twenty-four dollars now.

I pull my wallet out of my back pocket and take out a twenty.

"Here, pipsqueak, I have a feeling your mother is going to cost me a lot of money today," I tell her as she grabs the bill from my hand and shoves it into the front pocket of her jeans.

"Okay, fine," Gwen finally says with a sigh. "I guess I'll take that black and silver one right there."

I lean over her shoulder and see that she's pointing to a Kel-Tec 9mm.

"Good choice," I tell her with a nod as I signal the owner so he can get it out of the case.

Gwen turns her face towards me and our noses are practically touching. I can feel her breath on my face and I know if I don't move away, I'm going to be hard as a rock in two seconds. This woman drives me fucking insane, but she's also hot as hell and the strongest person I've ever been around considering what her life has been like lately. She also shoots down all the innuendoes I've thrown at her like she's swatting at house flies. There's nothing this woman does that *doesn't* turn me on.

"Since I can't use a pink gun today, can I get a pair of those ear muff thingies in pink for when I'm shooting? And do they have those with sparkles?"

I take that back.

388

Printed in Great Britain
by Amazon.co.uk, Ltd.,
Marston Gate.